Where I Belong...

Judy LeGrand

Copyright © 2024 Judy LeGrand
All rights reserved
First Edition

PAGE PUBLISHING
Conneaut Lake, PA

First originally published by Page Publishing 2024

ISBN 979-8-89157-761-9 (pbk)
ISBN 979-8-89157-776-3 (digital)

Printed in the United States of America

To Amanda and Zak.

CONTENTS

Maggie's Playlist vii
Acknowledgments ix

Chapter 1: Revelations (Always the Last to Know) 1
Chapter 2: The First Night Alone (The Sound of Silence) 14
Chapter 3: Not Just Another Day at the Office (I Heard
             It through the Grapevine) 18
Chapter 4: Rockaways (I've Got Friends in Low Places) 27
Chapter 5: Packing Clothes and Unpacking Emotions
             (Take Me Home, Country Roads) 33
Chapter 6: Escape to the Isle (Toes in the Water) 44
Chapter 7: A Brand-New Day (I Can See Clearly Now) 58
Chapter 8: Meeting the Family and Weaving Stories
             (Dream Weaver) 72
Chapter 9: Sunday Outing (Walking on Sunshine) 85
Chapter 10: D-Day Is Here—Sort Of (Landslide) 94
Chapter 11: Helping Turtles and Moonlit Walks
             (Waiting on the World to Change) 111
Chapter 12: Drafting a Book and a Photo Shoot (Hit Me
             with Your Best Shot) 118

Chapter 13: The Whirlwind That Is Debbie and Annette
           (You've Got a Friend) 131
Chapter 14: The Calm before the Storm (Patience) 145
Chapter 15: Uprooting a Home (The Winner Takes It All)........149
Chapter 16: Back Where I Belong (Here Comes the Sun!).........173
Chapter 17: When Time Stands Still (Anticipation)....................196
Chapter 18: It's a Wrap! (Go Your Own Way) 202
Chapter 19: Wedding Bells and Forever (A Thousand Years)......209

Epilogue..217

MAGGIE'S PLAYLIST

"Always the Last to Know" by Del Amitri
"The Sound of Silence" by Simon and Garfunkel
"I Heard It Through the Grapevine" by Marvin Gaye
"Friends in Low Places" by Garth Brooks
"Take Me Home, Country Roads" by John Denver
"Toes in the Water" by Zac Brown Band
"I Can See Clearly Now" by Jimmy Cliff
"Dream Weaver" by Gary Wright
"Walking on Sunshine" by Katrina and the Waves
"Landslide" by Fleetwood Mac
"Waiting on the World to Change" by John Mayer
"Hit Me with Your Best Shot" by Pat Benatar
"You've Got a Friend" by James Taylor
"Patience" by Guns N' Roses
"The Winner Takes It All" by ABBA
"Here Comes the Sun" by The Beatles
"Anticipation" by Carly Simon
"Go Your Own Way" by Fleetwood Mac
"A Thousand Years" by Christina Perri
"You're the One" by Greta Van Fleet

ACKNOWLEDGMENTS

I have wanted to write a book since high school. I have attempted to start it several times. Then in July 2021, four months before my sixtieth birthday, I decided to try one more time. I sat down and started writing. As I wrote, I found myself dreaming plotlines. I wrote this book in four months. It flowed. I hope another book will flow because this has been fun! I fell in love with my characters. (I am still waiting for my Liam to appear! He is out there, I just know it!)

In case you are wondering, I am not Maggie. Bill is not my ex-husband. Sam is not my daughter, and Maggie's boss is not any boss I have ever had, but wouldn't it be nice to have a boss who would let you stay at his beach house? There might be a couple of things that we have in common with the characters, but for the most part, the characters are all figures from dreams and my imagination. I set it in Isle of Palms because I grew up going to the beach there. I named restaurants after restaurants that may or may not still be there—again, dreams, imagination, and a few memories.

I want to thank my daughter for supporting me by reading the draft, helping with song titles, and encouraging me. I want to thank my grandson, Zak. His unconditional love makes life a lot brighter. I want to thank him for writing the turtle story for the character, David.

I want to thank Stephanie for reading the draft—from first draft to final. She is always there for support, constructive criticism, and encouragement to try new things, be a better version of me, and live life to the fullest. (She is looking for a Liam for me too. Keep looking!)

Judy LeGrand

I want to thank Becky, Carol, and Erin for reading the drafts and suggesting edits! Thank you all for your encouragement! Carol, I am so glad that you were a reading teacher; you were my stickler for details!

CHAPTER 1

Revelations (Always the Last to Know)

If I had been paying attention, I would have noticed that our marriage had ended. I was so busy with work that I failed to notice that we were basically just living—no more like coexisting in the same house. I had thrown myself into my job because that was where I found my happiness. Or maybe I was just so busy that I did not notice the big void in my life.

My friends kept trying to get me to go to dinner or out for drinks. I chose to work late and just go home to comfy pants and Netflix. I assumed Bill was just busy at work because he left early, stayed late, and traveled more than ever. Again, if I had been paying attention, I would have realized there was a void in his life too. Maybe on some level, I knew there was a void in both of our lives. I just assumed he was filling the void with work like I did.

Annette, Debbie, and I had been friends since high school. We stayed in touch now more by text and phone. We used to go to dinner and a movie or out for a drink monthly. We even took time for a quarterly girls' weekend getaway. At least we used to. I guess I was the one that stepped away from the girls' weekends. I guess I just got tired of all the negative comments about Bill. Bill and I had married right after high school, but Annette and Debbie both seemed to think I should have waited…or maybe I could have done better. It hurt me that they felt that way about my choices. I never made judgments about their choices. If we were honest, on a scale of one to ten…my choices were way better than theirs. But I kept that one to myself.

Then a couple of months ago, Debbie called me and begged for all of us to go to dinner. I agreed…probably to get her to stop asking. We went to a local dive, Rockaways, and it was fun! It was fun to reminisce about school and catch up on family. Debbie and Annette both had grown children, and they were divorced. Bill and I had one daughter, Sam, who was married and lived in Tennessee. Sam and her husband loved their jobs, traveling, and hiking, and I did not see grandchildren in my future. Debbie and Anette were both anxiously awaiting the arrival of grandchildren. I felt the divide on our common interests growing. But I could put all that aside because it was so great to be back together.

Then they started it. They made it through the first drink. They waited for the appetizer to arrive. Then it all began…like it always did.

"So," Annette said, "what is Bill up to these days? Doesn't it seem odd to you that he travels so much these days?"

Of course, I was defensive about him and said that he worked a lot…like I worked a lot. Debbie asked if I ever thought he might be seeing someone on the side. I could feel the heat in my face. I held my tongue and waited for the heat to pass. "You don't know anything about Bill."

Her response was "You are absolutely right. I don't know anything about Bill, but I do know what was happening with my husband when I thought he was working late and traveling." Debbie also said that she knew what Annette's husband was doing when everyone thought he was the poster child for "who's who of corporate America." They were both "doing someone" fifteen years younger and in better shape.

I was furious. I could not eat my dinner. When the waiter brought it, I just asked for a "to-go" box. I cut Debbie and Annette off, saying I had heard their accusations before and did not want to go there again. I said that I was going home. I paid my bill and got my to-go dinner. I had hoped that the two-block walk to my car would help me to cool off. No chance of that. I unlocked my car, and

I dropped into the driver's seat. I took a deep breath and started to think. *God, what if Debbie and Annette were right? What if he was not working overtime? When I said I was working overtime, I was working late.* I called his number. No answer. When I got home, I decided to look at his calendar on my computer. I hesitated, thinking I was overstepping. But as a wife, I reasoned I had a right to know.

There it was…6:00 p.m., Stacey. Who was Stacey? Maybe it was a client. Bill was an intelligent man. Wouldn't he be smart enough to hide an affair from me by keeping it off his calendar? However, it was his *personal* calendar. I decided to look back a few weeks on his calendar. Funny, he had an appointment with Stacey three days a week. I decided this might take some liquid courage, so I went to the kitchen. No beer—my liquid courage of choice—but we had some wine. I poured a glass. I took a few sips and kept searching. There it was…three months back. Her address. It did not look like a business address. I decided to use my GPS and find it. The address was for a residential neighborhood. It had to be business; otherwise, wouldn't a smart man hide it on his calendar? Again, personal calendar that he did not expect me to look at. On some level, I knew the truth. I kept arguing with myself, but in the end, I knew deep down what the truth had to be. If I was honest with myself, I had known what the truth was for quite some time. Something Debbie and Annette evidently suspected to be true for some time.

So before I drank more, I decided I needed to take a drive to check out his 6:00 p.m. appointment. I tried to make excuses and justifications for why I would not find his car there. I did this all the way there…until I turned onto her cul-de-sac. After all the excuses, there it was, his 2019 Mercedes SLC300. Black, full buyer package, just like he wanted. My heart sank into my stomach. Maybe there was some innocent reason he was there. Then I thought about all the appointments I had seen with "Stacey" on his calendar. Then I had to wonder…I had only looked back three months. How long had this really been going on?

My mind was flooded with questions. I felt like I was frozen in place staring at his car. Part of me felt like I should drive away, but part of me wanted to sit right there until he came outside. Maybe I could let the air out of his tires or scratch the side of his car with my key. An entire Carrie Underwood song lyric played through my head! But I just sat there. Then he walked outside the front door with her. I heard this noise that tried to break through my stupor. I felt like my mind was trying to work its way to the surface from a very deep ocean cave. I *knew* in my heart I was not suddenly in a deep-water cave in the ocean, but panic is a funny illogical thing. One side of my brain told me I was simply sitting in a car on a cul-de-sac. The illogical side made me feel like I was drowning. I tore at the collar of my T-shirt and felt like I could not breathe. I worked hard to grab hold of the part of my brain that knew this was a panic attack and that I was sitting in a car on a cul-de-sac.

I suddenly realized the noise I heard was the sound of me screaming. Then panic-attack me started to try to reason with logical me. You know…if you are screaming under water, you *will* drown. So panic-attack me stopped screaming. Logical me clawed at the door and finally managed to open it. I finally forced myself to climb out of the car that panic-attack me envisioned as an underwater cave. I took a deep breath. Panic-attack me was still a little leery, but logical me reasoned with her to just breathe…lean on the car for support…and relax.

So there I stood in front of what I assumed was Stacey and Bill's "love nest." Now that I had my panic attack under control and I had no fears of drowning in my car, the love nest did not seem so scary. I was standing there enjoying air (and breathing) and recovering from the edge of another panic attack. I could hear the muffled sound of their conversation and the very distinct sound of Bill's happy laughter. I will admit that in that moment, it was a sound I had not heard for years. In that moment, I realized it was a sound that I remembered from vacations in the early years of our marriage. It was a sound I heard when our daughter was growing up. They always just enjoyed each other's company, whether it was a trip, a video game, or a day at the beach. In that moment, I realized he had not sounded that happy with me…in years.

I heard his muffled reply, and I heard her carefree laughter in reply. I realized I had not seen him look that happy and at ease with me in years. If I were honest, I had not felt that happy with him in years. A sudden rush of sadness filled my heart, and without realizing it, I sighed out loud. Wow, it must have really been "out loud" because "the lovers," Bill and Stacey, looked up from their intense conversation and embrace on the front porch. If I had mentally prepared myself for what I would have seen, I would have avoided the loud sigh. But because my observation was detected, I missed any chance I might have had to see a whole lot more of their love story unfold in front of my eyes because my sigh cut them short of all that was about to happen. It was obvious that they had been involved for a while or it was one of those "love-at-first sight" moments. Who am I kidding…they had been involved for quite some time! They were just too comfortable. Man, I could try to explain it all away, but it was like I was standing on the outside watching a Lifetime or Hallmark movie. These two were soulmates who finally found each other. Suddenly, I felt like I was the obstacle standing in the way of true love. Then the thoughts of betrayal and anger moved in. How dare he feel this way about someone else. Why didn't he feel this way about me? Why didn't I feel this way about him?

With my overactive brain, I could have pondered this for hours. Unfortunately, my "bigger than life" sigh had made them all too aware of me. Bill and Stacey pulled away from their embrace, and Bill walked toward me. The closer he got, the more anger I saw in his eyes. There was no remorse for lying to me; there was no apology for the deception that I now realized I had been going through for quite some time.

He screamed and asked me what the hell I was doing there. *Me*…so he was going to be the victim in this, or maybe the knight in shining armor defending his princess…Stacey.

No. Panic-attack self and logical-self united. How dare he play the victim here. Panic and logic me took a deep breath and said, "Bill, you wait one minute. I came here because I had a feeling something was going on. I guess you were counting on me being so oblivious that I would not check your calendar, but I checked. Part of me *hoped* she was a client. The embrace and the deep-throat kiss you gave her on the front porch eliminated that theory.

"Really, Bill, how long have you been in love with Stacey? You can claim it is not love, but watching you two, I know that she has been your new love for quite some time. Can you honestly stand there and deny that?" He tried to muster up some words of denial, but they fell short. "Bill…I saw the two of you. You talked, caressed, and kissed like we once did. You cannot deny the feelings between you two, and neither can I."

More silence. "Bill, you will need to be free to be with Stacey, and I need to be free from your deception. I know you are a powerful businessman with many friends in the legal profession, and you could make me homeless. I must ask, after all that we have been through together, can't we end this on a civil note? Obviously, we were not happy together. If we had been happy, you would not be 'doing it' with Stacey. Am I wrong? I am thinking you two are 'doing it,' right?

"I was so busy going through the motions of working and keeping our home together that I did not notice you were looking elsewhere. I am sorry for that, but you could have said 'wake up or I am looking elsewhere!' So maybe we are both to blame. What do we do? I had pictured myself scratching your car or deflating your tires, but I knew that if I did that, I would be saying I was blameless, and I am not blameless. We grew apart…and you found someone to fill that void. I did not. I will not lie. It breaks my heart that you looked elsewhere. It makes me angry that you found someone. I wish I had been looking for 'a filler' myself because then I would not feel so empty and alone right now."

Bill said, "How can you be so gracious?"

I only had one answer. After seeing his calendar and suspecting what was going on, I was not gracious. No, not gracious at all. But when I saw the two of them, I could not be too angry. Because I knew the two of us had not felt that for some time. How could I fault love on the deepest level? I was jealous because what I saw between Bill and Stacey was what I had longed to feel for years.

"Bill, it is obvious that you have moved on. It is probably my fault for being so absorbed with our daughter then my job. I am sorry I did not see the warning signs. You deserve to be happy. I hope that you can look beyond 'legal speak' to see that I deserve that too. I wish you no ill. I hope that after all these years, and because of our daughter, you can feel the same way. Now, do I wish I could have found out another way? Yes, definitely yes! So what do we do now? I don't know. I don't think I can wrap my mind around a solution tonight. It is still too fresh. Well, I would like for you to pack your things and get out of the house tonight. Just your clothes and some personal items. I cannot watch you pack tonight. I will go somewhere and give you a few hours to get your personal stuff. We will meet and go through items later for each of us to take."

He said that he totally understood and that he would pack a couple of bags of clothes this evening along with his work stuff. I told him to take as long as he needed; I would not plan to get back to the house until around ten thirty. He said that he would pack just the essentials and leave the house key on the counter. He apologized again, saying how sorry he was for doing this to me.

"I am sorry too. I wish all of this could have ended differently."

In a moment of bravery, I asked where he and Stacey had met. He hung his head and sighed deeply. He looked up and said that they used to work together. When management started to suspect that they were more than just coworkers, they had moved her to another branch. Well…been there, done that! That was how Bill and I started dating. My mind was flooded with all those memories, replaying all the years.

Bill cleared his throat to bring me out of my musing. I knew that he knew where my mind had gone. We just stared at each other in silence. I really had no words. I said that I was heading out and I would be back home by eleven. He said that he would be gone by ten. He started to apologize again, and I just raised my hand to stop him. I had no words at this moment, and I was in no mood for his words. I got in my car and managed to crank the engine and pull away before the tears started to flow.

I needed to talk to someone. I could not call Debbie or Annette—the wound was too fresh for an "I told you so." I could not call our daughter, Sam, after all…this was *her* dad. He may have screwed me over big-time, but he was always a good dad. So who could I call at nine thirty at night to tell them my world had just imploded? I guess I could call my brother. Probably not because I wasn't in the mood for his "I told you so" either. He had never been too fond of Bill. I could not call anyone from work because I did not want to relive it at work tomorrow.

After weighing all my options, I thought it was best to call Debbie. She would be less likely to tell me "I told you so." My biggest problem would be keeping her from going to beat up Bill. So after weighing all the options, I took a deep breath and decided to call Debbie. I searched for her name/number on my phone and pressed send. Then I began praying that I had made the right choice. I needed a friend, not a judgmental confrontation. She answered on the first ring. I hoped that meant that she was not grabbing it before it could interrupt anything. With Debbie, you could never be sure!

I apologized for calling so late, and she promised I had not interrupted anything. She said she had just picked up her phone to check Facebook and Instagram. She said that she wished I had stayed for dinner, and she apologized for running Bill down. Well, I knew that she would retract the apology soon enough. I took a deep breath and spilled my guts about why I was calling. There was a moment of silence., and then she asked where I was.

"I just left 'her' house."

After a moment of silence, she insisted that I come right over. I let her know that it would take me about ten minutes to get there. She said the beer was chilled and she had some very high calorie snacks to see us through. I assured her that I would not be there too long because Bill would be out by ten thirty. She said that we would take beer and snacks and go back to my house. She said that I was not walking into that house alone after he left.

I pulled up into her driveway, shut off my car, and took a deep breath. There was no doubt that this woman was my best friend, but I still did not know if I could handle her commentary on my life at this moment. I braced myself for the worst and rang the doorbell.

She engulfed me in a huge, bear hug, and all my fears of condemnation vanished. She pulled me away, cupped my face, and assured me that she was there for me. She added, "Even if that meant disposing of a body!" I assured her that body disposal would not be necessary. I admitted to her that we were both at fault.

After her rousing "bullshit," I explained that I was just as much to blame for the failure of our marriage because I had been too busy to notice he had moved on. I then got the "until death do you part" speech, forsaking all others, blah, blah. It was all great in theory! So being the great friend, she agreed to put the "I told you so" speech aside.

Debbie pulled out two beers and a bowl of pretzels to get us started. I unloaded on her about my suspicions and my detective work on Bill's computer. I outlined the encounter in front of "the other woman's house" and where we had left it. She silently drank her beer during my synopsis of the night and the decided outcome.

I must admit that she kept her silence a lot longer than I thought she would. Then she took a deep breath and said, "Well, if it were me, I would have skinned the two of them alive. But if you can live with the outcome, I can support you. I just know that you deserve better, so we are going to start looking for better for you!"

I almost didn't know what to say. I had braced myself for the worst, for Debbie to chew me out for not seeing the signs sooner and for not standing up for myself. I just chugged the rest of beer number one and opened beer number two. My brain was foggy before the beer, maybe it was informational and emotional overload. Now, enter beer number two. The informational overload became silent. I could feel the emotional overload rising to the surface. I looked at my watch. It was already ten thirty. I hoped Bill was true to his word and would be leaving my house.

I insisted that I needed to get home. She said that she would drive me, but I insisted that was not necessary. I don't know why I thought I could win that argument. There was no telling her "no." I insisted that I needed to drive home to have my car there. She said that was fine and she would just follow me. So we set out for my house.

When we arrived, Bill was just leaving. Oh god, I was hoping Debbie would not get out of her car and confront him. I just was not up to the confrontation, whether Debbie thought he deserved it or not. He *did* deserve it, but I could wait for another day.

Thankfully, I got out of my car, and Debbie stayed in her car. I was very grateful for that. I walked up the sidewalk as Bill was locking the door. He unlocked it for me and gave me the keys. He turned to walk toward his car, but after a few steps, he stopped and turned to look at me. He looked at me and then looked down. He cleared his throat and said that he was sorry that he had hurt me. His voice cracked, and he said, "I know you may not believe this, but I really do love you. I just got lonely. I know that I was wrong, and you deserve better."

I knew that if I said much, I would lose it, so I kept it to "I love you too, and I am sorry we ended up here."

I turned and walked to my door. He turned to walk to his car. Debbie waited in her car until he was in his car. Now, I was praying fervently that she would stay in her car and then just get out and walk up the sidewalk to my front door. *Please let her walk passed his car, without stopping, and just come in. Come on…you are halfway there; keep walking, keep walking…* That was when she stopped dead in her tracks and turned to his car. My heart sank. *Please do not say anything, please.* Then she started screaming at his car. She called him a few choice names and then shouted to him that he did not deserve me. I could tell she was just getting warmed up. I stepped off the front steps and called for her to drop it and come inside before the neighbors called the cops. She hesitated but turned on her heels to come in. I was thankful that Bill stayed in his car and no porch lights came on.

Then I saw "Nosy" Nellie's curtain move. Great, if she had heard the commotion, it was only a matter of minutes before the phone chain would be activated and the news of the end of my marriage would make it halfway up the entire East Coast. I waved apologetically toward her window because I knew she would still be looking. Then I pulled Debbie inside the front door and cut off the porch light. Then I heard Bill crank up his car and back out of our driveway and out of my life. Debbie went straight to the kitchen and grabbed two beers and put the rest in the refrigerator. I wish I were one of those refined drinkers who would drown their sorrows with a wine spritzer or a red wine, but that just was not my style. I liked IPAs and preferably local craft IPAs.

I took off my shoes in the hall and hung my purse on the hall tree. As I walked toward the great room, I paused to look at Bill's study. His laptop and work folders were gone. I knew that I should have felt nothing but anger and disappointment toward him, but what I felt was a heavy sinking feeling of impending loneliness. I walked to the great room to join Debbie. I sank down on the sofa, and she handed me my beer. She even went so far as to pour it in a frosted glass from my freezer. She opened her mouth to say something, but I just threw up my hand to stop her. I was not up for a lecture or even a planning session to map out my next steps.

"I really appreciate you following me here so I don't have to face Bill alone if he cops an attitude. Luckily, his attitude so far had been apologetic. I need a few days to process my thoughts and emotions."

She asked me if I was going to tell Annette and my daughter, Sam, tonight.

"I am not calling anyone tonight. I will call Sam in a few days."

She said that I might not want to wait too long or Bill would tell her first.

"I will think about it. You can go ahead and tell Annette tomorrow. I just don't want to talk about it with anyone right now."

I turned on the TV and Netflix for background noise. It automatically went to the last show I had watched... *Virgin River*. Well, I was not up to seeing the twists and turns in the love life of the leading characters tonight, so I switched to the *Great British Baking Show*. It is always entertaining and lighthearted; well, at least to me. I guess if you are one of the contestants baking and getting kicked off the show, it probably did not feel too lighthearted! The bread and dessert creations always looked delicious, and if I was totally honest, Paul Hollywood was always good to look at. My mind wandered. Paul's cute, but maybe not good husband material either. I had looked him up on Google one time, and it talked about his marriages and affairs with younger women. Then I had an epiphany. *Maybe he was no different than Bill. Maybe he was lonely in his marriage. But why do they have to look for someone to fill the loneliness who is half their age? Are women their own age incapable of filling that void?*

Well, this was certainly an angle I had never thought about when watching the show before. Maybe all men were all the same. Maybe there would come a time when all the men would be involved with women twenty to thirty years younger than they were. Maybe all the older women could form a union or start a commune. Wonder what that would look like. Maybe tonight was not the night for me to develop a plan for a commune. Maybe I shouldn't be lumping all men into the same category with Bill right now. No, he was in a category all by himself.

Debbie cleared her throat and snapped me out of my daydream. She asked what I was thinking. Rather than go into the whole commune plan, I simply said that I was thinking about Paul Hollywood's deep blue eyes. She rolled her eyes because she knew there was more to it, but she was also the kind of friend who could step back and give me time to process. We finished our beer in silence, other than comments on the baking dishes.

She asked if I wanted another beer. I said that I really appreciated her coming over and hanging out with me, but I really needed to get to bed because I have work tomorrow. Well, work would be a fun time. She suggested that I take some time off. I assured her that I would in a few days. I had a few pressing deadlines that I needed to finalize. Luckily, work was a little slower right now.

We got up, and I put our glasses in the dishwasher. I walked Debbie to the door. I hugged her tightly. What would I do without my overprotective best friend?

"Be careful going home."

She insisted that I call her if I needed anything. I assured her that I would. Right now, I had to try to get through work tomorrow without one million questions and crying. Who was I kidding? Right now, I was going to have to try to get to sleep so I could make it to work. I walked her to her car.

She said that she would call Annette tomorrow and that I needed to be prepared for a dinner with the two of them tomorrow night. She promised that they would not lecture. She recommended

Where I Belong...

Rockaways. Since we had moved to Columbia a few years ago for work, Debbie, Annette, and I went there for a burger sometimes. Anyway, it might be a good place for a casual and quick dinner. Maybe if it were quick, it would be painless. I knew they meant well. I watched her drive away, and I went back inside to get ready for bed.

CHAPTER 2

The First Night Alone (The Sound of Silence)

When I came inside and closed the door, suddenly the house felt very quiet and very lonely. It was not like Bill and I were these great conversationalists, but at least he was a warm body here. So I cut the sound up on the TV to have it for background noise. I put together some food for lunch to take to work. Then I started the dishwasher. I cleaned the sink and countertops. Now on any other night, I would *not* have done all this, but right now I was trying to kill time. I guess I thought that if I stayed up until I was dead tired, I would just fall asleep when I got in bed.

I took a shower in case I did not sleep well and overslept in the morning. Whenever I had trouble sleeping, I would toss and turn until about five thirty in the morning; that was when the good sleep hit. Then I would hit the snooze button repeatedly until I was late for work. I convinced myself that I was planning for potential crisis in the morning. I put on a comfy pair of pajama bottoms and a baggy T-shirt. I pulled my hair back in a headband, washed my face, and brushed my teeth. As I left the bathroom, I took a quick glance in the full-length mirror. Well, I may have been comfortable, but there was nothing even remotely attractive about my outfit.

When Bill and I first got married, I had an array of sexy little nightgowns. Well, no nightgowns anymore because then I knew

I was long overdue to shave my legs. Hmm…that may have been one nail in the coffin that was my marriage. Now, I was not making excuses for Bill becoming involved with Stacey, but maybe I could have paid more attention to how I looked. Okay. Stop it, brain. I was staying up to get tired so I could go right to sleep, not to spend the time analyzing all the things that caused today's events. Well, not just today's events, just the event of me finding out about it.

Okay, I lived my life by making and completing lists. I loved the feeling of accomplishment I had when I was able to mark things off my list. In my twenties, Bill gave me an electronic notepad. This was back in the dark ages before we all had cell phones. I could keep my calendar on it and type out my daily to-do list. I remember it had little memory cards I could plug in that had games like monopoly and scrabble. I know, back in the dark ages! The problem was that when I put a check mark on my to-do list, it deleted the item from my list. Instead of feeling like I had accomplished a lot, I felt unproductive. I quickly had to retire it and go back to my notepad and pen. There were times that Bill and I would go to the grocery store together—dinner and grocery shopping was a good date night. He would hold the list and mark things off. One time I picked up an item that was not on the list. I stood there frozen in place for a bit. He laughed and asked if I wanted to write the item on the list so he could mark it off. He made fun of me many times over the years for my quirky list-making habit, but it was how I functioned. I still make a list at work. If I have any items left over at the end of the day, they go at the top of the new list for the next day.

So here I was at 1:00 a.m. making a list for tomorrow:

- Check and respond to work emails.
- Order lunches for the staff handbook committee.
- Register board of director members for the upcoming conference.
- Work on a job manual for my job as executive assistant (I keep hoping that I will win the lottery and be able to enjoy an early retirement. Part of being able to enjoy it was being able to walk away from my job because they would know

everything that my replacement would need to do. So far I had had absolutely no success at winning unless you considered an occasional $5, $7, or $11 win a success.).
- I needed to start working on the timeline for the company's annual business meeting. I oversaw pulling the meeting together. The meeting was not until December, but I usually started planning in August.

That was probably enough to get me through the day. There were always unexpected emergencies that came up that pulled me away. I just needed to make sure that I stayed extra busy so there would be no time to think about the impending doom of my marriage. I needed to stay locked away in my office so I would not be blindsided by seemingly innocent questions like "How's Bill?" "What are you and Bill doing tonight?" "What are you and Bill doing with the rest of your life?"

Yes, I was going to need to stay busy. Maybe I would take my lunch and go sit in the park to eat to get out of the office. I had a bad habit of working while I ate at my desk. I used to walk at lunch. When our office was downtown, my friend Vicky and I would walk at the Horseshoe on the University of South Carolina Campus every day. Well, that might be nail number two in the coffin: no sexy nightgowns with clean shaven legs and no daily exercise to lose weight and then keep it off. Okay, no more nail-talk tonight. No more coffin-talk tonight.

I cut off the TV in the great room and headed back to the bedroom. I picked out my outfit for tomorrow. Navy dress pants, pale blue sleeveless dress shirt, and a gray blazer. Here lately, I had been dressing down a bit too much, so I decided tomorrow would be a good day to dress up, maybe put on some makeup and some jewelry. Well, maybe I would go light on the makeup and jewelry. If I glam it up too much suddenly, that will raise more questions, and I was trying to avoid all questions tomorrow. I knew I would have to let my direct supervisor know about the new status of my marriage, but I did not think it had to happen tomorrow.

Where I Belong...

Okay. Still wired. I could not manage to keep my eyes closed if I taped them shut. So maybe I should read. I have not read my Bible in a while. I always find other things to distract me. Since I did not have a current Bible study I was working on, I decided to Google peace of Jesus. After all, after today's events, I felt I needed His peace more than anything else now. I read through a few verses in Psalms and Proverbs. Then I read John 14 and John 16. John 14:27 made me feel better. Jesus assured His disciples that he was going to leave them with His peace, a peace that passes our understanding. So after reading, I said my prayers. I thanked Jesus for His peace because my peace was not working right now. I asked Him to guide my steps and help me to know what to do. I added a revenge prayer for Bill and Stacey, but I quickly retracted it. I knew that wasn't something Jesus was going to do anyway.

CHAPTER 3

Not Just Another Day at the Office (I Heard It through the Grapevine)

The scripture and the prayer were the right combination. I put my Bible down, cut off all the lights except the small night-light, and fell asleep. Weird dreams and feelings of panic woke me up around five thirty. (I told you, it was like clockwork.) I tossed and turned until six thirty. My mind was racing, so there was no going back to sleep for me. I got up to start what I imagined would be a very long and emotional day. The good news was that I did not hit the snooze ten times. I washed my face and got dressed.

During this season of dressing down, my dress clothes had become a bit snug. The gray jacket I had picked was a little snug. I rehung it on the hanger and picked out another gray blazer with a different cut and style. This one fit better. I was going to have to work on getting off some weight, and in the meantime, I was going to need to pull the snug stuff and put it in a separate area of the closet. Then I went to the kitchen to fix some breakfast and much-needed coffee.

I scrambled two eggs with cheese and salsa. I put them on a low carb tortilla shell along with one-half of an avocado. Then I fixed a large mug of coffee with sugar-free creamer. I knew *what* I should eat; I just did not always do it. I was going to need to cut back on the creamer and try to cut it out altogether. But not today! I washed my dishes and frying pan since the dishes in the dishwasher were clean.

If I had been smart, I would have just unloaded the dishwasher, but I decided to leave that for tonight. I grabbed my lunch and fixed a large bottle of water. If I took that with me, maybe I could avoid some of the conversations at the water bottle filling station. I put my to-do list in my work bag, grabbed my purse and keys, and headed out the door.

I was leaving about ten minutes ahead of schedule thanks to the "no-snooze button" action this morning. So I should be able to get in and to my desk ahead of most of the crowd. It usually only took me seventeen minutes to get to work. It was a dream-commute for Columbia! I worked with people who drove 45–55 minutes from Lexington and beyond to get to the office. I had commuted from Sumter for four and a-half years. I had no desire for a long commute ever again!

Well, there was not much traffic, so I was able to get to work by seven forty-five. That gave me plenty of time to get my purse and lunch box stowed away in my filing cabinet. Then I decided to go get a cup of coffee from the breakroom before it filled up with coworkers. Tomorrow, I will bring a travel mug of coffee along with the bottle of water. I passed a couple of people as I headed back to my office, but I did not stop long enough to do a lot of talking. It was Thursday, so by this afternoon, all the questions would turn to plans for the upcoming weekend. My plan was to avoid those conversations at all costs.

I logged into my computer and pulled up my email. First things first, I deleted all the spam email. That cleared out about thirty emails. Then I started with the oldest email and responded about the availability of conference rooms and meeting rooms; I added meetings to the calendar. I sent the board chair a draft copy of the agenda for the next quarterly board meeting. I had a couple of emails requesting appointments with the executive director. I worked my way through these emails and added the meetings to his calendar. By the time I made it through all the emails that had come through since five thirty yesterday, I had killed one hour. So far so good. It was 9:00 a.m., and there had been no in-depth conversations with fellow employees.

My desk phone rang, and I answered without checking the number. It was Debbie. I probably should have let that one go to voicemail, but it was too late. She was calling to ask how I was feeling. I tried to convince her that I would be fine if she did not make me discuss my current marital situation. She gave me a mini lecture about how I was going to have to talk about it and think about it and make some decisions. I repeated my comments from last night: I would talk about it and think about it and make an entire life plan, but just not at this moment. I maintained that I had a lot of work to get done and I would have to let her go.

She let me know that she had called Annette and said that I could expect a call from her. That one, I would definitely let go to voicemail! Debbie asked if I would be able to go to dinner at five thirty. She had mentioned the idea of Rockaways to Annette, and she liked the idea.

I figured it would not be too busy at five thirty. I agreed to meet them at Rockaways, and I hung up so I could get back to my to-do list. Next, I went online and ordered boxed lunches from Schlotzskys Deli for the Staff Handbook Committee meeting. This committee was composed of a representative from each department. They were working their way through our employee handbook making updates and making sure it was current with recent policy manual changes. Man, just thinking about it was boring. I was thankful that I only had to order lunch for this one. They were meeting tomorrow at noon in the large meeting room. April, an assistant from my department, would be there for the meeting, and she would let me know if anything exciting happened. I ordered the lunches, along with sweet and unsweet tea and extra cookies. I figured the least we could do was make sure the group had plenty of sugar to keep them going if they had to work their way through the employee manual.

My boss was at a meeting downtown, so it was quiet. He would be in the office by eleven. I wanted to try to get as much done before he got back. He would want to discuss the upcoming Handbook Committee meeting and the national meeting that he and the officers would be attending in a little over a month. I went online and registered him, the president, and the vice president. After I got them registered, I booked their hotel rooms on the company credit card. I was glad that they each booked their own flights. Years ago, I used to have to book the flights. I would have to have their full name as it appeared on their driver's license, their date of birth, and the same information for their spouses if they were going. I had to guess where they preferred to sit on the plane. We finally decided that it was better for them to book their flights in case they wanted to use personal points to cover their spouse's tickets. Then I would reimburse them for their flight and other expenses. I was able to get all their hotel rooms booked. I emailed my boss and each officer with the confirmation numbers and check-in/check-out details.

I stopped to drink some water and go check the mail in the mail room. Again, I had a few encounters with staff, but there were no involved conversations. I had almost made it to lunchtime. I put the mail on my desk and went to the restroom. The thing I liked about our restroom was that each stall was totally walled in with doors, so no one knew who was in there. The thing I did not like about our restroom was that the stalls were totally walled in with doors. Today, I was in there minding my own business when two girls came in. They did not know anyone was in there, again because of those walls. They were whispering, but I was able to make out that they were talking about, me and Bill and Debbie screaming at him at the top of her lungs in my driveway. My first instinct was to scramble and dash out there to ask where they had heard their gossip, but I decided to stay quiet and just listen to see what I could learn. Wouldn't you know it...Tonya had a friend named Theresa who had an aunt who lived on my street—right across the street. You guessed it, Nosy Nellie. Damn, she was good. She really did have a phone chain. Well, if Tonya knew and was talking about this in the bathroom with Beth, odds were that the entire office knew. No wonder I had not had that many close encounters of the nosy question kind; they were avoiding me. I could feel the anger bubbling up and the heat rising from my neck to my face. I wanted to say something or scream or yell, but I decided to stand there in silence with my hands over my mouth until Beth and Tonya left. I then flushed, collected myself, washed my hands, and barricaded myself in my office.

Well, the good news was I probably would not get too many interruptions today. My cell phone rang. It was Annette. How could this day possibly get any worse! I decided to answer. I took a deep breath to prepare myself for her questions and her solution. If I knew Annette, her solution may have included disposal of a body too. Of course, the first question was about how I was doing.

I relayed the conversation that I overheard in the restroom and that if that were the worst thing the day held, I would be okay. She asked if I had notified my supervisor yet. I informed her that he would not be in for another thirty minutes but that if he went to the restroom today, chances were he would hear it from someone else before I said anything to him! To my surprise, she did not ask a whole lot of questions. She said that she loved me and she was there for me. I knew that she and Debbie would always be there for me, and I appreciated the gentleness of her demeanor today. Then she confirmed the dinner plans for Rockaways. I confirmed that I would be there.

Just as she was about to hang up, she said, "We can make a plan for disposing the body tonight during cocktails. See you tonight!" Then she hung up before I could give my reply. There was the Annette that I knew and loved. She was the type to help you out of any mess without asking too many questions. I bet she really did have a shovel in her trunk.

Of course, I was angry and hurt, but I did not want to dispose of Bill's body. Now, Stacey on the other hand…no. That would not solve anything. Bill would pine for his lost love, and I would go to prison. With my complexion, I could not spend my last days in an orange jumpsuit!

My boss made it in around eleven thirty. We talked about his calendar for the rest of the day and tomorrow. He had several phone calls to make, a Zoom meeting at one, and a conference call at three. I decided he had enough on his plate without me unloading on him about the fact that Bill and I were separated. I tried to reassure myself that I was doing him a favor when in fact I just did not want to talk about it. It had already come up on the phone with Debbie and Annette and in a bathroom gossip session. So he retreated to his office to check emails and return calls. I worked on the timeline for the annual business meeting and then decided to break for lunch at twelve thirty.

I decided to stick to my plan. I got my lunch out of the filing cabinet and went to my car to make the short drive to the park. It was a warm day, but there were picnic tables in a shaded area. I parked and made my way to a remote table. I must admit it felt weird *not* working while I ate my lunch. But I decided that this had to be part of my new ritual. I needed to get up from my desk and take a break other than walking to the postage meter or copying machine in the mail room. My lunch was not too exciting, but it was healthy. I had a large salad with grilled chicken and balsamic dressing. I had baked BBQ chips and a banana. I had my healthy bottle of water. So all in all, it was a diet-friendly lunch. Man, what I would not give for a soft, chewy chocolate chip cookie! I did not pack one, so at least for this hour, I would stick to a diet.

I finished eating and sat to enjoy the life of the park. Children were playing on the swing set while their moms talked on park benches. Some health nut was running around the walking trail. Who runs in the middle of the day when it is *hot* and *humid*? People like him with 10 percent body fat. He was cute, but I still think I would have preferred the chocolate chip cookie. I know, I know. With this mindset, I was doomed to be overweight for the rest of my life.

There were squirrels desperately searching for some lost snack. I guess with kids eating in the park, the odds were always high that they would find some tasty morsel! There were birds flitting around the fountain and bird feeders at the edge of the park. To look at this scene, life looked happy-go-lucky and peaceful. Anybody passing by seeing me sitting quietly at the picnic table would assume that my life was happy-go-lucky and peaceful. Well, it just goes to show you that you cannot always judge a book by its cover. Today's scene was the total opposite of the scene with Bill in front of Stacey's house and the scene between Debbie and Bill in my front yard. Yes, the scene that Nosy Nellie had shared with my coworkers. I did not want to go back to the office, but I knew I had to go. I packed up my lunch box and left some chips for the squirrels. I wonder if squirrels even like lower-calorie chips.

I got in my car, cranked the engine, and rolled down the windows to get some cooler air inside until the AC started feeling cooler. I turned up the radio to hear "Before He Cheats" by Carrie Underwood. I pushed the button for another reset station. "Whose Bed Have Your Boots Been Under" by Shania Twain. Really. I switched to another station to find "Lyin' Eyes" by The Eagles. Obviously, God was trying to speak to me through the radio today, and I just was not up for it. I cut the radio off. Maybe silence would be better. Luckily, it was a short drive back to the office, so my brain would not have time to start filling the silence. I knew that it was just a matter of time before the logical brain, the illogical brain, and God were going to have to have a long talk. That was a conversation for a lonely section of beach or a hiking trail; not here, not now. If I started that conversation, I would not be able to go back to work.

I only had to make it through four more hours, and I could put my first day at the office without Bill in my life behind me. I stopped by the restroom and the bottle filling station before heading to my desk. There were no gossipmongers in the restroom, and I thought that was a good sign. I spoke too soon. As soon as I sat down, Jill from HR stopped by. Jill never stopped by, but she stopped by today, and her first question was "How are you doing?"

"I am fine. How are you?"

She said that she had heard about Bill and she was so sorry. I insisted that I appreciated her concern, but that everything would be fine. She said that she would not pry, but that if I needed to talk to someone, all I had to do was stop by to see her.

Of course, she wanted to pry. If she had not wanted to pry, she would have kept walking past my door. I could feel myself getting angry, or maybe I was just embarrassed. I have known Jill long enough to know that she probably did mean well. She was just doing her "mental health check" job for HR. I took a deep breath and thanked her for stopping by. I assured her that if I needed someone to talk to, I knew where to find her. She left.

I worked on a few sections of the job manual for my position. I guess there was no real hurry because as of yesterday, I still had no winning lottery ticket, but I did want to get it done. I figured this could keep me busy for the rest of the afternoon. I was just about to attempt the procedures for setting up the annual business meeting when my boss, Dave, tapped on my door. He asked if I had a few minutes to talk. Well, it was obvious that the gossip grapevine had made it to his office.

He came in, shut my door, and said, "So how are you doing?"

Really. We need to find another opening line.

I said that I was fine. He had heard about what had happened with Bill. He asked if there was anything he could do. I assured him that there was really nothing that could be done. We just had to work our way through it and decide our next steps. He said that he would have never thought something like this would happen. He winked and hinted to me that he had some friends who could take care of the situation for me. He even offered his shovel. Well, that was two offers in the span of five hours. I assured him that would not be necessary.

He asked on a serious note what I needed. I admitted to him that I thought I needed to get away for a few days to think and process. He insisted that I should take all the time that I needed. He offered his house at Isle of Palms. He said it was nothing fancy, but it was second row from the beach with an awesome view of the ocean from the rooftop deck. I said that it was sweet of him to offer, but I could not impose. He said it was no imposition. He reminded me to keep in mind that it was a small beach shack, probably one of the few older homes left intact after Hurricane Hugo. It was simple, but it had two bedrooms in case I wanted to take my girlfriends. It was a really nice offer, and I appreciated it because I needed to spend some time alone to wrap my head around what would happen next. He asked if I wanted to go tomorrow or Saturday. He suggested that I plan to stay a week or so.

"If it's okay with you, I would like to go tomorrow. I am a little uncomfortable around here hearing the gossip in the bathroom and having people ask questions or, worse yet, avoid me because they did not know what to say."

He went to his office and came back with an envelope and handed it to me. The address was written on the envelope. He said that there were two keys inside—the big key for the front door and a smaller key for the shed in the backyard. He said there was a bike and some beach supplies in the shed. There was a great screened in porch and the rooftop deck. It also has a small pool and patio in the backyard. Again, nothing too fancy, but it's a great way to beat the summer heat.

"The TV has a Roku, so you can binge-watch Netflix, Hulu, or Discovery+. There is some bottled water in the fridge, but not much else. Make yourself at home and relax. You can walk one block to get to the Windjammer, the Dingy or the One-Eyed Parrot."

I thanked him for his generosity.

He said that he knew that I knew his cell phone number, but it was written on the envelope if I needed him.

"Do not hesitate to call if you need me." He said that he would not call and bug me because the work would wait until I came back.

I offered to take a laptop to be available to work, and he said he would not allow that because this was my time. He apologized that I had to go through something like this. He said that I could call him if I needed anything or could not figure out how something worked.

I asked if there was an alarm system that I had to worry about, and he just laughed. He said that I would understand when I saw the place; it was nothing fancy that needed to be armed…it was just comfortable and a home away from home. He suggested that I go ahead and go for the day so I could pack and get some groceries together. He said I could always wait and shop at IGA on the island, but it was a little more expensive than shopping in Columbia.

I thanked him and decided to take him up on his offer to go home early. I would not have time to pack since I was meeting Annette and Debbie at Rockaways at five thirty, but it was a chance to avoid any more well-intentioned or otherwise conversations at work today.

Chapter 4

Rockaways (I've Got Friends in Low Places)

When I left the office, I stopped to fill up my car, so by the time I got to Rockaways, it was almost five fifteen. I decided to have a beer before Annette and Debbie got there. I sat down and ordered a beer and looked around the room. I loved their food, but it really did remind me of Garth Brook's song "Friends in Low Places"! Funny, when I was in college, I had never gone to this college bar. The first time I had gone was when I was first married to Bill, and we went to a New Year's Eve party there with his brother and his girlfriend. The one and only time I had schnapps. I had two shots of peppermint schnapps. I remember thinking it tasted like mouthwash. *I know, I am definitely not a sophisticated drinker!* That seemed like a million years ago; it was before Sam was born.

It was not crowded. They put me in a booth near the back right corner across from Zoltar the fortune-teller machine. As soon as I sat down, he started talking. "Let me tell you your fortune. Yes, you. For a small fee, I can tell you your future." Blah, blah, blah.

"Really, Zoltar, where were you thirty years ago? I do not know if you can handle my present or my future. You might want to pipe down a bit."

This was probably not a good sign. I was on my first beer, and I was already back-talking Zoltar. This might be an interesting night. I reminded myself that it needed to be an early night so I could get home and pack to go to the beach. I know that I could get to the beach whenever I wanted to since I did not have a set check-in and check-out time, but the excitement of going to Isle of Palms made me want to get down there early. I reminded myself that an early night meant that I had to go easy on the beers. It was good that I had a chance to talk to myself before Annette and Debbie got there. I was pretty sure that pitchers and shots were going to be their solution for me to get over Bill. If I were strong, I could stand my ground. I had to pack for a week at the beach. Now, I know that I am going to go to the beach to regroup after something terrible, but it was *still* a trip to Isle of Palms. I could not help but be excited. I had been going to the Isle of Palms for summer vacations since I was a kid. That was where we always went for the Fourth of July week.

I was making a list in my head of things to pack when my cell phone rang. I looked down and the caller ID said Bill. Really? It was not bad enough that I had had to endure gossip under the bathroom stall, a talk with HR, a talk with my boss, and a phone call from Annette and Debbie to rehash all the events from last night. I thought I had done well to make it to five thirty. I contemplated voicemail, but I figured I might as well get it over with. I answered on the third ring.

He sounded surprised that I answered and said he thought he would be leaving a message. I gave him a nervous laugh, and then I was silent. That was all I could muster. He said he would not keep me because it sounded like I was in a restaurant.

"Yes, I am meeting Debbie and Annette for dinner, and I should probably get off the phone before they arrived."

He agreed, saying he did not want to relive the screaming match last night. He said that he wanted to meet and discuss next steps. He said that he was moving in with Stacey. He wanted to know if I wanted to keep the house or if I wanted to sell it and split the proceeds. Our house was nothing too fancy, but the mortgage had been paid off for a while. The market was doing well, so we stood to make a pretty good profit since it was in a good area and a good school district. He went on to say that he had contacted a lawyer about starting the process for a divorce. Since Sam was no longer a minor, there would be no child support, and since I had a really good job and would get money from the house, he did not really see any need for alimony.

Okay, I found out last night at eight thirty that he was having an affair, an affair that he had probably been having for a while. In twenty-one hours, he had already decided on the divorce and what I deserved in the settlement. I avoided conversations today because I was afraid that I would fall apart and cry, and he had the entire thirty-year marriage over and divorce planned in twenty-one hours. I had wandered off in my thoughts when something he said snapped me back to reality. It was something about Stacey being so glad that everything was finally out in the open that they could go on with their plans.

I chimed in sarcastically, "Well, I am so happy that Stacy is happy."

Funny, this did not sound a thing like the guy who had apologized for hurting me and stated his love for me on the sidewalk in front of our house. He continued talking about the divorce. I stopped him and said that I appreciated him taking care of all the preliminaries, but nothing would be finalized until I spoke to an attorney. I assured him that I would be back in touch in a few days, and I hung up. I shoved my phone in my purse and finished my beer just as Debbie and Annette were walking up. The waiter came over and took their drink order, and I ordered another one. Maybe it did not have to be such an early night after all.

When the waiter walked off, Debbie asked who I had been talking to. I indicated that Bill had called to talk about finalizing the details of our divorce. Her mouth dropped open; this was one of maybe only two times I had seen her speechless.

Annette, however, was not at a loss for words. She said she figured it was him because my face was so red and I had shoved my phone in my purse like I wanted to kill whoever was on the other end. She proceeded to let loose with a long diatribe of his faults, then she started in on her long list of all the things that deserved to happen to him.

I suggested she just drink her beer and save the list for some other time—when we were not in a crowd of people who could possibly know him and be called as witnesses at our hearing. The waiter came back with our drinks and asked if we were ready to order. I had not even looked at the menu, but Debbie answered for us all. She said "We wanted fried pickles and fried cauliflower as an appetizer" while we decided on our meals. I was guessing this was not going to be a low-calorie meal.

Annette took a few sips of her beer, took a deep breath, and asked what all Bill was proposing for this divorce that he needs immediately that no one knew about this time yesterday. I said that I did not want to go into it here, but we could go back to the house and talk. I insisted that I could not drink too much or stay out too late because I was planning to leave in the morning for the Isle of Palms. I let them know that my boss had offered his place to me.

Debbie asked if she and Annette could go with me for a girls' weekend. I insisted that I needed to go have some me time to come up with a plan, especially if he had already seen a lawyer. I needed to find an attorney I could call tomorrow to take my case. Annette said she might be able to help with the name of an attorney. She said that my boss might be a good resource for that.

I knew she was probably right. He had worked very closely with several attorneys from around the state on foundation business. I just did not know how many of those attorneys would have a specialty field of divorce since our foundation was a nonprofit foundation that offered educational grants for colleges and universities in the Southeast.

I said that they could plan to come down Wednesday or Thursday. That seemed to make them happy! The appetizers came, so we concentrated on eating for a while. My salad from lunch had left me hungry, but I did not want to fill up on fried pickles and cauliflower. The waiter came by to check on us. Debbie ordered another round for the table. I reminded them that this was my last one. The waiter asked if we wanted to put in an order of food. We all ordered the Rockaway pimento cheeseburger and fries. You really cannot eat at Rockaways without ordering the pimento cheeseburger. It is famous. The story goes that George W. Bush stopped by with his secret servicemen to get a pimento cheeseburger! If it is good enough for George W., it is good enough for me! I would not need any fried food for a month after these appetizers and main course!

We drank our beer and talked about the day. They asked if a lot of people asked questions. I admitted that it had not been too bad. I relayed the bathroom gossip incident. They both could not believe that someone from the office had heard about the events of the following evening from Nosy Nellie.

"That is why I had indicated that I wanted to be careful about what we said here."

I retold the story of the head of HR stopping by to check on me because she had heard the story through the grapevine. Then my boss had come to me at the end of the day. I speculated that more people did not stop by because they were afraid I would start sobbing or screaming or something. Except for Jill and Dave, everyone had taken a wide detour around me all day! The only people who had called about it were them and the beloved Bill.

The burgers arrived, and I ordered a Diet coke. Annette and Debbie said I should order another beer, but I reminded them that I had to get home and make a call to Dave for a suggestion of an attorney and then pack and make a shopping list. Annette texted her friend to get some suggestions for attorneys. They both said they would follow me to the house to help me pack. For a few minutes, we ate in silence, the only way to really appreciate the burger! Unfortunately, I had eaten both fried pickles and fried cauliflower, so I was full after half a burger. I pushed the plate aside and determined that the rest would have to go home with me. This could be my "power breakfast" before my road trip.

We finished our meal, packed our to-go containers, and Annette grabbed my check. I insisted that it was not necessary for her to buy my dinner. She laughed and said to me that I should probably save my money for my divorce attorney. I guess I had not given that aspect of the situation any thought. I was getting ready to embark on brand-new territory.

I sighed in nervous agreement and thanked her. We walked out to our cars. I admitted that I had soft drinks and coffee and maybe some wine at the house. I suggested that if they wanted something else, I could stop at the store. Debbie said she would stop by and get something to refresh us during our talking and packing session. I assured them that I was good with water because I had to be able to drive tomorrow! I said I would see them at the house.

CHAPTER 5

Packing Clothes and Unpacking Emotions (Take Me Home, Country Roads)

When I got home, I looked at my watch; it was seven. It should not be too late to call Dave about a suggestion for an attorney. He answered after the first ring. I caught him up on the major details of my conversation with Bill. He said he had a couple of suggestions. He said that he would make a couple of calls and give me a call in the morning.

I really appreciated his help because I had no idea what to ask or expect in this situation. I knew child support was not an option and probably no monthly alimony. But I thought there should be some compensation after almost thirty years of marriage. He told me not to worry and to drive carefully tomorrow. I thanked him and hung up. He had really been not only a wonderful boss but also a great friend over the past twenty years.

I got out of my car, and Annette pulled in right behind me. As I got out of my car, my eyes naturally looked toward Nellie's curtain. It was all dark inside her house; I guess she had gotten enough gossip for one week. Annette joined me and said that her friend had texted her back with a couple of suggestions for a divorce attorney. I wrote the names down and planned to ask Dave about them in the morning. We agreed that he would probably know them all, and I could rely on his recommendation.

We went inside. Annette was comfortable enough at my house to make herself at home while I went to go get into some yoga pants. I loved my job, but I do wish we could wear "comfy pants" there! Yoga pants or pajama pants were my outfit of choice. I changed and went to the kitchen. I asked Annette if she wanted any coffee. She said she could not drink coffee this late because she would be up all night. I did not really have that problem, but if this coffee kept me up, I had enough to think about while I was tossing and turning. I put a pot on to brew and fixed Annette a glass of wine.

She followed me to the great room. We were just about to plop on the sofa when there was a knock at the door. I went to answer it, assuming that it was Debbie. I opened the door and was surprised to find Nosy Nellie. I tried to wipe the shocked look off my face, but I was having a little difficulty.

She said she was sorry to come over so late, but she wanted to check on me. I assured her that I appreciated her concern, but I was fine. She said that she had seen the confrontation between my friend and Bill last night and saw that he left with suitcases.

I informed her I knew that she had seen and heard everything because her niece Theresa had shared the news with a friend at my office. I immediately regretted blurting this out in my anger because she dropped her head in embarrassment and began to cry.

She apologized and said that she had not meant for anything like that to happen. She said that she was upset by what she had seen and heard and she was worried about me. She wanted Tonya to make sure I was okay (so she had called Theresa). She had not intended for Theresa to tell everyone. She said if she had known that Theresa would have handled it that way, she would not have said anything.

I apologized for yelling at her and that it was okay and no real harm was done. I guess the truth had to come out sometime anyway. Maybe Theresa had saved me the trouble of calling a group meeting and making the announcement.

Nellie looked at me and said, "You know, I am so sorry that this happened to you and Bill. You two have been together for so long. If he is such a dog that he would do this to you, you are better off without him. You can do better."

I gave her a hug and thanked her. She asked if there was anything she could do. At first, I didn't think there was anything I needed her to do, but then I thought about it.

"Nellie, I am going to the beach tomorrow to get away and have some time to think about what I am going to do. Will you do me a big favor and keep an eye on the house?"

I knew with Nellie on duty, nothing would happen with the house. She agreed to keep an eye on the house and pick up the mail. She asked how long I would be gone. I let her know that I planned to come back next Friday. She hesitated a moment before she spoke and then asked if Bill was supposed to be there. I assured her that he was not supposed to be there because he had given me his key.

She cleared her throat and said, "Hmmm, well if I were you, I would change the alarm just in case he has a spare. What a dog he turned out to be!"

After thinking about it, I thought she might be right. We had a couple of friends who had keys, and it might be just like him to borrow a key.

Nellie said for me not to worry because she and Bernie would keep an eye on the place. Bernie was her German shepherd, so somehow, I felt everything would be fine. I hugged her and thanked her. She apologized again, and I assured her there was no need to apologize again. She asked what time I was going to get on the road.

"My plan is to get on the road around eight. I wanted to stop by the store and put a few things in the cooler before I got on the road for the Isle of Palms."

Nellie said, "Please be safe on the road and call if you need anything."

I thanked her, and she turned to go home. As she was walking down the sidewalk, Debbie pulled up and got out of the car with a six-pack. Nellie waved to her and kept walking.

Debbie walked up the sidewalk, and the two of us walked in the house. "Wasn't that your neighbor, Nellie? What on earth was she doing here?"

I confirmed that it was indeed Nellie and that perhaps I had judged her too harshly. I shared all that Nellie had said about telling Theresa. I assured her that Nellie now shared her and Annette's long-standing feelings for Bill!

Debbie said that was enough to warm her heart toward Nellie. I also relayed Nellie's suggestion about changing the alarm in case Bill decided to come by. Bill had no idea I was going to the beach, but he *did* think I would be at work all day during the week, so it was a definite possibility.

Well, Nellie now had two new members of her fan club! Debbie took the six-pack to the kitchen and put it in the fridge. She offered me one. I declined and reminded them that I was sticking with coffee. She opened her beer, and I pulled a frosted glass out of the freezer. I asked them if they minded sitting in the bedroom and talking while I pulled clothes together to pack. They followed me down the hall and both kicked off their shoes and jumped up on the bed to get comfortable.

I pulled down a large suitcase and opened it on the bench at the end of the bed. I pulled out two bathing suits and two cover-ups and put them in the bottom of the suitcase. This was the most important fashion ensemble for a week at the beach. Then I added some shorts and T-shirts. I next added one pair of jeans, one pair of capri pants, and a few dressier tops. I added one sundress, two pairs of pajama pants, five tank tops (because those can go with pj's, shorts, and jeans), two yoga pants, and then bras and underwear. I added some socks for good measure. I will wear shorts and a T-shirt and sandals. I would pack a pair of flip-flops, another pair of sandals, and my athletic shoes. With my clothes packed, I pulled out a toiletry bag and packed a brush, makeup, deodorant, shampoo, body wash, sunscreen, and Tylenol. I would fill my vitamin/pill box in the morning and add that to the suitcase.

I put my laptop and charger in the suitcase along with two good summer reads. I pulled out a couple of ball caps and a beach hat. I pulled out some beach towels. I will pack a beach chair in the car just in case there was not one there. Dave had said there were sheets and towels there. He had said there was a washer/dryer and plenty of detergent. He said that everything was there; all I would need to bring was myself, clothes, and food.

We made some small talk while I packed. Annette and Debbie asked me if I was planning to stay longer than a week with all that stuff. I would rather pack it and not need it than need it and not have it! They asked what I planned to do while I was there. I planned to walk on the beach and take some pictures; as I said that, I put my camera bag next to the suitcase so I would not forget it. I planned to come up with a game plan for the rest of my life and relax!

They both laughed. Debbie said it was going to be impossible to relax if I was planning the rest of my life, a divorce, walking on the beach, taking photos, and reading the two books she had watched me toss into the suitcase.

I sighed and admitted that they were probably right; I would probably think about the divorce and spend the rest of the week in my pajamas eating chocolate ice cream. Annette declared that I was allowed two days to wear pj's, wallow in depression, and eat junk food, but after that, I was required to eat right, get out and sightsee, eat at the local restaurants, and take care of me.

I assured her I liked her plan better than mine, and I would try. She said they would call and check on me, and if I was too deep into wallow mode, they were coming down to force me into action. I said that was fair enough.

We walked to the kitchen. Annette fixed herself another glass of wine, and Debbie grabbed a beer. I fixed a cup of coffee and found some chocolate delight in the fridge behind our to-go containers from Rockaways. I asked them if they wanted a little dessert to go along with all the fried food calories we had ingested. They both requested a small bowl, so I fixed three small bowls. We took our dessert and beverages into the great room.

I knew I could not put it off any longer. I decided that if I started the conversation about Bill and my next steps, I could direct the conversation, you know, be in charge of the conversation. Who was I kidding? I have known Annette since sixth grade and Debbie since ninth grade. We would end the conversation when they were ready! I took a deep breath and started.

"Well, it is obvious that Bill has been contemplating divorce for some time if he has already contacted an attorney. He said that he did not see child support or alimony as part of the package. He asked if I wanted to continue to live in the house or sell and split the proceeds. I informed him it was too much to take in after less than twenty-four hours after finding him with his girlfriend. I agree that child support and alimony are not an option. Sam has been out on her own and married for seven years. I have a good job, so I don't see any judge giving me alimony unless they just want to punish him for being the dog that he is." I stopped for a minute to drink coffee and catch my breath.

Debbie went to the kitchen and got another beer and frosted glass. She offered to get me one, but I reminded her that I had to drive in the morning, so coffee was my drink of choice tonight.

Now, I got to sit back and listen while Annette and Debbie gave their commentary. Both had been through a divorce, so they were the experts, and I was the novice. They both agreed on the child support and alimony thing. They did not think I should try to continue to live in the house because if I did, Bill's attorney would probably want me to pay Bill half of the equity. So selling and splitting the proceeds might be smart, especially since the market was looking so good right now. Unfortunately, that would mean I would have to buy something else at a high price. Annette did say I needed to talk to a lawyer about the years that I was the main breadwinner when Bill went back to school to change his major and career path. She said that would be worth some monetary compensation. They both looked at me and asked what I thought my next step would be.

I had no idea. Two days ago, I thought I was a happily married lady, well, married and secure in my future. Now, I had a good job, and that was about it. I admitted that I thought a lot would depend on what the attorney said. I had no idea where I would look for another house or town house or condo or apartment. Bill and I had lived in that house for twenty-five years. I had worked for Dave for twenty years. I had not ever thought of leaving, but I guess I could not really say I would not move to another town/job if I needed to. Man, too many decisions.

Annette and Debbie both said that if I sold the house before I had a place to move, I had a room with them. They said they would split custody so I would not wear out my welcome with either one too quickly. That was a nice offer, I think!

So I had the start of a game plan. Talk to an attorney tomorrow, more than likely sell the house, and then who knew what would happen after that. The three of us were satisfied with the level of life planning we had done. I am confident that the number of beers they had were part of the reason for their level of comfort with the plan. Otherwise, we would have rehashed it a few more times. I offered to let the two of them spend the night since we had all probably had more to drink than we should have to drive. They decided to take me up on it. I gave them both yoga pants and shirts to sleep in. I put their clothes in the washer just because no one should go home in the same outfit, but if they did, it should be clean! They took turns showering, and I put their clothes in the dryer when they were done.

I offered them each their own room or they could stay in one room. They decided to stay in the guest room together because it would be one less bed to strip or make. I reminded them to make themselves at home because I was turning in for the night. I asked them to help me remember to change the house alarm in the morning when we left just in case Nellie was right. I asked how early they wanted to get up. They both said seven so they could get home and change for work.

I thanked them for everything and promised them I would make sure they were up. I showered and got in bed. I was very lucky to have two very good friends who would look out for me. I had also learned I had a good neighbor in Nellie who would look out for me and the house. I hoped I would sleep well. I was tired from the long day, I was anxious about what lay ahead with this divorce thing, and I was excited to be able to breathe in the salt air at Isle of Palms. I squeezed my eyes closed and hoped for the best.

I woke up long before the alarm went off. Why is it that on your days off you can wake up at the "butt crack" of dawn without even trying but then on a workday you sleep through the alarm or hit the snooze at least five times? I am sure the answer would be revealed if I took time for some counseling or something. Who knows after this divorce, counseling might be in order? Deep down, I was hoping that an escape to Isle of Palms would solve all the mental issues! Well, at least some of them!

I got up and washed my face, pulled my hair back, and got dressed. I made my bed and headed to the kitchen to put on more coffee. I would make a full pot this morning because I am banking on Annette and Debbie drinking some or taking some for work! I put the last few items in my suitcase and put the suitcase, camera, and a chair in my car. I pulled out the cooler and wiped it out. I checked in my fridge and cabinets. I did not really have anything to pack in the cooler. Another nail in my marriage coffin; maybe I had not kept the food supply stocked as I should have. To be honest, I was happy with a TV dinner or grabbing a bite out, and Bill was working late or traveling (or so I thought) four nights a week. When I look back now, I should have had all these bells, whistles, alarms, etc. going off. Oh well, today was a new day.

I sat at the barstool and went through the mail that I had brought in last night. Nothing too exciting, mostly junk. This was the reason I liked to open the mail by the trash can. I derived pleasure from raking the mail into the trash can. There were a couple of bills that I also got online. I had to bring those bills so I could change to online paperless billing. Then I came across an envelope from someone I did not recognize. I opened it. A month ago, I had submitted a sample to this company and inquired about writing children's books. Writing had always been a dream of mine ever since my eleventh grade English teacher suggested to me I had a talent for it. Those hopes had been dashed at college when I got a D+ for sloppy writing, bordering on plagiarism. The grade and the comment had crushed me. My teacher explained that I was a good writer, but I needed to pay more attention to my quotes. I had missing quotation marks or they ended too soon. Anyway, after English 102 and that grade, I had put down the pen and paper for a long time. I had always hoped to get back into it. I thought maybe children's writing would be the way to go. Anyway, this letter said that they liked my sample and wanted a completed story in three weeks.

I felt a panic attack coming on; 6:00 a.m. was a little early for a panic attack. I must be getting used to them because I immediately started talking myself down. After all, I had five pages completed. I just had to finish the story in three weeks. I was getting ready to go to IOP—the land of magic. I could sit in Dave's house or at a table in the local bar and write for a few hours each day and knock it right out. This explanation was plausible. I could do this. Panic attack averted! I packed the letter and my writing materials in the pouch of my suitcase.

I started making a list. I planned on drinking a protein shake for one meal a day. Healthy and easy. I put my protein powder and super greens in a bag to take with me. I would pick up a gallon of almond milk on the way to the beach. Okay, now that I knew I had to write every day, I could plan to sit at the bar/restaurant and write every day. I could order lunch to justify using their table every day. Then I could plan for a simple supper at the house each night. I needed to be practical in that I did not want to buy too much and have to pack to bring it home. I could get a rotisserie chicken, a loaf of keto friendly bread, mayo, and maybe some meal bars to keep up the diet-friendly menu. Then yogurt and carrot sticks for snacks. Bottled water and coffee and coffee creamer. Maybe some limes to dress up the water. I knew I did not need to buy wine or beer for the house because I would drink too much. I needed to walk to the bar to get that. I had learned my lesson over the years! If I had to go drink it at a bar or restaurant, I would not drink too much because I had to drive home. If I had a twelve pack in the fridge, chances were I would convince myself that just one more beer would make me feel better until I had consumed six or eight or ten. Then I just felt like crap but had to go to work anyway. So at least I was making wiser choices! I know, I know. True wisdom would be no beers at all, but I am a work in progress.

Now I knew that I would want something sweet. Cannot keep that at the house either. I would go to the ice cream parlor...or get dessert at the restaurant or bar. I know you are saying... you need more willpower. You are probably right. I also know that right now, getting ready to face a divorce and the sale of my family home of twenty-five years was not the time to test my willpower. Baby steps.

I poured myself a cup of coffee, and I heard Debbie and Annette start to stir. They were not moving too fast. I will not judge, but I was thinking maybe too much beer/wine between Rockaways and here. I had pulled their clothes from the dryer, and they both got dressed and fixed coffee. I asked if they wanted eggs/bacon or a protein shake. They both opted for coffee only. They wanted to get home to change and get ready for work.

I asked them if they thought they would be able to come down to IOP Wednesday or Thursday for some "girl time." Debbie and Annette said that they could both come Wednesday. I suggested that we would have dinner at the house and have a fun night at the Windjammer. My plan was to come back Saturday afternoon. So we would have time all day Friday and most of the day Saturday.

I went online and changed the code on the alarm system. I made a note of the change so I would remember if they called! I was praying that Bill would not be mean enough or sneaky enough to come by while I was gone. Debbie and Annette asked if they needed to come by and check the house. I felt sure that "eagle-eyed Nellie" had it covered, so coming by wouldn't be necessary. I felt the least I could do was change her nickname! Afterall, I do believe that she meant well and thought she was looking out for my interests.

We finished our coffee, I washed out the pot, and washed our cups. I had washed a load in the dishwasher last night, so I put those up. I left the dishwasher cracked to dry out. The girls stripped the bed and made it with new sheets. I put the dirty sheets in the laundry basket. I walked around the house. I do not know why, but my mom had always taught me to leave the house looking clean and picked up in case you did not come back. Now if I did not come back, I am thinking that meant I would have died or gone to jail...do you think I would have cared about how the house looked? Nonetheless, I planned to leave it spotless. Otherwise, she might haunt me in my dreams!

I fixed a protein shake for the road. Lunch en route! I set the alarm, and we went out the front door together. I hugged them both. I knew I would see them before the end of next week, but suddenly, I felt terribly alone. We gave each other an extra squeeze and promised to talk by phone in a couple of days. They wanted to give me time to get settled in. I was given orders to call before then if I needed anything. How could I be so lucky to have two friends like this? I was blessed and very grateful!

They each backed out of the driveway and headed to work. I put the empty cooler in my car and walked across the street to speak to Nellie who was waiting at the end of her driveway. I thanked her for her help and assured her that I had changed the alarm code. I gave her a piece of paper with my cell phone number, the alarm company's number, along with Debbie and Annette's names and numbers. I assured her I would be back next Saturday, but I was just a phone call away anytime.

She stated that she would keep an eye on the place but would not bother me because I needed the time to get my plans worked out. I squeezed her hand and thanked her for being so understanding.

I walked to my car and closed the garage door. I put my protein shake and coffee cups in their respective compartments. I hooked my seat belt and cranked my car. I put it in reverse and started on the next phase of my life's adventure. I had no idea what the next step would be. I was terrified, but I felt that with the support of Annette, Debbie, my boss, and now Nellie…I could make this work.

CHAPTER 6

Escape to the Isle (Toes in the Water)

I stopped at Food Lion on the way out and purchased my food items and a bag of ice. I packed the cooler and placed the three bags with nonperishable food items in the back beside the cooler. I hooked my seat belt and cranked the car. I said "On your mark, set, go" and put it in drive. I was on my way. It was a straight shot from Columbia, I-26, to 526, a 112 miles. I put my flash drive in so I could listen to my Isle of Palm mix! Beach music, country music, rock from the '70s and '80s...*my music*!

I had filled up the day before, so I had plenty of gas to get there. I would have to fill up on the island if I planned to drive to Sullivan's or into Charleston, but I would take care of that later. There was not too much traffic for nine in the morning on a Friday. I knew by noon the traffic would get terrible from Summerville on I-26 and then all the way on 526. I hoped I was ahead of the traffic curve.

I was about forty-five minutes into the drive when my phone rang. It was my boss, Dave. I picked up. He asked if I was on the way to Isle of Palms. I said, "Yes, do I need to come back?"

He assured me that I did not need to come back. He said that he had placed a bet with his wife that I would leave at 7:00 or 8:00 a.m. because I was so anxious to get to the beach.

"Well, you would have won that bet because I left the grocery store parking lot at nine. I probably would have left earlier except that Debbie and Annette had spent the night with me to keep me company."

He said that was nice of them to do that and that he hoped they were coming to the beach. I said that Debbie was coming Wednesday night and Annette was coming Friday night. He was pleased they would be there to keep me company. I asked him if he needed me to be on call for work while I was there; I assured him that I had my laptop. He said that he insisted that I *not* be available. He said that anything could wait until the following week.

I expressed my sincere appreciation for his understanding and the generous offer of his house. He said that he was glad to do it and that the house was not much, but he hoped I would enjoy the time to relax and be close to the ocean.

I asked if he had given thought to a possible attorney for my divorce.

He said he had called George Weinstein last night. "He is really the best in the Columbia area. Weinstein had agreed to work on the case. He did some investigating last night and found out that Bill had hired Robert Bloom, another excellent divorce lawyer in the area. Weinstein said that he was going to do some investigative work and give you a call Monday. I gave him your cell number. I hope that was okay."

"Yes, it was fine, I just hope I can afford his fees."

"You don't have to worry about it because Weinstein owes me for several cases I had given him over the years."

"I really appreciate it, but I don't expect you to cash in one of your favors to help me!"

He said he would not have it any other way, that I shouldn't worry but enjoy the weekend, and to touch base with him after I had talked to Weinstein on Monday. He said not to take any calls from Bill between now and then because Weinstein would be in touch with Bloom.

"Thank you! I'll try not to worry. This entire thing just makes my head hurt."

He said, "That was what Isle of Palms was for! Walk down to the ocean…dig your toes into the sand…and just relax!"

That was something I could do!

I sipped on my protein shake and coffee for the duration of the trip. When I crossed over on to Isle of Palms, I was glad I was almost there because I needed a restroom. I drove down to the Windjammer and then took a right. One block up on the corner, my GPS indicated that I was there. Okay, it was smaller than the houses on the ocean front that had been rebuilt because of Hugo, but it was not the dump that Dave described. It was up on stilts so I could park underneath. It was a single-story house with a rooftop deck. I parked. I got out and stretched my legs. I decided to go up and unlock the door so I could use the restroom before I unloaded the car.

I walked up, unlocked the door, and stepped inside. It was homey and not glamorous, but it was beautiful. I made my way down the hall to the restroom. Now that I had used the restroom, I could comfortably look around. It had a great kitchen with an eating area, a large living room, two bedrooms, and two bathrooms. There was a laundry room with a full-sized washer and dryer and sink. There was a screened-in porch with chairs, tables, a hammock, and a swing. There was a door off the porch with a landing and stairs up to a sundeck. It was covered and had four chairs and a table where you could sit and enjoy a rooftop view of the ocean. I came back down and walked through the screened-in porch into the house. I walked through the living room to the kitchen and out a back door. There was a small deck with stairs down to a patio that led to a pool. A very nice pool. Dave made his house sound like some fishing cabin off the grid. This was wonderful. It was not Olympic size, maybe that was why he thought it was not all that fancy. It was perfect. There was a small kitchen area underneath the house and an outdoor shower. I saw the small shed in the corner that he had mentioned. I unlocked it and found lots of pool floats and noodles, a grill, and a golf cart. A golf cart…really. Good to know it was there, but for a week and the short distance to the ocean and the main drag, I would not need the golf cart.

I locked the shed and went back through the house and down the stairs to get my suitcase and grocery bags. I took those in one trip. Then I came back and got my camera and the cooler. I am glad that

I had not brought any more stuff. It was not a long haul, but it was a haul up the stairs and into the house, *but* I was grateful for every step. What a place for a retreat! I put my suitcase in the bedroom, toiletries in the bathroom, and went to the kitchen to unload the cooler. I put the other food items in the pantry. Man, this was a nice kitchen; it was not fancy, but the layout was great. It would be a great place to cook and entertain unless you wanted to cook on the grill and entertain at the pool! I wonder why he did not just live down here. *I would!*

Anyway, I sent him a text to let him know I had arrived safely. I also mentioned that it was a great place, not the fishing shack picture he had painted. I asked if there were any maintenance rules I needed to know for the pool. I knew absolutely nothing about pools and chemical balance or cleaning or anything. I had no more than pressed send when he called.

He said that he was glad I had made it okay and was settled. "Of course, feel free to use the pool, and there were no maintenance issues to worry about. The pool guy would come to clean it Monday morning. His name is Ricky. So do not be surprised when a guy shows up Monday to clean the pool. Truck would be a giveaway anyway, Ricky's Pool Service."

I thanked him again! He said that I deserved it and to look for a call from the attorney Monday. He also said that if I wanted to, and felt comfortable doing it, I could call him about what the attorney said before I moved forward. He shared that unfortunately, this attorney had helped him in a divorce twenty years ago…so he knew that he was a good attorney from firsthand experience.

"I really appreciate everything. I will be in touch."

When I hung up, I had to wonder that in this divorce twenty years ago, was my boss "me" or "Bill"? Oh, well. I was not going to dwell on that. I will hear from the attorney Monday. I was hoping for a peaceful Friday, Saturday, and Sunday while I waited.

I decided I was going to be the total beach tourist. I put on my bathing suit and cover-up. I put sunscreen on and put the tube in a beach bag. I put two beach towels, a bottle of water, and my laptop in the bag. I put my cash, credit cards, and ID in a small bag along with the house keys and put those in the bag. I locked up the house and headed out for lunch and then the beach. I hoped I could eat and type for a while inside a cool bar then head out to the beach around four thirty or five. I am fair-skinned, so intense sunbathing was out of the question for me.

It was a very short walk, about one half of a block to the main drag. I walked past the Windjammer, and suddenly all kinds of college and post-college memories flooded my head. Back in those days, you could drink at eighteen. I remember a dark room, the smell of stale beer, and very loud music. Then later, I went to an Edwin McCain Concert there with Bill and Sam. I remember standing for the concert for almost three hours. There was beer and great music and lots of great memories. I would have to stop in there during my stay here! I am sure that Debbie and Annette will insist on a visit while they are here.

I walked down to the One-Eyed Parrot. It is and will always be my favorite beachfront dive, but I have always loved it. One time I took my mother there. I think she was around eighty-nine at the time. She wanted to go to the beach, so we stayed in a hotel with an ocean view. We walked down for her to see the ocean, and then we ate a cheeseburger at the One-Eyed Parrot. She loved it. I walked in and found a table inside with a view of the ocean. Memories of my mom flooded my memory.

It was not busy at all. It was me, the bartender, and four other customers. Maybe I was ahead of the busy rush. The bartender walked over and took my order. I ordered a local IPA on draft and a cheeseburger and fries. So much for not needing any more fried food for a month after Rockaways. Oh well, this was vacation. Those calories don't count, right?

He brought my beer, and I asked him if it would be okay if I sat here for a while and typed on my laptop, and I added that I would keep ordering beer.

He looked at me and said, "Sugar, you do whatever you want as long as you keep ordering beers."

I started to make a smart-ass comment about the whole "sugar" thing, but I decided a table inside out of the direct sun would be great for typing. So instead of fighting back to stand up for feminine rights, I said thanks. I must admit, as he walked back to the bar, I thought he was cute. He looked to be around fifty, so we were close to the same age.

I finished my lunch, which was delicious. I drank a couple of beers and then started typing. I started by pulling up the sample I had submitted. I had to figure out how to make that sample into an entire children's book. So I did what I did best. I made a list but this time in the form of an outline. If I went by the outline, I was about 35 percent through the entire children's story. So I set my laptop for a double screen so I could follow the outline, and I began adding to the story. This process sounded a lot easier than it was. I sat there for forty-five minutes and just stared at the screen. Mr. Personality the Bartender came by and asked if I wanted another beer.

I said, "Yes and thank you."

I looked at my watch; it was two. The sun was still bright for this pale face to go out in the direct sun, so I decided to try to work for at least an hour or two. They did not seem too busy, just a few people that seemed to be locals or regulars. I guess the tourists went to Coconut Joes. I was busy typing a new train of thought, and I did not notice the bartender come up behind me. He put the beer down and startled me.

He looked at me and said, "Talking turtles…really, is that what you are typing about?"

He caught me off guard, and without thinking, I said, "Yes, I am typing about talking turtles…not that it is any of your business!"

He proceeded to tell me that I was typing in his bar, so it was his business.

I held my breath for a minute and then told him I was working on a children's book. He looked surprised, and I felt he didn't believe me. I asked him who else would be reading about talking turtles.

He said it may have been a children's book subject, but the sentences he read sounded too grown-up for any child to want to read them.

"You know, you probably should not read other people's stuff on their laptops."

He grinned and shrugged his shoulders. He asked if I had ever written a children's book before.

"No, I haven't, have you?"

He said he had not written one, but if he had seen that book as a child, he would not have read it. He could tell that I was offended. He quickly apologized and said that he meant no offense, but maybe I should look at the book for a child's point of view. He asked if I had children.

"I have a daughter, not that it is any of your business."

He said that maybe I should try to write it like it was a bedtime story I was telling her. He added "I'm just sayin'" and walked away.

Well, this was twice in one week that I had been angry at a man. First Bill and now this guy, a bartender that I did not even know his name. I slammed my laptop shut and drank my beer. I finished my beer, and I decided that I needed to pack up my things and go look at the ocean. I finished my beer, and he came by and asked if I was ready for the check.

I asked him for the check. He started to walk away but turned back toward me and said, "Listen, I didn't mean to offend you. I was just suggesting a different way to look at the story. I wish you the best in your writing. Are you in town for a while?"

I told him I was staying here for the week. He invited me to come by and write each day if I wanted a change of scenery from the house. He said that he opened at ten thirty and I could type and then eat lunch and go to the beach. He added that I would need lots of sunscreen with my fair skin.

I decided not to jump down his throat for the fair-skinned comment because I was pale…very pale. I took a deep breath and thanked him for the offer. I thanked him and said that I would be by tomorrow and I would take his idea for a storyline into consideration.

He smiled and took my credit card. He came back with the bill. He smiled and said that his name was William. I thanked him for lunch and said my name was Maggie.

As I walked out the door, he shouted, "See you tomorrow, Maggie. I can't wait to hear about those turtle adventures."

There were a few customers in the bar, and they all looked at us like we were crazy.

I simply smiled, waved, and said, "Yes, see you tomorrow."

He stopped me and asked if I was going down to the beach with a laptop. I asked if he had a problem with that. He said the heat and sun were not all that good for a laptop. He asked if I wanted to leave the laptop with him behind the bar while I went to the beach.

I looked at him with a puzzled look. "I don't know you that well. Why would I leave my laptop with you?"

He said that he was just offering to keep it safe while I went to sunbath and play in the ocean.

Now I knew he was making fun. I look nothing like someone who sunbathes. "I just want to go look at the ocean and stick my toes in the water."

He smirked and said, "And your ass in the sand."

I should have known he would know my Zac Brown reference! I smiled and said, "Something like that!"

He suggested I go dip my toes in the water and feel the sand beneath my toes, sit, and relax for a while. He said that I could come back for dinner. I thanked him but declined since I was staying nearby, and I had chicken and salad there to throw together for dinner.

He said that I could stop by for a beer or two and get my laptop and then go eat at home. Again, I said that I was not sure because I did not know him from Adam. He promised to guard my laptop. I asked him to guard it with his very life because if I lost the start of my turtle story, I would not be able to finish it.

He offered to finish the turtle story while I was gone. "Ha, ha. You are a bartender, what do you know about turtles?" He informed me that the sea turtles hatched here every year.

I felt silly that I did not know that. I had come to the beach since I was a child, but I must admit I was never there during turtle-hatching season. "My apologies. You are more than qualified to complete my story, but I want a chance to try. I tell you what. I am going down to look at the ocean. It is four thirty. I am going to look at the sea, sand, and sky, contemplate life, and then I will be back here at five thirty for two beers."

He laughed and said that he was really impressed that I could do all that in just over an hour.

"Well, I'm a fast worker!"

He winked and said, "That's good to know!"

I felt a witty comeback on the tip of my tongue, but I thought it was best to keep it to myself. I thanked him and handed him my laptop. I was so glad that this was my smaller laptop from work with no personal files on it. I had my personal laptop in my suitcase.

He gave me a wink and insisted that it would be safe with him right here behind the bar when I came back at five thirty. He said that if I decided to eat dinner there, he had grilled chicken and salad that he could serve me, and there would be no dirty dishes for me to wash.

"It's a very tempting offer, and I will contemplate while I was contemplating life at the seashore!"

He suggested I walk out the back to the deck and then use the bar's boardwalk down to the ocean.

I nodded, waved, and walked toward the back deck. I put my sunshades on and paused on the deck. I had to let my eyes adjust from being inside the bar. It was dark and cool, a great retreat from the hot sun of July on the Isle of Palms, but to be honest, a vampire could live in there 24-7. It was that dark. Of course, then my mind wandered to a *Twilight* moment…how the Cullen family would glisten and shimmer when they stepped outside the bar onto the deck. Wow, my mind could wander. This was one of the many times I was grateful no one could read my thoughts!

I walked down the boardwalk and stepped onto the beach. It was beautiful. The sky was bright blue with a few fluffy white clouds. The sky met the ocean. It looked blue green today. There were people out riding the waves and floating. Families were out on blankets and under umbrellas all over the sand. It was low tide, so there was a huge sandy beach area. The dunes were bleached white, and then there were yards of darker wet sand. I have to say as I stood there and took in the scene, it took my breath away. The beach was alive with laughter and the sound of crashing waves, but it was peaceful all at the same time. I walked out on the sand. I kept my flip-flops on until I got to the wet sand because I knew that the bleached white sand was glistening in the sun because it was scorching hot! I stepped onto the wet sand and picked up my shoes. I walked straight down to ocean so I could feel the water.

Now anyone who knows me knew I enjoyed looking at the ocean and feeling it up to about knee level. I preferred a pool to a lake or the ocean because you could see if there was anything in there swimming around your knees waiting to take a bite out of you. I knew that may be overdramatic, but I had watched *Shark Week* and *Jaws* enough to know they were out there lurking just under the surface. But I stepped out into the water. It felt so cool and refreshing. I walked along the edge enjoying the feel of the water and enjoying the sound of all the beachgoers enjoying the sun. There were plenty of sun worshippers out there baking in the sun. That was something I did as a teen but not anymore. I was paying for those teen years of sun worship now with precancerous spots here and there.

I walked for a while and noticed a large piece of driftwood up on the beach under the pier. I thought this would be a great place to sit and think without being in the direct sun. I made my way up and sat down. It was so peaceful watching the waves crash into the shore. It was so much better than being at work dealing with deadlines and staff crises. I loved my job, and I was very thankful to have it, especially now that my future with Bill had ended abruptly. But in the back of my mind, I had always wished for a Publishers Clearing House or lottery win to see me through.

Well, my thoughts had broached the subject I had been trying to avoid. Bill. What was I going to do? I guess there was not a whole lot to think about until I talked to an attorney. I think it was going to be a logical decision for us to sell the house and split the proceeds. After that, where would I move? Sitting here, drinking in the sun and scenery, here seemed like a good choice. I laughed out loud to myself because a move to the beach was not going to be an option when my job was in Columbia. I decided that all this could wait until Monday or Tuesday.

As I sat there, my phone rang. I fished around for it in my tote bag. It was Debbie. I guess I knew that before I even looked at it. I answered.

"What ya doing?'" were the first words out of her mouth.

I chuckled and said that I was sitting on a piece of driftwood under the pier looking at the ocean. She asked if there were any hot guys there.

Without thinking, I said, "Well, not on the beach." Without meaning to, I had peaked her attention.

She asked *where* I had seen some hot guys if it was not on the beach. I tried to brush it off by saying that she misunderstood me, that I meant I had not seen any. She pressed.

"Fine, I ate lunch and typed a bit at the One-Eyed Parrot. The bartender was a little interesting."

She literally squealed in excitement. I warned her not to make something out of nothing, after all technically, I was still a married woman. She added that my husband was currently shacking up with his girlfriend and filing for divorce, so she thought it was okay to make something out of it.

"Just drop it. How is work going?"

She said, "It was boring but busy."

She was not going to be able to get away until Thursday, but she would be there Thursday morning if it were still okay. I said that it would be great!

"Dave really downplayed his house too much. It is great, and it has a pool."

She said that would be great and she was looking forward to it. She said she had to go but added, "If you need me before Thursday, call. Are you sure you are okay?"

"All things considered, I'm fine. I love you, and I'll see you Thursday."

"You better text me if something, anything, happens with the bartender. What's his name?"

"His name was William."

"Oh, William…Liam… Good name! keep me posted."

"Stop it! I'll see you Thursday!"

I looked at my watch; it was five thirty. Time flies when you are in the presence of the ocean. I stood up and started the walk back to the One-Eyed Parrot. When I got up on the deck, I rinsed my feet and put my flip-flops back on. I walked into the bar, took off my sunglasses, and waited for my eyes to adjust.

William waved and called out, "Welcome back! Grab a table, and I'll bring you your laptop and a beer."

I found a table in the corner, and he placed the beer and my laptop in front of me.

"Hey, no need to worry because I kept the laptop safe. I even finished the turtle story for you!"

I guess my mouth dropped open because he laughed and told me not to worry, the story was still waiting for me to finish. I laughed and confessed that I might need some suggestions when I started back on it tomorrow. He said that he would be ready and willing to help with all his turtle expertise.

I thanked him for the beer and relaxed in the chair. I guess I did not realize how tired I was. Yesterday had been a long day, followed by a long night with Debbie and Annette. Then I started my day early with the drive down here.

There was a guy playing guitar and singing in the corner. I was enjoying listening and relaxing.

William came back and asked if the beer was okay.

"It's fine, but I'm going to stop with just the one beer."

He asked if I wanted some dinner.

"I appreciate the offer, but I'll just fix something at home."

He said he did not mean to pry but asked if I had driven in today.

"Yes, I drove in from Columbia this morning."

He suggested a salad and grilled chicken from here for tonight. He said that the food I had in the fridge would be there tomorrow.

I did not need much convincing. I agreed to the salad with grilled chicken with balsamic dressing. I asked for a Diet Coke. He went to put my food order in and brought me a Diet Coke. I thanked him and asked about the singer.

He said, "He was a local guy from Sullivan's Island."

"I really like the music!"

"Good, you just sit, relax, and enjoy, and your salad will be ready in a minute."

He was true to his word. He brought the salad and asked if I needed anything else.

"No, thank you, the salad looked perfect, and I don't need anything else."

I ate my salad and listened to the music. He finished his first set at seven, and I had finished my dinner. William came by to see if I needed anything else.

"Just the check." I paid my bill and thanked him for guarding my laptop and providing dinner! I got up to leave.

He asked where I was staying.

"Just down the road."

He asked if I wanted a ride; he offered to drive me home in his golf cart.

"That won't be necessary."

He said that Larry would watch the bar, he could drive me to my door, and then he would come back to finish the dinner service and close.

I did not know what it was about this guy, but I felt comfortable with him. Besides, it was a golf cart and not a car. I could jump out if I needed to.

"Thank you, I'll take you up on your offer. It's been a long day, and I guess I am a little more tired than I thought."

He called Larry to tell him that he would be right back. We walked out to the cart, and I directed him to drive toward the Windjammer and turn right. The house was on the corner one block down. We drove there, and he pulled up in front of the stairs.

He looked at me and said, "So you are staying at Dave Nelson's place? How do you know Dave?"

"I work for Dave. How do you know Dave?"

He said that he had gone to school with Dave. He said all the islanders knew Dave and his family. The house had belonged to Dave's parents.

All I could think to say was "It's a small world" and laughed. I thanked him for the ride.

He said that he would wait to see that I got inside okay.

"You really don't have to stay, I'll be fine."

He said that he would make sure. He said there were just so many people on the island this time of year that he wanted to make sure I was home safely. "Well, 'home' for now anyway if you know what I mean. So are you still planning to come sit at the bar and type tomorrow? I'll be glad to help you with your turtle facts!"

"I will come by around eleven tomorrow to type. Thank you for your hospitality at the bar, a great dinner, and the ride home."

I turned and went upstairs. I unlocked the door, turned to wave good night, and went inside. Well, today had been a very interesting day. I had not sulked about my divorce, and I had not gotten any work done on my children's book either. But I had stuck my toes in the water and the sand and met a very interesting turtle expert.

I was going to take a shower to get all the sunscreen and sand off, then I was going to bed. Maybe tomorrow I will text my boss and ask him about his former classmate.

CHAPTER 7

A Brand-New Day (I Can See Clearly Now)

I should not have been surprised that I woke up early. After all, I was on vacation, sort of. I know the real reason I was here was to make plans for the divorce, but for the weekend at least, I was going to pretend it was a vacation. I was going to go for a walk on the beach this morning then come back and drink a protein shake. I would put a pot of coffee on so it would be ready when I got back from my walk. I would take my camera so I could take pictures of anything exciting on the beach.

Now that I had my mental to-do list complete, I could get up. I crawled out of bed and dressed for a walk. It was going to be a hot day, so shorts and a tank top would be in order. I pulled my hair back in a ponytail and put a baseball cap on. The sun was just coming up, but I knew I had to put some sunscreen on. I started the coffee, grabbed a bottle or water, my camera, and my keys. I decided to take the camera with one lens without the heavy bag.

I decided to go down the path to the beach behind the Windjammer. I did not want to go down to the One-Eyed Parrot in case William was there. I did not want him to think I was stalking him. I felt comfortable with him, but I had to try to keep everything on a friendly level. I did not have time for complications. It was high tide, so there was less beach than yesterday afternoon. There was still plenty for a walk. There were already people out on the beach jogging, riding bikes, and walking dogs. I decided to go left and walk out past the pier. I took a few pictures of the sunrise and the pier. As I walked, I took pictures of the little sandpipers playing at the water's edge. I took a few pictures of dogs playing in the water. It was a beautiful morning early enough that the temperature was comfortable. I decided to cut off my camera and concentrate on getting some steps in. It had been quite some time since I had walked, so I was going to have to get used to it. I knew that no matter how much or how little I walked, I would be a little sore tomorrow. Maybe I could start with a mile and a half today.

Without the distraction of taking pictures, I had plenty of time to think about my situation. Today was Saturday, and I knew that the attorney would be calling Monday. I wonder how much he has been able to find out about Bill's lawyer and their intentions. Then my mind drifted to the house. If we put it on the market, we were going to have to figure out what we each wanted to take from the house. There were twenty-five years' worth of memories and "junk" there. Luckily, we had cleaned out the attic and garage last summer, so there was less "junk" than there had been. Where would I go? Another house or a condo? Maybe a town house or an apartment. Everything but another house would mean that someone else could do the yard work. That sounded like a good option. What if Bill wanted the house? I guess he would have to pay me my portion of the value. If he bought the house, that would mean he would move Stacey into the house. I do not know how I felt about her being in my house… in my bedroom. I guess that part was not up to me.

I checked my Garmin. All my thinking had taken my mind off the walk. I had walked almost a mile. I decided to drink some water and turn around. The final walk would be closer to two miles. Now I just had to make it back! There were more and more people coming out to walk. Now I can speak to people and pet dogs and use that as a distraction from the walk and the divorce. It worked well. When I looked up at the shore, I was already back to the condos and the One-Eyed Parrot. It looked like William was on the back deck hosing it off. I guess that was part of his morning ritual. I wonder if he just worked there or if he owned it. I wonder if there was a Mrs. William. I wonder what his last name was. While I was pondering all my "William" questions, I had unconsciously made my way up closer to the boardwalk.

He turned and saw me and waved. I waved back. He dropped the hose and walked out on the boardwalk. "Good morning, Maggie. Are you out doing research for your turtle book?"

"Very funny. No research, just an early morning walk and a few photos."

He pointed to my camera and commented that it looked like a nice camera. I thanked him and said that I had taken a photography certificate course from TEC a few years ago and the camera and a couple of lenses had been my graduation present to me.

He said that I would have to bring the camera with me when I came to write so he could look at the photos.

"I'll bring it. Well, I will see you later. It is time for me to get back to some much-needed caffeine. I'll see you around eleven or eleven thirty, is that okay?"

"That will be fine. Your table and the coffee will be ready by ten thirty when we open."

I thanked him and headed down the beach to the path behind the Windjammer.

I walked up the path and around the building to the main road. I tried to stomp my feet a bit to get rid of some of the sand. I headed toward the house. I went upstairs, took my shoes off on the porch, and went to the kitchen. I took the baseball cap off and poured a cup of coffee and added my sugar-free Italian cream coffee creamer. I put it on the counter and went to check my hair.

All I can say was that I was glad I did not take the hat off in front of William. I stopped brushing my hair and looked in the mirror. *What was I saying? It did not matter what he thought of my hair. I barely knew him. To be honest, I knew nothing about him except that he went to school with my boss. What did it matter what he thought? Why was I so happy to see him on the deck this morning?* I was asking myself entirely too many questions before my first cup of coffee had even started to kick in.

I decided it was best to table those thoughts, finish my coffee, and fix my protein shake. I decided to check emails while I drank my breakfast. Nothing much but spam in my personal email mailbox. I checked work email out of habit. I replied to a couple of them and forwarded one to Dave that he needed to follow up on.

In less than five minutes, I had a reply email from Dave. It simply said, "Why are you checking your work email? Stop. Enjoy the beach. Relax."

I wrote back, "It's just habit. I will stop. I am enjoying the beach. I took a two-mile walk this morning. I am more relaxed than I have been in a while. Thanks again for the use of the house. By the way, do you know a guy named William who bartends at the One-Eyed Parrot? He may be the owner. I did not get his last name or ask his job title. He said he went to school with you. Anyway, call me if you need anything at the office."

I had stopped to finish my protein shake and pour another cup of coffee when my cell phone rang. It was Dave. I picked up the call. He asked if I was having fun and if everything was okay with the house. I told him it was great to be back at the beach and the house was wonderful.

"About William. Did you two talk at the bar?"

"I ate dinner there, and we talked." I decided to leave out the part about me typing there all afternoon and the ride in the golf cart just in case he was getting ready to tell me he was a serial killer or something.

He laughed and said that William's last name was Riley. He had graduated from high school with him in Mt. Pleasant. He said that he was a nice guy and he owned the bar. I sighed and admitted that I think I called him a bartender to his face. He laughed and said that he was a very good bartender.

"Maggie, I am glad you met him. He will be a good friend. Just be careful."

"What do you mean be careful?"

"Well, to be honest, if you were to get involved with someone, Bill would probably try to use it against you. Even though the fact that he has moved in with a girlfriend would not help his case."

"I appreciate the advice. I have no intention of getting involved."

He encouraged me to enjoy the weekend and do some sightseeing in Charleston. "I know you probably brought that camera of yours! Go to a plantation or down to the market. Be a tourist! Monday, let me know what the attorney says and stop checking your emails!"

I thanked him and hung up. William Riley. Wonder if he was related to the former mayor? Oh well, do not ponder. Do not get involved.

I rinsed my cup and glass and put them in the dishwasher. I cut off the coffee. I would warm up another cup later. I made the bed and looked at the photos I had taken. The sunrise photos were pretty good! I had a couple of good shots of a black Lab and the sandpipers. It was only nine, so I decided to sit in the swing on the front porch and read one of the books I brought. I had just grabbed two off the shelf. Both were murder mysteries. Maybe a murder mystery was not such a good idea since I was staying in a strange house all by myself. I decided that I would go to the store later and get some magazines or a romance novel. That would not be scary! Or maybe a romance novel would be a bad idea. What were these feelings I was starting to have for William? I was hoping it was just friendship, but then Dave have given me that ominous warning.

Anyway, I checked my laptop. It needed charging. So I put it on to charge so it would be ready by eleven thirty. While it charged, I decided to call Sam. When I looked at my watch, I realized it was an hour earlier there. She would be teaching a class. I decided to send her a text to ask her to give me a call this afternoon. I needed to talk to her about Bill and the divorce. I hoped that he had not beat me to it. I hoped that she would have called if he had said something to her.

I checked my texts. Debbie and Annette had both sent me a text while I was on my walk. I guess they felt like they needed to call or text every day to make sure I had not fallen into a deep depression or something. I responded that I was fine and that I had gone for a walk and was going to try to work on the children's book for a bit today. I assured them I would call them tomorrow.

At eleven thirty, I gathered my laptop and a notebook and pen to head out for the One-Eyed Parrot to work on my children's book. I said a few prayers that the ideas would flow today. The publisher had given me until next week to get them a first draft. William was right; I guess, I was overthinking it. It needed to be like a bedtime story in print. I would work from the outline that I had submitted and try to come up with something today. Today was Saturday; that was plenty of time to meet the deadline, right? It was not like I was writing the great American novel; it was a children's story.

I had taken one last look in the mirror before walking out the door. I brushed my hair and put on lip gloss. Now, I have not put on lip gloss in years. Why suddenly was it so important that I have on lip gloss? My brain knew the answer. I was becoming attracted to William. How could this have happened in one day? Maybe it was because I had been so lonely for so long. Still not a good reason. I had to remember what Dave had said. "Be careful." I argued back and forth with myself all the way to the bar. When I opened the door, William was there to meet me. In that instant, all the logical reasons for not getting involved slipped out of my mind.

We exchanged greetings, and he pointed to "my table" in the corner. He had it cleared off so I would have room for my laptop and notes. He followed me to the table with a cup of coffee and creamer. I thanked him and said that I could get used to this kind of red-carpet treatment.

He took a bow and said, "Just doing my part, ma'am. I don't want anything to stand in the way of the great turtle story!"

I smiled. Coffee would probably help, or at least it would not hurt! He said to yell when I got hungry or if I needed anything. Otherwise, he was going to give me space for the creative juices to flow.

I opened the laptop to a blank page and stared at my notes. What did I have so far? I had Tilly the Turtle who lived in a pond on Farmer Brown's farm. So far I had Tilly, a pond, and a farm. Why had they selected me to write a children's book? I had submitted a short paragraph about a turtle finding out how important it was to listen to her parents. They said they wanted me to expand on the idea and submit a draft in a couple of weeks. What was I thinking? I stared at the blank screen and just sighed. William chuckled and asked if

I needed anything. I confessed that I needed him to write a story about a turtle who found out how important it was to listen to her parents…by Thursday!

He told me that he thought I was still just overthinking it. I admitted that maybe I just had too much on my mind with the whole separation, divorce, selling the house, figure out what I am going to do with my life thing!

"Wow, it's just a lot to wrap your head around!" He agreed that all that might be suppressing the creative juices. He asked when I was supposed to hear from the attorney.

"He is supposed to call Monday."

"I think you need to have a vacation day to loosen up and enjoy yourself, then you would be better prepared to settle down and write. Have you ever written down your thoughts and feelings about the separation/divorce and all that went along with it?"

"Well, since I only found out Wednesday night that my husband of twenty-seven years has been having an affair and I only found out yesterday that he had already contacted an attorney to file for divorce, no I have not written down my thoughts and feelings."

"Wow, I had no idea it was all that 'new.'" I am sorry. That is why you cannot write right now. I know when I went through my divorce, it helped me to write it all down in a letter. My sister suggested that I journal because when she divorced her husband, her counselor had suggested she write a letter and then burn the letter."

I told him that I was sorry to hear he had gone through that and that I did not realize he was divorced.

"Well, we just met yesterday, so there are lots of things you don't know about me. However, today is not the day for *my* story! I'll save that one for another day." He leaned in and said that he had an idea. "How about for now, I get you a piece of chocolate cake. You work on a letter to Bill or a diary entry, however you want to frame it. Then you and I take an outing to clear your head."

Well, since I have never been someone to turn down anything chocolate, it sounded like a plan. "William, you had me at the word 'chocolate,' but what kind of outing did you have in mind? Don't you have to work?"

He smiled and put his hand on his chest and said, "Well, since I own the place, I think I can take some time off."

He yelled over to Larry at the bar and asked if he thought he and Stewart could handle it. Larry said they would be fine and if it got busy, he could call one of the girls to come in and wait tables.

William thanked him and smiled at me. "See, it is covered."

I smiled and said that we had the chocolate and the restaurant covered, but I still did not know what he had in mind for the outing. He paused a moment and said, "I think that we should go out to Middleton Place Plantation today for lunch. You can bring your camera, and we can go on a garden tour or walk around. They have lots of plants, trees, and animals for you to photograph. Then we can go out to my sister's place. I have been promising my niece and nephew I would come visit. Maybe we can have story time and give you an idea for your story. They love to make up stories, and I bet my niece, Kristie, can come up with a good turtle story. We can eat there tonight. Tomorrow, we could go to the aquarium so you can see some turtles and go to the market. How does that sound?"

It sounded great, but I was not sure how William's sister would feel about us dropping in on her and staying for dinner. William gave me a sheepish grin and admitted that he had talked to his sister about the idea last night.

"Well, it sounds like you have a plan, and I am looking forward to it. Since we have lunch and dinner on the agenda, I will save the calories by skipping the chocolate cake, but I reserve the right to get a piece of cake later during my stay."

So with the bar covered and a plan in place. I gathered up my laptop and notes. He said he would drive me to the house so I could get my camera. He pulled in behind my car, and I invited him to come in while I got my camera. He suggested that I throw a bathing suit and a change of clothes in a bag because his sister had a pool. I must have had a terrified look on my face because he asked me what was wrong. I took a deep breath and admitted that I was nervous enough with the thought of being in a bathing suit around him since I did not know him that well then on top of that I had no idea who I was going to meet at his sister's.

He shook his said and said, "It would be fine. Stop overthinking *everything* and pack the bag."

So with my marching orders, I packed a bathing suit, beach towel, cover-up, sunscreen, hat, and a change of clothes. I put a few toiletries in the bag. I put the bag on the chair closest to the door along with my camera bag. I put my laptop and notes down into the bag with my bathing suit so it would not look like I was moving in. I threw the laptop charger in too. I asked him if he wanted any water or Diet Coke. I apologized that those two were the only options unless he wanted coffee. He said he would take a bottle of water for the road.

He said that the place looked nice and that he had not been inside since high school. He laughed and said it was pretty much the same except newer furniture. I told him he was welcome to walk around and look. He took a brief tour before walking out to look at the pool.

"Between the pool and that front screened-in porch, you can vacation right here without even walking to the beach."

I did agree that it was a great place. We were getting ready to walk out the door when my phone rang. It was Sam.

"I better take the call because it is my daughter."

"Of course, take the call and take your time."

I walked into the bedroom and answered. We chitchatted for a bit about the classes she was teaching at the university. We talked about my job. She asked about her dad, and my heart stopped. I did not go into any details, but I simply said that he had moved out and wanted a divorce.

She was quiet, but when she spoke, she said that she was not all that surprised. She said he had seemed distant for a long time and that we both seemed to be living apart under the same roof. That statement hit me hard. I knew it was not an ideal marriage, but had it been that bad? Had it been that obvious to everyone but me? She asked if I was okay.

"I am in shock more than anything else. Dave offered his house at Isle of Palms to me for the week to collect my thoughts and myself. I am just sorry that things have ended the way they have."

"I am sorry, too, but I will always love you both no matter what. I wanted to call to make sure everything was okay, but I have to go to my next class. It is a lecture on sea turtles."

We told each other that we loved each other and agreed to talk Monday after I talked to the attorney. When I hung up, I made a mental note that she was another resource I would have to confer with for my turtle book!

I walked back out to the living room, and William was checking his phone. I apologized for the delay. He asked if everything was alright.

"Sure, everything will be fine." I cleared my throat and added, "Obviously, I was the only person in the state that did not realize my marriage had been over for quite some time."

He chuckled and said that if it made me feel any better, he had not suspected, so that was two of us. He gave me a wink and a devilish grin! He grabbed the bags, and I picked up the two waters. He held the door for me and set it to lock.

He opened my door and put the bags in the back seat. He hopped in and said "Let the adventure begin" as he backed out of the driveway. He asked if I had ever been to Middleton Place.

"I went to a luncheon there when I was twelve, so pretty much it's a first-time visit!"

He said, "We could eat at the restaurant and then take a garden tour. It did not matter what season, there would always be flowers in bloom."

He suggested that maybe next week we could go to Cypress Gardens or Magnolia Plantation. I said that sounded like a good plan.

When we pulled in, I could not help but gasp. He asked if something was wrong. I assured him that nothing was wrong; it was just that the buildings were beautiful. I confessed that I loved to take pictures of old buildings.

"Then it's a good thing you are in Charleston. You may have to stay another week or two or four to photograph it all!"

Even though that sounded wonderful, I knew that I had to get back to Columbia next week and deal with next steps on the house.

I just smiled and nodded; there were too many thoughts rolling around in my head to try and respond. He encouraged me to bring my camera into the restaurant because the architecture was too pretty to miss a photo opportunity! I am glad that I had switched to a small crossbody bag instead of my usual humongous purse. He parked and got out to open my door. I walked beside him, and he grabbed my elbow as we were going up the steps. I looked at him with a puzzled look.

"I am sorry, ma'am, I am a Southern gentleman, and with these uneven steps, I have to be ready to protect and defend."

I just shook my head and added, "Why, William, I do declare you spoil a girl so!"

We both had to laugh at our perfect *Gone with the Wind* moment. When we walked in, they greeted him by name and walked us to a private room. He leaned down and told me not to worry because there would be time for pictures. The waiter pulled my chair out and put the napkin in my lap. I suddenly felt that with my shorts and tank top, I was terribly underdressed. Of course, he was in khaki shorts and a One-Eyed Parrot T-shirt, so it was okay. The waiter said that he would give us a minute to look at the menu and would return.

William looked at me and said, "Well, first, I guess I never divulged my last name. It is Riley. Yes, old Charleston name. I know you are wondering about my relatives. I am only a very distant relative of Governor Riley. There are just a lot of us 'Rileys' around these parts. Now, your next question, how did they know we were coming? While you were on the phone with your daughter, I called so we could have a table ready. I also lined up a tour after lunch."

"I see. So if you are not directly related to the governor, how do they know you here? Sounds like you might be more than a bar/restaurant owner on the Isle of Palms. Yes, Dave disclosed your last name and that you owned the One-Eyed Parrot. I felt terrible about calling you just a bartender when I was questioning your vast knowledge of sea turtles. I am thinking you probably know a lot more about sea turtles and about Charleston in general than I do."

He laughed and added that there was no need to feel bad about calling him a bartender. He said that he was a bartender who owned a restaurant, worked for a local foundation, *and* knew a great deal about sea turtles and Charleston, but there was still a lot for both of us to learn.

"Now what would you like for lunch?"

"What would you recommend?"

He suggested the blackened catfish with collards and macaroni and cheese.

"That sounds delicious and truly Southern."

He asked if I wanted sweet tea, a beer, wine, or water. I assured him that water with lemon would be fine. So when the waiter came back. He ordered for both of us. A woman could get used to this royal treatment. Bill had never been the "knight in shining armor" type. When we first started dating, he would always insist on walking on the outside of the sidewalk closest to the road for protection. Over the years, he had dropped that chivalrous act and let me walk on the outside. Maybe he was waiting for the moment to push me in front of a car. William cleared his throat and asked what I was thinking about. I did not want to go into the details, so I simply said that I was thinking about how refreshing it was to be in the company of a true Southern gentleman.

"I have to say, I had no idea you worked for a foundation. It's funny Dave had not mentioned that since Dave is the executive director for a charitable foundation."

He asked what I was doing checking up on him with Dave. I assured him. "I had just asked him your last name because you had not mentioned it."

William stated that there was a simple explanation why Dave had not mentioned the foundation because he had not seen Dave since a class reunion five years ago, and at that time, he was not that active with the foundation. It was one of those things where an uncle and his father informed him that he would be involved. He said that it was okay because he really enjoyed working with them.

Our food came, and it was delicious. I could not tell you the last time I had collards. We ate and enjoyed some small talk. We both passed on dessert so we could get started. I wanted to take a few pictures around the restaurant. Then we walked outside for me to take a shot of the outside of the building. There was a golf cart near the door. William looked at me and took my hand to help me into the cart.

"My lady, your chariot awaits." He said that this way, we could see most of the gardens. He said for me to let him know when I wanted to stop for a photo. He wanted me to see the gardens and the stables.

"After that, there is a great gift shop if you are interested."

"I never pass on an opportunity to look even if I did not buy anything. I should get something for Dave as a 'thank you' for letting me stay at the house."

We started down the path. He stopped to let me take pictures of the main house and the smaller gardens. He asked if I wanted to tour the House Museum. I was fine with just touring the outside unless he wanted to go in. He assured me that he had seen it many times. Next, we rode through the gardens. The hydrangeas were beautiful.

"Hydrangeas were one of my favorite flowers." He asked what else I liked. "Black-eyed Susan, tulips, and roses are my favorites, but I think I just like them all!"

We parked the cart and walked down to the tiered bank of what was once the rice field. It was just so beautiful and peaceful. I took a lot of pictures. I insisted that if I was getting on his nerves, I could stop. He insisted that I take as many photos as I wanted. When I felt I had captured everything, we walked back to the cart.

Next, we drove to the blacksmith shop. We got out and walked through the blacksmith shop, the carpentry shop, the pottery shop, and the textile shop. We walked through Eliza's House. This house was a Reconstruction-era freedman's house that has an exhibit that documents the story of slavery in South Carolina. There was so much history here, and the craftsmen were so talented. I took lots of pictures, and then we walked back to the cart for our last stop—the gift shop. They had a lot of nice things, but nothing really jumped out at me as a good gift for Dave.

William bought us some water. He asked if there was anything else I wanted to see before we drove to his sister's house on Sullivan's Island. I assured him that I had enough memories and photos to last me for a while. I stopped by the restroom before we headed back to the car. In this area, you never know when you are going to be stuck in traffic, so it pays to be prepared.

CHAPTER 8

Meeting the Family and Weaving Stories (Dream Weaver)

The traffic was not too bad. I asked him who all would be there just so I could be prepared. He said that his sister Susan would be there along with her husband, Artie. They had two children, Kristie, age eight, and David, age five. He said they had a Lab named Rhett and a cat named Scarlett. I had to laugh at the pet names! He warned me to get it out of my system now because they were very serious about their Southern traditions. I thanked him for the warning. Just as he ended his warning, we turned into their driveway.

Wow. Two-story house on the ocean. Not too shabby. I did not realize it, but my mouth had dropped open. William laughed and reassured me that they were very down-to-earth. Down to-earth. Right. He cut off the engine and walked around to get me. He grabbed my bag with clothes and suggested that I bring my notebook in case I got any ideas for my story.

We went around to the back because they were all out at the pool. I hesitated and took a deep breath. He grabbed my hand and reassured me that they would love me. I asserted that they did not have to love me, but it would be great if they did not hate me. We walked on to the patio, and all we could hear was the squealing of Kristie and David calling for their uncle and running to hug him. He scooped them both up in a bear hug. It was great to see how much they obviously loved him. He put them down, and Kristie looked at me.

She said, "Hello, I am Kristie, and this is my brother, David. You must be Maggie. We are so glad you are here!"

I waved hello and said that I was very glad to be here and very glad to meet them. Susan and Artie walked over. They were happy to see William but not quite as enthusiastic as the kids. William introduced us, and we shook hands; although I was thinking that if the kids knew who I was, the adults probably did too. Susan motioned us toward the patio to seats under a covered awning. At this time of day and year, the shade felt good. William motioned me to a seat. He asked if I wanted something to drink. He took one look at my face and could tell I was just a little overwhelmed. He chuckled and said he would bring me a beer. Susan told him to have a seat and she would bring two.

We talked for a few minutes, and they asked all the typical work questions and questions about Columbia. They avoided husband and family questions, so I could tell they had been coached. I did offer that I had a daughter who taught at the University of Tennessee at Chattanooga. She was a biology major and taught courses in biology, earth science, geology. I looked at William and filled him in about her lecture today on sea turtles.

William laughed, and in unison, we said, "Another expert!"

Susan looked puzzled. William explained that I was working on a children's story about sea turtles. "I offered my expertise, and now Sam can contribute too!"

Susan said that she knew Kristie would want to contribute because she loved sea turtles. Kristie's ears perked up, and she ran over to us.

"What about sea turtles? They are my favorite."

William told her I was working on a story about turtles and hoped that she and David could help with the story!

She was so excited. "What kind of story? Can it be a story about us helping the sea turtles to stay safe until they hatch? Then we could watch them walk out to the sea. I just love to watch them march out to sea. There are so many of them. We must help protect the nests so bad people do not dig them up. Then when they hatch, we stand out there and wave our arms to keep the seagulls from diving down and eating them."

I smiled and said it sounded like she had the story; I just had to write it down.

David walked over and said, "Hey, what about me? I want to tell a story too."

I insisted that they could both tell the story. Susan suggested we wait until after dinner.

William asked Kristie and David if they wanted to go play kickball. They invited me to join them, but I declined saying that I would just watch if it was okay. Kristie pulled William up from his chair, and they were off to play.

Susan looked at me and smiled. "They love their uncle William!"

It was pretty obvious that they loved each other. She thanked me for including Kristie and David in the storytelling adventure. I confessed I needed their help because I was having a case of writer's block. I asked if there was anything I could do to help with dinner.

She said that she had the salad ready, and Artie was grilling the steak and potatoes, so she thought we were set. We turned our attention to the kickball game. Kristie and David were teaming up on William. It looked like he did not stand a chance.

Artie announced that dinner was ready. Susan directed Kristie and David to go wash their hands. She looked at William and suggested that he probably could stand to wash up after the game! She instructed him to show me where the restroom was in case I needed to know later! We walked in and went to the powder room off the great room. We took turns washing hands. The kids came running to the door. I winked at William and congratulated Kristie and David on their victory in the kickball game. David beamed with pride. Kristie giggled.

William tickled them both and said, "I never stood a chance! Come on, let's go eat so we can play in the pool and write a story!"

The sun had gone down enough that it was comfortable out on the patio. Dinner was delicious, and I complimented both chefs. We talked about the foundation work that I did in Columbia. Susan worked with the family foundation with William. She discussed ideas for fundraisers and celebration ceremonies.

Susan smiled and suggested that I was a good resource to have for ideas for the foundation and that she was glad he had found me. William agreed that I was a "good find." I could feel the heat rising on my face, and I knew I was blushing before William pointed it out; you know, in case anyone missed it!

We finished dinner, and I helped clear dishes. Susan signaled for me to go sit, but I insisted that after the delicious meal and their hospitality, the least I could do was help clean up and wash dishes. We cleared the patio table, put away leftovers, and I rinsed plates and put them in the dishwasher. She wiped down the counter and said we should join the kids and the guys at the pool. I made a stop by the powder room before joining them. On the way to the pool, I grabbed my notepad out of my bag just in case Kristie and David were ready for their turtle story.

I sat in a chair beside William, and he asked if I was okay. I told him I was fine. Kristie was sitting at the end of William's lounge chair. She saw the notebook and asked if I was ready to write down the story. I grabbed my pencil, opened the notebook, and indicated that I was ready when she and David were ready.

David wanted to tell his story first. "When baby sea turtles are born, they are really cute, except for one because that turtle has a hole in his shell showing his heart. The man walking on the beach found the turtle and knew he had to rescue it. If the little baby sea turtle were not saved, it would die. He was a vet, and he took the sea turtle to his home and put it in a fish tank that was just the right size and just the right temperature. The water was just right for the turtle's heart. The turtle had a home, so he would be just fine in time. The end."

I thanked David for his great turtle-rescue story. William looked at Kristie and told her it was her turn.

Kristie cleared her throat and began her story. "Once upon a time, there was an island princess named Kristie. (David added, "And a prince named David.") She lived by the sea and watched over the sea turtles. She made the people pick up trash on the beach. She commanded that no plastic bags were allowed in the kingdom because the plastic trapped the turtles. She commanded that they could not have those plastic things around soft drinks either. The mama and daddy turtles laid their eggs up on the beach every year. When the eggs were buried on the beach, Princess Kristie (she looked at David and added) and Prince David would not let the people shine flashlights or bright lights on the beach because the lights disturbed the turtles. She had the lifeguards sit on their tall chairs and watch for the hatching.

"When the eggs hatched, she had her subjects stand on the beach and wave their arms to keep the seagulls from diving down and grabbing the babies. She wanted them to be able to make it to the water. Some people stood back and made loud noises so the coyotes would not come and grab the babies. The turtles were able to make it out to sea and find all the mama and daddy turtles. They swam all day and would rest at night. The turtles were happy, and Princess Kristie and Prince David were glad the subjects of the island were able to keep them safe. The end."

I kept writing for a bit so I could get it all down, then I looked up. "Both of those are great stories. May I combine the two stories to make one story?"

They approved of the idea. Kristie said the vet could be one of her subjects who saved a turtle who had a hole in his shell. She said a seagull probably bit the turtle and made the hole. I agreed that this was probably what happened.

William praised them for the great job of storytelling. Kristie asked if they could draw the pictures to go along with the story. William hesitated because he did not know if I needed pictures, but I thought pictures were a great idea.

"Today is Saturday, is there any way you could draw me some pictures tomorrow?" I will scan them into the computer and write the story down at the bottom of each picture page.

Susan said she would help them get the pictures drawn tomorrow. William said that he could hardly wait to see their art masterpieces. He asked if I had enough for a children's book. I told him I thought it would be perfect.

"I think this book needs to be typed by Maggie Nelson as narrated and illustrated by Kristie and David Smith."

Kristie beamed with joy!

William asked Kristie and David if they were ready to play in the pool. I hope he was not expecting a "no" because Kristie lifted her sundress to show that she was already in a bathing suit. David was already wearing swim trunks, and he was out of his shirt and in the water before William could comment on Kristie's swimsuit. Kristie jumped in, and William got up to go put on a suit. He asked if I was going to get in the pool or sit on the side and overthink the book.

"Ha, ha. No need to overthink it. It is written! But I think I will just watch."

He pointed to the floating basketball goal in the water and suggested that I was just afraid I would get beat. Susan laughed and indicated that I better get in there and defend that challenge.

William took me by the hand and pulled me up. "Come on, let's go change." He leaned over and told me not to be shy or self-conscious. "You're beautiful, and Kristie, David, and I all know it!"

Again I blushed. I was not quite sure what this "thing" was between William and me. We had just met on Friday, but I felt like we had been lifelong friends. Something tugged at my heart and intimated that I thought of him as more than a friend. Occasionally, I thought he felt something too. Then again it was just friendship. I tried to convince myself to concentrate on the friendship and not overthink this relationship!

We played basketball for about an hour. Kristie and David had a great time. I must admit I did too. The water was really refreshing after a long day. It was about seven thirty when Susan informed the kids they had to take a bath. They wanted to stay and play with us, well, mostly William. William convinced them to go ahead and take a bath because we were going to have to go too. They hugged each of us, and William said that we would see them Monday or Tuesday to get their turtle drawings.

We got out and showered off using the outdoor shower. Then we changed in the pool house. I thanked Susan and Artie for a wonderful evening. William hugged his sister and brother-in-law, and we walked to the car. He held my door for me, then he got in. He turned to me and asked if I had a good time. I assured him it had been a wonderful night.

It had been a great day. Middleton Place was beautiful, and the time with his family had been fun and relaxing. It was a bonus that the kids had helped me with a turtle story. I do not know if it was what the publisher wanted, but I know that they had fun. If nothing else, I would get it printed for them to have.

William asked if it would be okay if we stopped by the One-Eyed Parrot so he could check on things. That would be fine because a beer might be good to help me sleep. Although after all the walking and swimming today, sleep would probably not be a problem.

We pulled up in front of the bar and went inside. It was busy for nine. Larry, Stewart, and one waitress were there working. Stewart was back and forth bringing food orders from the kitchen. Larry was bartending, and the waitress was balancing all the tables.

William motioned for me to sit at the bar. I asked if I could work on my laptop at the bar, and he said he would make an exception for me. I opened a blank document and started typing the story that Kristie and David had told us tonight. I would decide how to divide up the text when I saw their pictures. William brought me a beer. After I finished with the turtle story, I opened the diary I had started the other day. It had been a good suggestion. I had written down my feelings about Bill and the divorce situation. I had also written down some of my fears about my next steps. I still did not know what I was going to do about the house. I guess I would make that decision after I talked to my attorney Monday.

I wrote an entry about all the fun I had had today. Everything seemed so easy with William. He had been a big help distracting me from all that had happened this week. As I typed, I still could not believe that it had only been Wednesday when I had found out about Bill and Stacey. It all seemed so long ago. I saved my notes and logged out of my computer.

I took a few sips of beer and figured I had better check my emails and text messages on my phone. I had a few work emails but nothing urgent. Most of them were for information not really requiring any action before I went back to work the following week. I had been enjoying being on vacation. It was going to be hard to go back. I checked my personal email. I had an email from Sam, just checking in. I responded and wrote about my day. I thought she would get a kick out of the turtle story. Maybe I could get her to give me some scientific facts to include at the back of the book. I closed out the email by telling her that I loved her and that I would give her a call Monday after I talked to the lawyer. I had my daily texts from Debbie and Annette. I let them know I was fine. I shared with them about the plantation and dinner with William's family. I promised that I would be in touch tomorrow.

Having caught up on all my electronic communications, I took a quick look at Facebook and Instagram. I do not know why, but I decided to check Bill's Facebook. Stacey was plastered all over it. I decided to click on her name and look at her page. As soon as I did, I knew that I should have not gone there. Stacey was pregnant, four months pregnant. It was right there; she and Bill Nelson were expecting a baby boy. It made me angry. Not that I had wanted a baby at this stage in our lives, but I had wanted a second child when Sam was young. He had insisted that he was finished raising children. Now he was involved with someone twenty-five years younger, and they were starting a family. I closed Facebook. I chose not to look at Instagram.

I decided to send a quick text to my attorney. I guess it did not really matter, but I thought he should know. This would explain why Bill was suddenly in a hurry to get the divorce. I sent the email and put my phone in my purse. I worked on my beer. William came over and asked if I was okay. I asserted that I had just seen some news on Facebook that had surprised me, but everything was fine. I did not want to unload on him, especially sitting here at the bar. He asked if I wanted another beer, and I said yes. I know that I tend to drink too much when I am upset or angry or sad. I know self-medicating was not the answer, but tonight, numb would feel good.

William helped at the bar for a little while. He said that he was going to go check on a few emails and phone messages. He said that he would be right back. Larry assured him he would keep an eye on me and keep my glass full. William did not look like he liked that idea. Before I had finished that beer, Larry brought me another one. I finished one and handed him the empty glass. He looked surprised, but impressed, that I could drink that much beer. William came back out and worked the bar for a while. He asked if I was okay, and I said I was fine. Unfortunately, the beer was starting to kick in. I was feeling *fine* and numb all at the same time.

While I was drinking my beer, some guy came in and sat next to me. He started talking, and then he asked if he could buy me a beer. Before I could answer, William informed him that he could not buy me a beer. The guy asked William if I was with him, and he said no. Well, not that I thought we were dating or anything, but I had just spent all day with him, so when he said no, that made me angry. I should have kept my mouth shut, but liquid courage forced me to say, "Well, if I am not with you, he should be able to buy me a beer."

William shot me a look that told me I had crossed a line.

The guy smiled and said, "Great, get her another one of whatever she is drinking."

I shot him a look. At this point, I think he and William were both confused. I pulled out money to pay for the three I drank and put it on the bar. I turned to him and said, "Thank you for the offer. I just thought you should be able to offer. I am done for the evening." I drank the rest of my beer, put my laptop and purse in my tote bag, stood up, and left.

When I left, William, Larry, and the stranger were all staring with their mouths open. The air felt good on my face. The beer was making me feel warm, and the unexplained and unwarranted anger with William were making me angrier. The walk to the house did me good. I had cooled off by the time I got to the stairs. I headed upstairs, unlocked the door, and went in.

I was about to get in the shower when there was a knock on the door. Before I could get there, it went from a knock to a bang. That confirmed that it was William and I had made him mad. I switched on the light, looked out to make sure, and opened the door. He asked if he could come in.

I motioned him in, and he took one step in turned and shouted, "What the hell was that?"

I was surprised that he yelled. I apologized and said that his comment had just hit me the wrong way.

"You acted like you did not like him offering to buy me a drink, but you indicated to him that I was not with you. For some reason, that stung more than it should have." I took a deep breath and turned away. "I know we are not together, but I guess I get mixed signals from you. We have spent all day together. We have spent a great deal of time together over the last two days. When you talk, I feel like you are flirting. I guess I misunderstood. I guess I just feel too comfortable with you. I am sorry if I misunderstood. So why didn't you just let him buy me a drink?"

"Because I didn't want him to buy you a drink. I want us to be together, but we are not because you are still married. I guess I do send mixed signals because I it scares me how comfortable I feel with you. I have only known you for two days, but I feel like I have known you for years. It scares me that I can feel that way about someone. I do not think I even felt that way about my ex-wife. For some reason, you and I seem to fit, and it scares me. Now, maybe if you weren't married, it would be different."

I just stared at him. "Well, I guess after Monday, that will not be a problem. I found out why Bill is pushing for this divorce to be finalized so fast. Seems Stacey is four months pregnant."

He took a step toward me and reached out for me. He hugged me and apologized. He asked how I knew that, then he stopped and said, "Is that what you found on Facebook?"

I nodded my head yes. I looked into his eyes and said, "Listen, I am sorry if I misunderstood your feelings for me, but you have to understand, I don't know why, but I felt something between us the first time I saw you. When you told me your name, I had to laugh. Husband, Bill. Guy who I am undeniably attracted to is William. Although, I did like the idea of having 'Liam' as my nickname for you. Yes, I am attracted to you. You make me laugh, you make me feel loved and confident, and I know it was just me reading the love into it. Every time we are together and you leave, I cannot wait until I can see you again. I know that by saying all of this, I have probably ruined the chances of keeping this friendship. I am sorry I messed it up. I am sorry if I embarrassed you at the bar. Please tell Larry and that guy that I apologize."

He took my face in his hands and pulled me closer to him, and he kissed me. It was a kiss that felt like more than friendship. The kiss proved to me that he had the same unexplainable feelings about me. We kissed for a long time, then he took a step back. He kept his arms around me.

"We are not just friends. I do not know why or how, but I feel like we were meant to be together. I want to be with you, and as soon as you have those divorce papers in your hands, if you will have me, I am yours. You can call me Liam anytime. I like it. You do not owe Larry an apology. He told me I better come check on you because something was not right. You don't owe Roy an apology either, and please don't let him buy you any drinks."

"Roy? That's the guy at the bar?"

He laughed. "Yes, Roy is an old friend of mine. He is a fireman, and he is always trying to pick up beautiful women. You are beautiful, but I want you to be my beautiful woman. I guess I said you were not with me when he asked because I wanted to protect you since you are still married. I am sorry that it came across as if I did not want us to be together. I don't know how it happened so fast, but, Maggie, I do believe I am falling in love with you." With that, he pulled me close again and kissed me.

He took my hands and walked me to the couch. "You know, if I could, I would make love to you now, but I don't want to risk causing you any problems in the divorce. Although if you do not mind me saying so, if Bill got Stacey pregnant four months ago, he has no room to cast any stones. He is a dog, and you don't deserve to be treated this way."

I knew he was right about waiting. I could not risk it. It felt so good to be in his arms. He looked down at me and smiled.

"So, Liam. I like that." I blushed.

He looked at me and cleared his throat. "You know I haven't asked you a lot of questions about Bill. I didn't want to pry, and I didn't want to make it any harder on you by talking about him, but I have to ask. Bill…please tell me you never called him William or Liam!"

I laughed. "No, his name is Bill. It is Bill on his birth certificate because his mother did not like the name William. He is definitely not a Liam either. We were very young when we got married. I think we were both looking for a way out of living at home. I think we loved each other, but it just did not last. We both focused on Sam, then when she was gone, I threw myself into work. I think he has been throwing himself in to 'other distractions.' When I found him at her house Wednesday night, I think I was angrier and more hurt than anything else. It is not that I wanted to fight for us to stay together. We have been living apart…under the same roof for a long time."

He hugged me tighter and kissed the top of my head. "If you are going to call me Liam, I am going to have to call you Maggie Mae… after one of my favorite Rod Stewart songs!"

I laughed and said that I could live with that. I looked at him. "I am sorry for how I behaved at the bar. I should not have drunk the beer to numb my feelings. When my feelings are numb, my brain can do stupid things. Do you forgive me? Are we okay? If we need to start over, I can come in and sit at a table tomorrow and introduce myself."

He kissed me lightly. "We are more than okay. Our feelings are out in the open. Do you know how much I wanted to grab you and kiss you in the pool today? Do you know how much I wanted to hold your hand at lunch, in the car, and in the golf cart? I'm still going to have trouble keeping my hands off you, but at least now I know you feel the same way!" He kissed me again. "Now do you want to get breakfast before we go to the aquarium tomorrow? We need to look at your pictures tomorrow."

I told him that would be great. He stood up and hugged me and kissed me again. He pulled away and said, "You take a shower to get the pool water off and get a good night's sleep. What time should I come by in the morning?"

I winked and suggested that he could come by as early as he liked. He said that he would be here at eight. He kissed me again, and I wanted to tell him to stay.

"Let me go before I convince myself to stay."

I grabbed his hand. "Liam, are Larry and Stewart going to resent you being away from the bar so much? I don't want to cause a problem."

He laughed and winked. "Maggie Mae, I own the bar. They manage it most of the time. I would rather spend my time with you. *They* would rather me spend my time with you because I am a happier person with you! Now get some sleep."

And with that, he was gone. I locked up, took a shower, rinsed out my bathing suit, and hung it out on the back porch. I took some Tylenol so I would not have a headache in the morning and got into bed. I was exhausted, but I doubted very seriously if I would get any sleep tonight. I wonder if I could push to get the divorce finalized *early* Monday! Oh, well. Tomorrow promised to be another fun day.

CHAPTER 9

Sunday Outing (Walking on Sunshine)

I had set the clock for six thirty, but I was up at five. I had tossed and turned for about an hour, and then I went to sleep and dreamed about Liam's kisses. When I woke up at five, I had a smile on my face. I cut my clock off and got up to get dressed. I know he said we were going to the aquarium then possibly the market. He had mentioned a possible carriage ride and eating at Poogan's Porch. I decided on a sundress and flat espadrilles. I knew I was going to need sunscreen. My face was a little pink from walking around the gardens at Middleton Place. I transferred my camera and the things from my purse into a small backpack. I decided against the entire camera case, or maybe I could leave it in the car in the event I wanted to change lenses.

    I fixed some coffee and took my allergy medicine and vitamins with a glass of water. The Tylenol was a good call last night. Note to self, no more than two beers…*ever*. I decided to sit out on the front porch to drink my coffee and read and write in my journal. I needed to get back to spending more time reading the Bible; this was a good morning to start. I opened my laptop to write in my journal; yesterday had been a highpoint in the journaling! Well, one low point, Stacey was pregnant. But all the rest was good!

    I decided to see if Debbie, Annette, Sam, or my attorney had responded to emails and/or texts. I had a "hi and see you soon" from Debbie and Annette. Sam had sent a short list of facts about turtles to fulfill her portion of my book! The attorney had simply said that he had heard about Stacey, and he would call me Monday. Well, that could not be good. If it were good, he could have just typed it, right? Not going to dwell on it today or drink any beer because of it.

I went in to fix another cup of coffee, and I had a text from William, "Ok, I cannot sleep or stay away any longer, is it ok if I come over?" I replied, "Meet you at the door with coffee!" He did not drink nearly as much coffee as me, but I had seen him drink it, always black. So I found a mug, poured a cup, and went to the door. When I opened it to go on the porch, he was there. He took both cups of coffee and set them on the table. Then he took me in his arms and kissed me. He pulled away briefly to say "Good morning, Maggie Mae" and kissed me again. I could get used to this.

He pulled away and said, "Okay, we need to drink some coffee. Now!"

We sat on the porch swing and sipped the coffee. He asked if breakfast at Saffron Restaurant & Bakery on East Bay would be okay. He said that they had a great breakfast selection and some wonderful pastries. He said that they opened at 7:00 a.m. so we could plan on breakfast at seven thirty and then get to the aquarium. He asked if I had packed my camera.

I assured him that I had it in my backpack. I asked if he thought the camera case would be okay in the car if I decided to change a lens. He said that he could hide it in the spare tire compartment. He said, "I know when we go to the aquarium, we are going to have to spend some time researching the sea turtles."

I laughed and told him that Sam had sent me a list of facts in an email, but more research was always a good idea.

He said, "We could walk around the market and go for a light lunch and a drink or two, no more than two, at Tommy Condon's Irish Pub." He winked when he said it, and I stated that I agreed on no more than two beers at a sitting. He asked how I would feel about a carriage tour.

I assured him that would be fun, but I did not expect him to spend so much money on me. He insisted that he had it to spend, and I was who he wanted to spend it on. He kissed my hand, and I blushed. I had blushed more in three days with this man than I think I have in my entire life.

He said, "Then we could go to Poogan's Porch."

"I went to College of Charleston for one year and have always wanted to go to Poogan's but have never been. If I see a ghost in the bathroom, legend has it that it is haunted. I am leaving without dessert!"

He said that at one point we needed to take a stroll along the Battery and through the park. Then when we came back to the island, we could come back to my house to look at photos, or we could go to his house. I said that either would be fine.

I kissed him and looked into his eyes. "Now I know I confessed to you that I am a list maker. The outline of the day sounds wonderful. Did you give me an outline because you are a list maker too, or is this for my benefit?"

He gave me a sheepish grin and said that he was a list maker to a certain extent but that today's list was for my benefit. He said that later, he would surprise me with a totally impromptu date!

We finished our coffee, and we set out on today's adventure. Saffron. We decided to share a stack of pancakes so we could share a pastry. It was delicious. He informed me that he had heard from his sister last night. She loved me, and the kids could not stop talking about how much fun it was to come up with a story and do the illustrations. She said they were going to draw pictures today.

I was pleased that the dinner and visit had gone so well. They were all so easy to like. The coffee was great. I took a few pictures before we left. We walked to the car holding hands. We drove to the aquarium. He said that he would save the walking for the market and the Battery.

I admitted to him that I appreciated it since I was wearing sandals. I had to smile, and he demanded an explanation. "Well, I had to laugh because Bill refused to come to Charleston with me after a few visits. He said I tried to walk his legs off every time. One of the last times, we parked in front of a restaurant at the market. I pointed out to him it was a two-hour limit. He said it would be fine. As we were coming back, we were getting ticket number two. He cussed all the way home. It took him five years to come back after that. He did learn the perks of parking in a parking garage though!"

He smiled and said, "If we are going to walk that much, we both wear athletic shoes and come in the late fall." Both were excellent ideas!

We got to the aquarium right as they were opening. We walked through and looked at every exhibit and tank. I took a few pictures. We stopped by the café to get two bottles of water and set off for the sea turtle exhibit. It was very informative. I professed that I wanted to be down here to see them hatch and make their way to the water. It was something I had only seen on videos.

He said that he could make that happen! We went by the gift shop, and I was looking at things, hoping I could find something for Dave. I still did not see anything. I took my time browsing, and William wandered off to the other side of the store. After a while, he came back and asked if I had found anything.

I confessed that I had no idea what to get for Dave as a "thank you" for allowing me to use his house. William said that he thought Dave would like some cigars. He said there was a shop at the market, and he would help me pick something out.

I thought cigars were a perfect idea. We decided to go to the market to walk for a bit. We stopped at every vendor table in the open-air market. I saw several Charleston paintings that I liked. I had a couple—*The Storm, St. Phillips*. I would see if I got to keep them after the divorce. We found the cigar shop, and William helped me pick out some for Dave. I did love the smell of a good cigar, so shopping in there was pleasant. They were giving out spoon-sized samples at the ice cream shop, and we each got a spoon.

There was a dress shop that had some beautiful formal dresses in the window. I commented that they were pretty. I admitted that I liked looking at dresses, but I never bought them. I had one little black dress and one semiformal that I wore to foundation dinners and fundraisers. He asked if we ever had dancing at the dinners. I said that we did and that I had taken ballroom dancing so I would be able to dance. He asked if Bill liked to dance. I had to laugh.

"I wouldn't say he liked to dance. We danced when we first dated, but he would never take ballroom or shag lessons with me. Do they have dances for your foundation?"

"Yes, they do have dances. I am going to have to bring you so I can have a dance partner."

I chuckled and insisted that I was sure he did not have any problems finding a dance partner.

He stopped me and kissed my hand and said, "I don't just want a partner that I can dance with. I want you." He leaned over and kissed me on the cheek. He whispered that I better be glad we were in public or we would not be finishing our list of stops on our adventure.

Again I blushed, and I whispered, "I would be okay with changing the list!"

He shook his head, and we started walking.

"Are there any other shops you would like to stop in, or are you ready for lunch?"

I assured him that I thought lunch would be fine because I believed I had walked off my half stack of pancakes and half pastry. We got to Tommy Condon's just before noon, so it was not crowded.

He asked if I wanted to sit outside or inside. I asked if we could sit inside. I would reserve outdoor eating in downtown Charleston for late fall. He whispered something to the host, and we followed him back to a small side room. We had it all to ourselves.

It felt good to sit down, and it was nice to have him all to myself. The waiter appeared and handed us a drink menu. William asked if I wanted my usual. I nodded, and he ordered a local IPA. The waiter said he would be right back with the drinks and to take our orders.

William asked if I knew what I wanted. I smiled and said that my traditional Tommy Condon's order was shepherd's pie. He complimented me on my good taste. When the waiter returned with our drinks, he asked if we were ready to order. William ordered two shepherd's pie entrées. The waiter asked if we wanted bread, and William ordered a basket of sourdough bread with butter.

We talked about the aquarium. We talked about sea turtles. We talked about the market. He even asked about the Charleston prints I had looked at. I could not believe how observant he was. I explained to him that I had several Charleston prints, but I did not know how many I would get to keep. He said not to worry that if Bill insisted on one that I wanted, it could be replaced. I squeezed his hand and said we would worry about that another day.

The food came. The shepherd's pie was delicious as always. I made it at home sometimes, but it was not the same. William said that was probably because I did not add Guinness to it when I cooked. No, I had to admit, I never cooked with Guinness! The bread was soft and warm and delicious. The waiter asked if we wanted anything else to drink or dessert. I reassured William I was fine but he could order something if he wanted to. He asked the waiter to bring us each a cup of coffee. A man after my own heart! The waiter brought coffee and cream. We drank coffee and talked about what was next on the agenda. He asked if I was still up to a carriage ride and walk at the Battery. It sounded great to me.

He reached in his pocket and pulled out a little black velvet drawstring bag. He put it in front of me and confessed that when he saw it, it made him think of me and he had to get it. I told him that he should not have done this. I opened it. It was a sterling silver chain with a sea turtle on it. I could not believe he had bought it.

"It is so beautiful. Thank you." He offered to put it on for me. I could not help it, I had to kiss him.

He touched the necklace and said, "You're welcome."

We left Tommy Condon's and walked over to the carriage tour reservation desk. William got our tickets, and they led us over to a carriage. We got in, and the tour guide started the tour. I looked at him because I couldn't believe it was just the two of us on the carriage.

He said, "I wanted to have you all to myself. You better get your camera out to be ready."

It had probably been twenty years since I had been on a tour, so it was great to hear the history. The best part was that William would signal him to stop so I could take pictures. When we got down to the Battery, the carriage even waited for us to walk along the Battery and through the park.

I reminisced that when Sam was a little girl, we had visited this park. I had a picture of a young, skinny me holding her. I had joked to Bill that the next time I got married, I wanted to get married in this gazebo.

William looked at me and said that this could probably be arranged. I was sure that he would not have any problems arranging it, but now that I was older and wiser, a simple wedding on the beach at Isle of Palms would be nice...in fall or winter! He leaned over and kissed my cheek and said that he had to agree!

We got back on the carriage and finished the tour. He stopped, and I took pictures of houses all along the way. I had no idea what William must have had to pay for this tour. But it was the best tour I had ever had! When we got back, William and I thanked the tour guide. William gave him a tip. It must have been a good one because he thanked him repeatedly.

William asked if I wanted to go to Poogan's Porch or go back to his house and he would cook. I conceded that if he did not mind, I would like to go back to the beach, put on some comfortable shorts, and eat there. I had not been to his house, so I wondered what it would be like. He assured me that he had shorts and a T-shirt for me.

We pulled up in his driveway. His house was beautiful. Not as big as his sister's house, but it was very nice. It looked like there was a pool in the back. It was on the ocean. We went in, and he took me to his room. He pulled out a T-shirt and shorts. He said that they were from his thinner days and did not fit him now. He said that with the drawstring, we could make them work for me. He showed me to the bathroom and got out a towel and washcloth. He said there was shampoo and body wash in the shower. He also said that he was going to make a salad, take a shower, and then he would put some salmon on the grill. He suggested we eat on the screened-in porch since the sun was going down and it was cooler.

After walking around in Charleston in July, it felt good to shower. I washed my hair and washed off all the sunscreen. I got out and got dressed. Again I got a little sun, but it was not too bad. Well...no underwear. Hmm... We were going to be good until my divorce was final, so I could do this! I put my dirty clothes in a plastic bag from the kitchen.

William was out of the shower and marinading the salmon. I walked over, and he grabbed me. He gave me a kiss and joked that his shorts had never looked so good. He squeezed my waist and ran his hands up my back. He looked at me with a devilish grin and apologized. He smiled, continued to caress me through his T-shirt, and kissed me.

"Man, I don't know if I have the willpower for this or not."

I just smiled and said that I knew we could both be strong! I pulled away and asked if there was anything I could do to help him in the kitchen. He pointed to the cabinet and asked me to get plates and salad bowls. I found the silverware and napkins. I set the table on the porch. He pulled two beers from the refrigerator, opened them, and handed them to me to carry out to the patio. He put the salmon on to cook, and I handed him a beer.

It was a beautiful night. Dinner was great. We talked and laughed and just enjoyed each other's company. We worked together to clear the table and clean up the kitchen. William cleaned the grill. He asked if I wanted to go home. I assured him that I really wanted to stay but that if we wanted to "be strong" until the divorce was signed, I had to go home.

He smiled and pulled me up from the sofa. "Okay, then if we are going to go, we better go now!"

It was a quick drive. He opened my door and walked me up the stairs. He took my key and opened the door. He insisted on carrying my camera case and tote bag. I asked him if he wanted to have a seat. He pulled me toward him and kissed me. The kiss indicated that he wanted to stay. He pulled away and held my face close to his.

"You know I want to stay, but you know I have to leave. Tomorrow is a big day. What time do you expect to hear from your attorney?"

"The attorney had planned to call at eight."

He hugged me and kissed me good night. "Call me in the morning if you need me. I will be at the bar by eight. I will work unless you need me here. Let me know what he says. Remember, do not panic. I will be by your side to help you through. Sleep well." With one final kiss, he walked to his car.

Yeah, right. Sleep. The good news was that I was not really thinking about the call from my attorney.

CHAPTER 10

D-Day Is Here—Sort Of (Landslide)

Well, Sunday was a lot of fun, and I slept well. I had set my clock for six thirty so I could take a shower, fix coffee, eat breakfast, and get mentally prepared for the call from my attorney. I woke up before the alarm, so I went ahead and got up. I had my shower, made my bed, and went to fix coffee. I decided to have my usual protein shake. I sat down on the front porch with my coffee and shake to check emails.

The phone rang at seven thirty. It was William. He wanted to say good morning before my call. He was going to be working at the bar this morning. He asked me to come by after my call because he wanted to know what was happening. He said that Susan had texted him last night to say that Kristie and David had done about ten or twelve pictures. William indicated that we would come get them at some point today. He said he could tell that I was nervous because my voice sounded different.

"It is just the fear of the unknown. I want this call to be behind me. I will call you after I talk to the attorney."

When I hung up the phone, it immediately rang. It was my attorney. The fact that he was calling at seven forty-five was either good news or really bad news. We exchanged a few pleasantries, but he said he knew that I would want to get down to business. He said that Bill's attorney had contacted the judge about Stacey's condition. The attorney said that if I was filing for a divorce on grounds of adultery, there was no need to wait.

"Bill said he was willing to file with that status. The only thing standing in the way is finalizing the house. Bill wants to sell the house and split the proceeds fifty-fifty. Once there is a contract/closing date on the house, the judge will call a hearing to finalize the divorce."

I said, "Okay. So I guess I must put the house on the market."

He sighed and said, "Well, Bill's attorney said that he has someone who wants to buy the house for a cash offer at 5 percent above market value, as is, if they can close in two weeks. The judge said that sounded like the wisest way to move forward because if you wait to list, you may have to accept less."

My head was spinning. Two weeks to clear out all the items in the house, find a place to live. Two weeks.

"Two weeks from today?"

He said it was two weeks from Friday because he had informed the judge I was out of town. He suggested that I take today to think about it, but he really thought it was the best thing to do. I asked if there was anything to do about his pension. He said that by quitting his job and becoming a consultant, he had worked his way around the loophole of my getting any portion of his pension.

I asked him to give me a few hours and I would call him back. I assured him I did not have a problem with Bill coming and getting his stuff out of the house. Sam would need to get what she wanted. I could put my belongings in storage until I could find a place to live, and we could donate or trash what was left. The one unknown was where I would live. I asked if he could find out what my portion of the sales price and what expenses I would have (like his fee) to subtract from that money so I could have some idea about what I would have to put down on a house or condo. He indicated that he would contact Bill's attorney and get a figure for me. He confessed to me that he was sorry that this was where we were, but he said he was glad we did not have to drag it out.

I decided to walk over to the One-Eyed Parrot to talk to William. I put sunscreen and a hat in a backpack in case he was busy and I needed to go for a walk to process on my own. I walked in, and Larry was cleaning off the tables. They did not open until ten thirty, so it was just staff now. I said good morning and asked if William was around. He said that he had gone to make a deposit but would be back in just a few minutes. I told Larry I was going to go for a walk on the beach and I would come back by later. He asked if everything was okay. I assured him that everything was going to be fine. I asked him if he had any coffee ready. He motioned for me to have a seat and he would bring me a cup to drink before my walk. I went ahead and took a seat at "my table." He brought a cup and some creamer. He brought a Danish along with it.

"Thank you so much. You are a sweetheart!"

He smiled and started to walk away. I stopped him and said, "Listen, I am sorry about Saturday night. I am sorry if I was a jerk. Life just got the best of me, and I had a few too many beers. Maybe it was not that I had too many beers, I just did not handle them well. I am sorry if I was rude to you or Roy or Stewart."

He hugged me unexpectedly and assured me that I never had to apologize because he understood all too well how life could feel overwhelming.

I drank my coffee and looked at emails and texts. I had my "check-in texts" from Annette and Debbie. They were both planning to come Wednesday because they had rearranged their work schedule. I guess I would call them tonight if all that was going to have to change so I could pack up the house. Dave had sent me an email to ask how things were going with the attorney. I was going to have to call him this afternoon. What was I going to tell him?

I had a text from Bill about coming by this weekend to get some things out of the house. He had also sent an email to my personal and work emails. He had also left a voice message. What was his hurry? Was she giving birth this week? Jerk. Jerk. Jerk. Without realizing it, I had said the last "jerk" out loud. It was at that moment that William walked up behind me and put his hands on my shoulders. I jumped.

He said, "Well, I'm hoping you weren't talking about me!"

I stood up and threw my arms around his neck and said, "Of course not. Sorry." I held him tight, and he held me closer.

"Hey…are you okay? I am guessing you talked to the attorney. Talk to me. Come back to the office with me." He took me by the hand, and we walked back to the office. He closed the door and swept me up in his arms and gave me a kiss. He took my face in his hands and looked into my eyes. "You do realize whatever the attorney disclosed, you do not have to face it alone. I am here to help you."

I nodded my head and said that I knew that. He kissed me again. I pulled away and confessed that if he did not stop now, I would not be able to tell him about the call. He laughed and said it was tempting but that he would let me talk. We sat on the sofa.

I took a deep breath and shared that the good news was that I would be divorced in two weeks. He smiled and said that was great to hear. "So what's the bad news."

I looked at him and said, "I am not sure if it's bad news. It's just contingent on getting a lot done in a short amount of time. The divorce is contingent on a signed contract on the sale of our house. Bill has someone who wants to buy the house for 5 percent above market price, as is, for cash as long as we can close two weeks from Monday. They evidently want to be in the house so their kids can start school. I guess it is the beauty of being in an excellent school district. The attorney considers it to be the best we can do because if we put it on the market, we would probably get less or they would do an inspection and require us to make repairs. We will split the proceeds fifty-fifty. I have no idea how much I will clear after attorney fees."

He looked at me and held me. "Well, I know it's a lot to think about."

I laughed nervously. "Yes, I have no problem with the divorce being over. I really do not mind having to sell the house. It is just that I have two weeks for Bill to get his things out. Two weeks for Sam to get her belongings out. Two weeks to figure out what I want to keep. Two weeks to trash or donate all that was left behind. I just do not know where I will go. If I cannot find a place that quickly, I will have to store furniture. I will have to be working while I do all of this because I have been off all this week."

William took a deep breath and said, "That is a lot, but you know that between Bill, Sam, you, me, Annette, and Debbie, we can get all that done. You know that Dave will work with you too. What else if causing the anxiety? What is making you hesitate?"

I stood up and looked out the window. He walked up behind me. He hesitated and turned me around so he could look at me. "I probably shouldn't say this, but I am hoping you are hesitating because you don't want to go back to Columbia. I want you here... with me. You know, I bet Dave would let you continue to work for him remotely. You could work with him on the foundation programming. You could work with *me* on our foundation. Dave would probably let you continue to stay in his house. He could rent it to you if he isn't willing to sell it."

I looked at him. "I doubt I would make enough money from the proceeds of our house in Columbia, well, my portion of the proceeds, to buy a beach house on the Isle of Palms. But my real hesitation was that I *didn't* want to go back to Columbia. I know I have only known you since Friday, but I just do not want to be apart from you. I guess it scares me that I feel that way."

"Then don't go back. Sell the house and move back here. If Dave will not rent his house to you, move in with me. Hell, even if he is willing to rent it to you, move in with me. Work part-time for Dave or work part-time for me. Or do volunteer work and stay with me. I guess what I am saying is stay with me. If you *know* that you have a place to live and you know that you do not have to worry about having a job right away or ever, can you have a feeling of peace about selling the house and being back here in two weeks or in a few days if we get everything taken care of with clearing out the house?"

He hugged me and pulled me closer for a kiss. He kissed me for a long time and then pulled away and held my face close to his. "I guess what I'm saying in a roundabout way is I am not falling in love with you, I am already in love with you, and I don't want to lose you. At this point, if you tell me you are moving back to Columbia, I will move to Columbia to be with you."

My eyes were filled with tears, and I hugged him. "It scares me to say it, but I love you too. It scares me because it happened so fast. But I feel like I have known you for a lifetime."

We kissed, and he caressed my back. "So I guess your decision is are you moving to Isle of Palms or am I moving to Columbia?"

I looked at him and insisted that I could not make him leave this bar or his home or his family. I confessed that I had been happier with him in four days than I had been in twenty-five years in Columbia.

He beamed with joy. "So does that mean you are moving in with me? I would *love* to have you as a roommate!"

"Liam, I believe I would love to be your roommate too. However, I think we need to date a little longer before we jump that quickly. Don't you agree?"

He gave me a devilish smile and said, "Maggie Mae, we'll take this as slow as you want as long as you promise we'll be together." Then he pulled me closer for a kiss.

I felt like I could stay in his arms forever. How could I argue with that smile? Or those kisses? I pulled away. "I have got to decide. I guess that I should tell my attorney that I will move forward on the sale of the house. I will need to arrange for Bill to be there Saturday and Sunday to go through his stuff and get it out. I am selfish because I am not willing to give up the rest of my week here. I want to be with you. I want you to have a chance to meet Annette and Debbie. I need to talk to Sam and see if she can come this weekend. It would help if she and Bill could be there at the same time. I just do not know if she is at a point in the semester where she can be here. I will get the rest of my clothes and personal items. There are a few pieces of furniture that were my mom's that I really want to keep. The stuff that Bill and I bought together, I have no strong feelings about keeping them or him taking them or setting them on fire. So the house is not the big issue. I can make that work.

"It's my job with Dave and his house. How can I ask him to let me work for him part-time just doing the foundation work and ask if I can rent his house at the same time? I think that is a little presumptuous of me, and I would think he might think it's a *lot* presumptuous."

William hugged me and suggested that I might be selling Dave short. He seemed to be just as much of friend as a boss. William suggested that I give Dave a call first and see where that went. "Besides, if he is not willing to let you work remotely or stay in the house, you'll find something else. You will not be homeless or in need of an income!"

William suggested that we go out front so I could finish my coffee. Too many conversations to be had with too little caffeine! So we stepped out of the office. Larry asked if I was still planning to go walk on the beach because it was warming up quickly. I changed my mind and decided that I would just walk back to the house and make a few phone calls. He offered to fix my coffee and Danish in a to-go container. I thanked him for being such a sweetheart.

William winked at us and said, "Hey, you two, I'm standing right here!"

William let Larry know that he was going to walk me home, and he would be right back.

We walked to the house hand in hand in silence. I was really dreading all the phone calls I had to make. William seemed to sense what I was thinking. He squeezed my hand and suggested that I make a list of all the calls I had to make and just start marking them off. I smiled. He offered to bring me some lunch. I invited him to come eat some chicken salad, cucumbers, and tomatoes at my place. I assured him that I had not finished the groceries I brought, and I was *not* taking them back with me! He asked exactly how much rotisserie chicken I had. I was pretty sure there was about 80 percent of the whole chicken left! He said that he would bring some fixings and pasta over and we would fix a chicken casserole to put in the freezer to eat when Debbie and Annette got there. Then we could make salad to go with the casserole. It sounded like a great plan! He said he would bring something for lunch.

He walked me up the stairs and unlocked the door for me. He walked me in. He leaned in and gave me a kiss. It was one of those kisses that really could have led to something much, much more, but he smiled and said that he was not going to keep me from my phone calls. He left and reminded me that he was just a phone call away if I needed anything.

I made my list: attorney, Bill, Sam, Dave, Debbie, and Annette. I knew that no matter what, the house had to sell, so getting it emptied was priority. Then I would decide if my stuff went into storage

Where I Belong...

or here. I dialed my attorney. I got his voicemail. I asked him to give me a call as soon as he could but that my decision was to go forward with selling the house with a closing date of two weeks from Monday.

While I waited for him to call, I decided to call Bill. I guess 9:00 a.m. was too early for a shot of something strong. I knew the answer to that, so I settled for finishing my coffee from the bar and fixing a pot. I figured it was going to be a long morning. I dialed Bill's number and hoped for voicemail. He answered on the second ring. I recapped all that my attorney had said about moving forward with selling the house for the cash offer with a closing in two weeks. I asked if he would be able to come to the house Saturday or Sunday to get what furniture and items he wanted. I planned to see if Sam could come get what items she wanted. He said he could be there Saturday. I told him that I'll call him and let him know when Sam was coming because the two of them might want to discuss some of the items. He asked what I was going to take.

"I am going to take my clothes and personal items. I want to take the few pieces of furniture that were my mom's and a few pictures."

He asked what we were going to do with the stuff that none of us wanted with a sarcastic tone.

"We can donate it or throw it away, it just had to be out of the house in two weeks." I guess my harsh tone bothered him, but I did not want to get into this today. "I have to go, but I will text about when Sam would be there."

Then he softened his tone and offered to bring doughnuts Saturday morning. I told him to bring whatever he wanted to eat and hung up. I know it was rude. I guess I was aggravated that this was all happening the way he wanted and on his timetable. It was sad that after twenty-seven years of marriage, I was not sad about the divorce, I was aggravated that I had to deal with him on his terms. Yes, after this was over, counseling was probably going to be a very good idea!

When I hung up the phone, it rang. It was my attorney calling back. He was glad that I had decided to move forward. He said the good news was that I would have the divorce behind me in just over two weeks. He said that he had done some checking, and I should be able to walk away with approximately $200,000. This was not a bad sum of money, but I guess I was hoping for a little more to go toward another place to live. Anyway, no need to dwell on it. He asked where I was going to move. I admitted that I was still working out the details, but if I did not have a place to go right away, I would put my furniture and miscellaneous items in storage. He told me that he hoped I would be able to work something out quickly. I thanked him for his help. I indicated that I would be at the house Friday and we were going to start dividing up all the stuff on Saturday. He stated that he would be in touch and added that if I needed him, I should not hesitate to call.

I admitted that I had one question. I asked if it would be a bad idea if William came to the house to help me move some items. He seemed to feel that since Bill had already agreed to file on the grounds of adultery and since his girlfriend was four months pregnant, it would not be a problem. He said that if Bill tried to make it a problem, call him.

I fixed another cup of coffee and ate the Danish. I wish I had taken two Danish pastries because then I could put off the call to Sam just a little longer. Since I only had one Danish, I made the call. She answered on the first ring. She said she was in her office on campus grading some papers. I thanked her for the facts about sea turtles. She was very excited about my idea to publish the book with the children's pictures and their story. She suggested I get in touch with the foundation down on Sullivan's Island that worked to protect the sea turtles. I was pretty sure that Susan and the kids were involved with the foundation, so I felt we had an in! Sam had made a small crocheted sea turtle for an event in Tennessee, and she offered to send me a picture. Maybe the foundation could work a deal to sell the books and the crocheted turtles as a fundraiser. She said she would be glad to make some. She also said that the pattern was simple and I could make some. She said that the ladies in the foundation might be willing to help too.

I loved her idea and asked her to send the photo of the crocheted turtle today since we were going to see Susan and the kids this afternoon. We both paused, and she said that she knew I did not call just to talk about turtles. She asked what was going on.

I informed her that the divorce was going to be settled quickly. She admitted that her dad had called her and spilled the beans about Stacey being pregnant. I asked how she felt about that. She said that right now, she just did not want to talk about it. She asked about the house.

"The good news was that your dad had found someone who wanted to buy it for cash if they could close two weeks from Monday."

She was stunned that it was all happening so quickly. I had to agree with her on this one. I asked if she would be available to come down this weekend to get what she wanted from the house. I knew that it was terribly short notice. She said that the timing was actually pretty good. She and Thomas were going to be on spring break next week. They could drive their truck and trailer down to get items out for me and for them. She asked what I was doing with my furniture. I had to make a phone call to see if I was taking what I wanted to Isle of Palms or putting it in storage. I hoped that Dave would allow me to rent the beach house and I could bring the stuff here. I was hoping he would allow me to work remotely. She asked if the reason I wanted to stay in Isle of Palms was the man I had met.

I admitted that I cared for him deeply and, yes, he was one of the main reasons I wanted to stay down here. She insisted that if the beach and William made me happy, I should do what I could to make it work. She said that her dad was not doing anything but securing his happiness, and I should not be any different. I insisted that *if* I got to stay in Dave's house, I wanted her to come visit. She said she would like to see the house and she had to meet William and give him her seal of approval!

I thanked her for being so understanding. She said that she was not being understanding, she just loved me and wanted to see me happy. I indicated that I was going to be at the beach through Thursday because Debbie and Annette were coming down. She laughed and said that she would check with them to see if he met their seal of approval! She said that she and Thomas would drive down Friday afternoon and stay at the house. They would stay if I needed them to be there. She asked when her father was coming to get his things, and I stated that he would be there bright and early

Saturday and he was bringing doughnuts. She mumbled something under her breath about him choking on a doughnut. I thought it best to let that one go.

I reminded her about how much I loved her and I was looking forward to seeing them both Friday. She said that *maybe* Thomas would drive the truck back and she would stay and go to the beach with me. I really liked the sound of that! We promised to talk Thursday.

Now, I had to call Debbie and Annette. I thought it would be best if we could get on the line at the same time so they could hear it at the same time, mostly so I would not have to repeat it twice! I texted both. They said they could do a video call at eleven. I suggested that they call me when they were ready!

It was ten, and I had made it through the easy calls, well easier. I do not think I would lump Bill in the easy category. I decided to take my coffee out on the back patio. You know, I had been here since Friday morning, and I had only been in this pool once. I had seen the pool guy come by, and he said he would be back in a week. I really should get in the pool. Now, I was trying to distract myself. I had to finish these calls. I could swim later.

Just then, my cell phone rang. It was William. I answered, and all he said was, "Well, how is it going?"

I reported that I had talked to the attorney, Bill, and Sam. The only calls left were Debbie, Annette, and Dave, and we were going to do a video call at eleven.

"We decided on a video call, so I only had to tell the story once."

Then there was a long pause, and he said, "Well, when are you going to call Dave?"

"Well, I am drinking coffee now and looking at the pool. When I hang up from you, I will call Dave and get it over with."

He told me he loved me and asked me to text when I had an answer from Dave.

"Liam…before you go, may I ask a favor?"

"You know you don't have to ask if you can ask me anything. Just name it!"

I took a deep breath and asked if he was willing to go to Columbia with me Friday to be there to meet Sam and her husband. He said that he would be glad too. He asked when Bill was coming, and I told him he would be there Saturday morning. He asked if I thought that would be a problem. I assured him that the attorney said it would not cause any problems with the divorce.

"Well, then, of course, I will be there. I will stay if you need me. I have a trailer I can bring to help with furniture. I am looking forward to meeting Sam, Bill not so much!"

"I really appreciate you being willing to go. Tell Larry and Stewart I will plan to wash dishes or tend bar next week to make it up to them."

He laughed. "See, you have a job waiting for you here no matter what Dave says! Now, go make that phone call! I will see you around twelve thirty with lunch. Then this afternoon, we can go see Susan and the kids."

I hung up and went back inside to get comfortable for the phone call that I was dreading most of all. I sat at the table and dialed Dave's cell phone. I got his voice message, so I left a message for him to call me back because I had talked to the lawyer today. I decided to start a load of clothes and make the bed while I waited. I got the load of clothes started, and my phone rang. I thought about letting it go to voicemail, but I knew there was no putting this off.

Dave said he was so glad to hear from me and asked what was going on with the divorce. I gave him all the details about the divorce being finalized two weeks from Monday on the condition that we had a signed contract and closing on the house. He asked if I thought we would be able to sell it that quickly. I shared that Bill had found someone who wanted to buy it for cash if they could close two weeks from Monday, probably so their children could start school in the district. He asked what I was going to do about a place to live. There was a long silence.

Dave finally said, "Maggie, just tell me what's on your mind. You know I will do what I can to help you."

I took a deep breath and asked him if he would be willing to let me work remotely on the foundation side of the business. He said that would not be a problem. He said that Amy could take on the executive assistant duties without a problem, but she just did not know the foundation side of the business well enough. He explained that he could only afford to justify twenty hours a week and then extra when we have functions.

"The most I could pay you is $500 per week and then extra for the functions. Would that work?"

I said, "That would depend on the answer to the next question."

He said, "Okay, go ahead and ask me."

I took a couple of deep breaths. "Would you be willing to let me rent the beach house from you so I could stay at the Isle of Palms?"

He laughed. "That's no problem at all. Remember, my wife hates that house. She says it is like a fishing shack. I keep trying to tell her the fishing shack has a nice pool. Anyway. Would you be willing to pay $700 per month? That would cover rent, pool, electricity, water, and internet. Could you swing that with a part-time salary and your settlement from the sale of your house?"

I insisted that I could make it work and I really appreciated it. "Now, here's the thing."

He laughed and said, "Oh, there's more!"

"Bill and Sam will be at the house this weekend packing up all that they want. I have a few furniture items and some personal things that I will want to bring to the beach. Is it okay to bring what I wanted from the house and put it in the house *and* may I have next week off to get everything moved out and the stuff that Bill and Sam leave donated to charity or trashed? I could start working part-time the following week."

"Of course, you can bring your furniture to the beach house. If you need me to get anything out to make room for your things, let me know. Our furniture can be stored downstairs in that storage room off the carport. As far as the job goes, could you work about ten hours next week and the following week? Then after your divorce is finalized, you can start the twenty hours a week. I will pay you for twenty hours a week for the next two weeks because you have so much overtime and vacation hours accumulated. Would you be willing to assist Amy via phone or Zoom if she needs any training?"

Where I Belong...

I had to stop myself from squealing! I suddenly felt like a giant weight had been lifted off my shoulders! I had a job, and I had a place to live. I could be frugal and make the money from the settlement last.

"Dave, I don't know how I can ever thank you. I really appreciate the fact that you are a wonderful friend and a wonderful boss. How can I ever repay you?"

He laughed. "I am glad to help. How about when you and William Riley get married, you and William work with me on some joint ventures for the two foundations!" I was silent and he added, "Don't you try to tell me that you two didn't hit it off. I could tell the last couple of times that I talked to you, and even from your emails, that there was something other than the sand, ocean, and salt air that was drawing you to Isle of Palms! Maggie, he is a great guy! I wish you all the happiness in the world!"

"Dave, I could just kiss you! Thank you!"

He said there was no need to thank or kiss him! He asked when I was coming into town.

"William and I will be at the house Friday morning. Sam and her husband are coming in Friday, and Bill is showing up, with doughnuts, Saturday."

He laughed and said he would stop by to see us Friday but he would be avoiding Saturday like the plague! "I will even come by Sunday if you need some help if you promise me Bill won't be there."

I said that I was sure Bill would spend as little time there as he possibly could. Dave laughed and said, "Just don't worry because everything is going to work out fine! You relax and enjoy the beach… and tell William hello for me."

I hung up from that call, and my video call request came through. I hoped they would be okay with me going to get a cup of coffee and a banana. This talking to all the world on the phone was getting tiring. I picked up the call, and we all had a few minutes of small talk while I refilled my coffee. They asked me what was going on, so I decided to just cut to the chase. I laid out the plan to divide the contents of the house this weekend, the sale of the house two weeks from Monday, the case settlement, and a finalized divorce.

They were both sitting there with their mouths hanging open, but they were not silent for long. They started with all the questions.

I assured them that it had all worked out. I was getting a settlement that I could frugally use. I was going to rent the house at the beach and stay there, and I was going to work remotely for Dave. They asked how I could work remotely with my current job for the long-term. I explained that I was changing jobs and would be handling the administrative aspects of the foundation work. That raised more questions. When I could get a word in, I informed them that I was going to work twenty hours a week for the foundation. My rent was reasonable enough that I could make it work for now.

I should have stopped without adding the "for now." They asked if I had other plans for the long-term and did they involve William? I admitted that I was seeing William, we were involved, we were going to play it day by day, and that was all they needed to know for now.

They both laughed, and Debbie said, "So you think you can get away with that answer with us? You know we will be there Wednesday. We are going to meet this William in person and see if he meets our approval."

"I am looking forward to your visit. We can all get together, and you can let me know what you think of William."

I assured them that I had a feeling of peace about the future. I was happy to be staying on the Isle of Palms and happy to be working part-time. I explained that the foundation work was my favorite part of my job. This way I did not have to deal with staff issues or board of director issues.

"I will be at the house in Columbia Friday, and Sam and her husband are coming in to help clear out the house this weekend. You two are welcome to come lend a hand and window shop the remnants! I know it's short notice, but come if you can." They both agreed they would try.

"Be sure to bring bathing suits Wednesday because there is a pool at the house, and we were a block from the ocean."

They asked if they should bring anything else.

"You may want to bring some dessert or a few snacks. Plan on a night at the Windjammer."

They said they were more interested in a night at William's place. I assured them that they would get a chance to meet him but I didn't know how much time he would be able to spend away from the bar.

"Ladies, I love you both so much, and I appreciate your friendship over all these years."

Annette said, "It sounded like someone was dying."

I apologized for sounding sappy, but I just wanted to make sure she knew how I felt about them both.

We were just finishing up the call when William walked in. Eagle-eye Debbie heard the door open and called him over. He came over and spoke to them both and said that he was looking forward to meeting them because he had heard so much about them. Debbie begged him not to believe everything he heard unless it was a story about me. He laughed and voiced his excitement about hearing all their "Maggie" stories!

I instructed them to have a good afternoon at work because I was going to go to Sullivan's Island. They said they would get to Isle of Palms around ten thirty and I better have the blender ready. I had a blender, but I was pretty sure I would have to buy blender materials.

I hung up and jumped up and wrapped my arms around William's neck. He hugged me back and took me over to the sofa. "I am assuming after that greeting that the final phone call with Dave went well."

"Yes, it went better than I expected. I am going to be able to rent the beach house and work remotely for the foundation twenty hours a week." I won't get rich, but it will allow me time to "play" with him and save the turtles!

He pulled me up into his lap and kissed me. I wrapped my fingers in his hair and settled in for a long kiss. He pulled away and grinned. He said he could tell that I was relieved because that was the most relaxed kiss I had given him all week. I confessed that when Dave said I could live here and work here, it felt like a huge weight had been lifted from my shoulders.

William asked if Dave had said anything about him. I hesitated and said that he said to tell him hello. He asked if there was anything else. He lifted my chin so our eyes met. "Maggie…anything else?"

"He said he would see you Friday." I went to get up, and he pulled me back down.

"And…"

I rolled my eyes and said, "Dave said, 'When you and William Riley get married. Maybe we can work on some joint ventures with the two foundations.'"

William grinned and kissed me. "That sounds like a really great idea!"

"Which part?"

He laughed and helped me up from the sofa. "I'm thinking both parts sound pretty good! Now let's eat some lunch and go get started on our part to save the turtles."

CHAPTER 11

Helping Turtles and Moonlit Walks (Waiting on the World to Change)

When we arrived at Susan and Artie's house, everyone was in the family room watching a Disney movie. William knocked on the door, and I could hear Kristie yelling, "They're here, they're here!" She opened the door and hugged her uncle! Susan walked into the entry and ushered us in. She asked Kristie to go get their artwork and we would gather at the table. She asked if anyone wanted some tea or a soft drink. We had just eaten lunch, so we didn't need anything.

I pulled out my note pages and my laptop. Kristie and David walked in with their artwork for the project. There were ten large drawings. Each had used crayons and watercolors to tell their stories about the Isle of the Sea Turtles. There were ten 11×17 drawings. William and I looked at each one. They were perfect. I asked if he had a scanner at the office.

He said, "If the one at the restaurant would not work, the one at the foundation office would take care of the job."

I stated that tomorrow, I would work on scanning their artwork and putting text on each page.

I shared with Susan that my daughter, Sam, had sent some scientific facts about sea turtles that I planned to incorporate in the back. William added that Sam had suggested partnering with the foundation on Sullivan's Island and maybe the coastal state parks who worked to protect the turtles to see if they could offer the books in the gift store or for sale online.

"Maybe the publisher would be willing to work out a deal to donate some of the proceeds to the turtle project." I added, "Sam had made a small crocheted turtle as a fundraising project for a science club on campus. She thought we could make some and have a package deal, book and turtle. Sam would be sending me a picture, and I would get her to bring one Friday."

The kids were excited about their pictures being in a book. Susan and Artie thought the fundraising idea sounded very promising. We talked for a while and then excused ourselves so they could get back to their movie. They asked us to stay, but William said he had a couple of errands to run. I had no idea what he was planning. I promised to keep them posted on the process. I hoped to get the draft to the publisher Wednesday. I still had one week left on my deadline, so I could have time for edits. I had plenty of time if they approved the idea.

We walked to the car, and William opened the door for me. I asked what errands he had to run. He winked and said that I would have to wait and see. I asked him for some hints, but he said that I would see when we got there. We were driving into Charleston. We turned into a parking lot, and I noticed the SC DEPARTMENT OF NATURAL RESOURCES sign. We parked, and he came around to open my door. We walked in, and he gave the guard our names and said that we had an appointment. The guard gave William a pass and directed us to the elevator. He said that the office was on the second floor. We walked to the elevator, and I declared that he was full of surprises. He smiled, and the elevator door opened, and I saw the sign: SEA TURTLE PROGRAM.

A DNR officer met us in the hall. We exchanged introductions, and he walked us to a conference room. He explained that William had called yesterday and explained a little bit about my idea for the book and fundraising idea. He gave us a brief overview of the program for the state. He said, "South Carolina has been a leader in sea turtle conservation efforts. In 1988, South Carolina became the first state to require Turtle Excluder Devices (TEDs), which prevented turtles from being caught in trawling nets. TEDs became a federal requirement in 1991."

It was nice to hear that South Carolina was a leader in something. It seemed like we always struggled to keep out of last place in education and road conditions just to name a few of our low points. We seemed to be first in things like domestic violence. He gave us a list of participating beaches, and when I skimmed the list, I saw that Edisto, Folly, Isle of Palms, and Sullivan's Island were all on the list. I saw that Bull Island was also on the list. He said that each beach had a volunteer coordinator, and those names and contact information were on the list. He said that the SC Aquarium had a Sea Turtle Care Center to help with sick and hurt turtles. I told him that we had seen it at the aquarium on Saturday.

He assured me that he appreciated any help that we would be willing to offer. He said that our work with foundations in South Carolina would make transition to working with the sea turtle conservation program an easy one.

"I look forward to learning more about the program and helping to make a difference."

He recommended taking a trip to Edisto State Park to see their program. He suggested that I work with the group on Isle of Palms or Sullivan's Island during hatching season. I gave him a little bit more information about the book and crocheted turtle idea. He said that it was possible that it could be picked up in all the coastal state parks by making the book and turtle available in gift stores on the properties and online.

I thanked him for all the information. He said that he knew it was a lot of information to take in all at one time.

"Yes, I am experiencing a little bit of information overload at the moment!"

He gave William a packet with two passes for Edisto. It included a water map if we wanted to make the trip by boat. He said that one of the park rangers would meet us and walk us through their program. William assured him that we would make the trip in a few weeks because the next couple of weeks were a little overbooked. I had to laugh because overbooked was an understatement: write a book by next week, clear out a house this weekend, sell a house in two weeks, get divorced, and transition to working for the foundation remotely. Add to that learning how to crochet a turtle and get a book published and picked up as a fundraiser effort for the SC Sea Turtle Management Program. No pressure at all.

We thanked him for his time. William assured him we would be in touch, and we made our way to the elevator and down to the car. He looked at me and asked if I was interested in that dinner at Poogan's Porch that we had missed the other night. I thought it sounded like a great idea. We parked and walked a bit and made our way to the restaurant. I asked him if I was dressed okay. He looked at my shorts and pointed to his shorts and said that we were wearing the perfect tourist attire!

We ordered a beer and an appetizer. He asked what I wanted for dinner, and I decided that I was going to stick with a salad because I had eaten more in the last four days than I had in over a year. He looked at me in disbelief.

"I decided just over a year ago that I had let myself go, so I started watching what I ate, did some walking, and then added some strength training. I hate to admit that I had that much to lose, but I lost eighty pounds. I still have one pants size that I want to drop."

He said that he was proud of me for what I had done because it took a lot of willpower. He said that he had started cutting back on the amount of beer he drank about a year ago and had dropped some weight. I admitted that I did not drink as much as I used to, but I still had my moments when I gave in; I still self-medicated with IPAs when life got to be a bit much. He said that maybe we could keep each other in check in that area because self-medicating was not a smart thing to do. I had to agree with him. Part of you says the beer will dull the pain. I guess briefly it does, but the side effects were not worth the momentary reprieve. So when it was all said and done, you still had the "blah" feelings then the headache and depression from the alcohol.

I thanked him for reaching out to the DNR people about the turtles. "When on earth did you have time to do that?"

He laughed and said, "It was amazing what you could get done at work at a bar at nine in the morning using Google and the 'contact us' feature on any website."

I really appreciated him taking the time to do it even though he was busy with work.

"Oh, this is just as much my project as it is yours now. I figure I will be crocheting turtles at the bar before it's all said and done."

I laughed. Maybe we could have a contest and ask people to crochet a turtle to get a free pint. He laughed and added, "That will work for the first pint. After that, I hate to think what the turtles would look like with a bunch of tipsy people crocheting them!"

I ate a salad, and he ate salmon. We skipped dessert and took a walk after dinner. We were both busy talking, so we were at the Battery before we knew it. We paused to look at the moonlight streaming down on the water. We stood there, arm in arm, silent. I felt a peace and happiness that I had not felt in years. Subconsciously, I reached up and touched his face and kissed him. He returned the kiss. After a minute, he looked at me. He touched my face.

"Why do you look so serious, almost sad?"

I assured him it was nothing, but he insisted that I talk. "I don't know, have you ever felt so happy that you were afraid it was all a dream and you were either going to wake up or it was going to turn into a nightmare or something?"

He said that he had wondered if it was a dream, but when he thought about it, it just seemed right.

I looked at him, and I was almost afraid to ask, but I decided I was going to be honest. "I have talked to you about Bill. What happened with your marriage? All I know is that you divorced, and your sister suggested you write a letter to get the feelings out in the open."

He did not release his tight grip around my arms, but he looked out at the moon and water. He sighed and paused for a moment. "It's a long story." I insisted that I had the time to listen.

"Well, Abbey and I met at school in New York. I went there for business school. We were both eighteen. It was my first time that far away from home for an extended time. She was from New York. I guess I found her liberal, free-spirited nature exciting. We were physically attracted to each other. We moved too quickly. I felt like we should get married, so one weekend, we did. Later I found out that she had been seeing a friend of mine on the side. She failed to stop that relationship even after we got married. I confronted her. I informed her I was moving back to SC because I thought if we moved and they had some distance, we could make it work. She came down here for a weekend trip, and she left in the middle of the night. She said she could not live down here in this backward area. She asked for a divorce and threatened to take me to the cleaners, which looking back was funny. I was nineteen, there was nothing for her to get. Everything was tied up in family investments and money. I declared that I would not give her a divorce, that we could just stay married. I stayed here and took over the One-Eyed Parrot and went to College of Charleston part-time. I got my bachelor's degree in business, but I learned so much more running the business. I was able to buy the business in about five years. I did not hear from her for two years. Then I received the paperwork where she was filing for divorce because she was going to marry my friend. So I agreed to the divorce, she married, and they have lived happily ever after in New York City ever since."

"Wow, I am sorry that she cheated on you. I know that had to hurt."

He said that when he looked back on it, they never really loved each other. "It was very young, naive, and superficial." He turned to face me and kissed me. "What I feel for you and the chemistry I feel between us is something I have never felt before."

I had to agree because I felt the same chemistry. "I know that Bill and I were married a long time. But for the last fifteen years, we had been living separate lives. Probably for seven years before that, we just went through the motions for appearance's sake, and for Sam. I am embarrassed to say that we lived out a lie for so many years. It hurts me to know that if I think back over the last five years, he has probably been involved with other women over all that time."

William hugged me and kissed me. "I think we are very fortunate to have found each other because we both deserve better. I promise that I will do everything in my power to make you feel loved, appreciated, and taken care of for the rest of my life if you will let me."

I smiled and threw my arms around his neck. "I think that sounds like the perfect way for us to spend the rest of our lives!"

He looked at his watch and said that we should probably get back home because it was going to be a busy day tomorrow. I had an entire book to write and pictures to scan since Debbie and Annette were coming on Wednesday. I agreed. He said that I could work in his office at the bar. If the scanner did not work, he would take me to the foundation office in Charleston. So we turned and walked hand in hand to the car.

We rode back in silence, but he never released my hand. Then he parked at my house and opened my door. He walked me to the door, unlocked the door, and came inside to check out the inside. I chuckled. He said that he wanted to make sure everything was okay before he left. He was going to go home and get a good night's rest so he would be mentally prepared to help me write this book if I needed his expert advice! I admitted that I appreciated him being on standby since this was my first attempt at writing. He said that between the two of us, Sam, Kristie, and David, we would have a bestseller!

He kissed me good night. I could feel myself wishing that his kisses and caresses never had to end, but I knew that he wanted to wait until the divorce was final. My head knew that he was smart and that it was the right thing to do. My heart and every other part of me wanted to throw caution to the wind. I pulled away, took a deep breath, and listened to my head.

CHAPTER 12

Drafting a Book and a Photo Shoot (Hit Me with Your Best Shot)

Again, I woke up before the clock went off. I took a shower and fixed a cup of coffee. I decided against the traditional protein shake and opted for a piece of toast with peanut butter and honey. I dressed casually because I planned to be sitting at a desk all day. I wore shorts and a T-shirt. I pulled my hair up and put on my best Clemson baseball cap. I gathered my laptop and power cord, my notebook, and Kristie's and David's drawings. I had my phone and the charger. I do not know why, but I decided to take my camera in case I needed a break from writing. I started to put a bottle of water into a plastic bag to take with me, and then I thought about all the implications the plastic products had for the sea turtles. Well, I guess this project would make me rethink how I did some things. I had reusable shopping bags at home. I had reusable water bottles. I had been used to no straws at the zoo in Columbia for years. You either had to do without or bring/buy a reusable straw. These were small changes, but if enough people made the changes, we could make a difference.

I had everything loaded in my arms and was opening the door when William appeared. "Good morning, Maggie Mae. Your chariot awaits!"

I kissed him good morning and insisted that I could walk. He said that I didn't need to walk since he was here. He took the tote bag and camera bag. I locked the door, and we walked to the car. I knew to wait for him to open the door. Bill had not opened the door for me in twenty-five years; this had been a refreshing change. Maybe I was more old-fashioned that I thought!

We drove and parked in front of the bar. I asked him how he knew that I would be ready to go that early. He said he knew that I had heard him say that he got to the bar at nine. We both just laughed at each other. He unlocked the door, cut off the alarm, and turned on the lights. We walked back to the office. He moved a few things off the desk to make room for my laptop and my notebook. He connected his scanner/printer to my laptop and loaded it with paper. I put my water glass and coffee cup down. He picked up my water glass to fill it with water. He came back with some fruit from the kitchen. He checked to make sure I had an internet connection and that the printer was working. He pulled the chair out and motioned for me to sit. When I sat down, he held on to the arms of the chair and pulled me toward him for a kiss. I reminded him that if he kept that up, we would not get any work done on this book. He released the arms and placed my chair in front of my laptop. He motioned for me to get busy but reminded me that if I needed more coffee, water, or to stretch my legs, he and the bar would be just beyond that door. He asked if I needed any background noise to block out the restaurant noise. I assured him if I did, I could pull up some music on my phone or on YouTube. He gave me one more kiss on the forehead and left me to work.

I decided that the first thing I would do was scan the pictures. I scanned each one, did a few edits, and saved as a separate picture file. When I had all of them scanned and saved, I opened a Word document and began with the title page: *Life on Turtle Isle*. Kristie had done the perfect picture of waves, sand, and turtles for the title page. I inserted the photo and the title. Next came the byline: As told by Kristie and David Smith. Transcribed by Maggie Nelson. All original artwork by Kristie and David Smith. I decided to do a dedication page: To Uncle William for bringing us together to complete this project!

Then I inserted a picture on each page and inserted the story Kristie and David had told word for word. After the final "and they lived happily ever after" page, I decided this was the perfect place for some of the facts about sea turtles that Sam had sent me. Then I included a page about the DNR program to save the turtles from extinction. I included a page with the beaches that had programs to assist in the preservation efforts along with contact information. I tried to keep this general instead of to a specific person in case the contact changed over the years. I was trying to think long-term for the book.

I saved the file as "Life on Turtle Isle Draft 1" and printed a copy. William had a color printer, so it turned out looking pretty good. I decided I needed to stand up and stretch. I went down the hall to the restroom. I grabbed my water cup and coffee cup and went into the bar for a refill. William was working behind the bar. He looked up and gave me a smile and a wink and asked how it was going. I reported that I had a first draft. He looked as happy as I did to have that first step complete. I informed him that I was going to go sit out on the deck before reading the draft. He asked if he could read the draft. I hesitated. Part of me wanted to at least do a first read, but I gave in. I figured he had as much riding on this project as I did. I left my water and coffee cups with him while I went back to his office to retrieve the draft copy. I brought a red marker for him to make edits.

I traded the coffee and water for the draft copy and pen. I instructed him to be brutally honest but in a kind way. I asked him to read it from the point of view of a child who was a princess of a land called Turtle Isle.

I left him to read and went out to the patio. It was about ten thirty, so I retrieved my sunscreen from my backpack and coated my face and arms. I had fair skin, and at forty-nine, I had already had enough "suspicious" spots frozen or cut off to make me very respectful for what the sun could do. Unfortunately, I had spent my teen years tanning, many times with baby oil all over my skin and lemon juice in my hair. I was paying the price for that now.

Where I Belong...

Some people were flying kites and playing volleyball, so I came back in to get my camera bag. I decided I needed to take some photos for a little change of pace. I took a few shots of kites—just the kites with the blue sky and puffy white clouds as a backdrop. There were rainbow kites, Spider-Man kites, and a few kites with streamers that reminded me of a Chinese dragon. Next, I changed lenses so I could get a landscape of the kites with their fliers on the beach. I took a few landscape shots of the volleyball game. Then I switched to get shots of the volleyball players and kite fliers with all the facial expressions. I walked out on the beach and took a few shots of sandpipers and seagulls. I took some shots of children playing in the waves. I loved taking photographs because it felt like I was capturing a specific moment in time for all eternity. I could have stayed out here all day, but I decided I better get back to the task at hand: getting a first draft to the publisher.

I turned to go back in, and William was leaning on the railing of the deck watching me. I smiled and walked up to him. He confessed that he could watch me take photos for hours because I seemed to escape into whatever world I was photographing. He said that he did not know if that made sense, but it was just magical to watch. I concurred that it made sense to me because I felt like I was in the moment capturing it for all eternity. I wish I had the power to read the thoughts of the people I was photographing because I thought the combination of their words and the captured expressions on their faces could tell a story. He suggested that maybe *that* needed to be my next project—a photo book or photo collection.

I argued that there were so many photographers that could capture so much more in a photo, that my work did not compare. He encouraged me not to sell myself short. He reminded me that he had asked to look at my photos before. I suggested that we could have a photo slideshow tonight if he wanted to. I downloaded my photos into folders on my laptop. I had several years' worth of photography on there. I had to download this week's photos, and I would do that today. I asked him how the draft looked. He said that he would not change a thing unless he could give me more credit. He said that I had given credit to Kristie, David, and even him. I assured him I gave credit where credit was due! When I submitted the sample to the publisher, my goal was to get *them* published. After talking to him and the kids and talking to DNR, I felt that the ones who needed to be recognized were the sea turtles and the people who were trying to save them.

We walked back inside. I got my water, and he poured me a cup of coffee. I looked at him. He said that he knew not to pour it right away if I was going out to take photos. I just smiled. It always amazed me how well he seemed to know and understand me. He carried my coffee and followed me back to the office.

"So what changes do I need to make to the draft? I will make them and submit it to the publisher."

He said, "It was perfect because it captured the storyline that Kristie and David wanted to tell."

I told him if he were sure, I would go ahead and submit a week ahead of the deadline! He encouraged me to go for it, and then he wanted me to download the pictures from this week so he could look at them. Then he wanted to look at photos from my state park trips.

So I insisted that he go back to work. I would submit the draft to the publisher. I asked if I should send a copy to Susan's email. He said that would be great and gave me her address. I emailed the publisher and attached the draft. I offered to submit individual .jpg files of the drawings if she needed them. I stated that I knew it was a different direction from my original proposal, but I felt that this was a direction I needed to follow. I outlined the idea of using it as an awareness campaign and fundraiser for the DNR and volunteer programs in South Carolina to save the sea turtles. I reread the email a few times before pressing "send." I had done all that I could do unless they turned it down. Then we would have to self-print. That was an option we could explore.

Next, I emailed Susan and attached a copy of Kristie and David's book. I let her know that I had sent it to the publisher. I indicated that if this publisher did not accept it, I would check with other publishers, then we could always self-publish and go through the volunteer groups or DNR as a fundraising vehicle. I asked her to let me or William know what she and the kids thought.

That project was marked off my list. I uploaded my photos from my week in Charleston and Isle of Palms. I still felt like I had known William and been here more than a week. I created a folder and uploaded the photos. Then I looked at each photo; if they were blurry or just not any good, I deleted them. When I finished, I had 140 photographs from my visit. Some of the best ones were those from the kite flying and volleyball game today. The Middleton Place shots were good too. I closed the folders and put my camera on to charge.

I drank some coffee and checked emails. The usual routine: work, home, then texts. I responded to a few. I looked at my phone, and I had a missed call from Bill. He must have called while I was outside, or he just sent it directly to voicemail so he did not have to talk to me. I punched in my code and listened. He was just confirming that he would be there Saturday morning to pack up a few things. He said that he wanted a few pieces of furniture from the den and his office then some personal items and clothes. He requested the bedroom set and the yard tools. I replayed the message a second time. I shook my head. I called him back and sent a message straight to voicemail that said, "See you Saturday. Take what you want." I was hanging up and mumbling under my breath when William came in. He asked who I was mad at.

I admitted that I was not mad, not even disappointed, just aggravated. I played the message for him. I looked at him and sighed, "I know it is nothing to be aggravated about, I guess he just ticks me off by just breathing."

He asked what my reply had been.

"I left a message that simply said, 'Take what you want and see you Saturday.'" I sighed again. I hated that hearing his voice and talking about him just seemed to grate on my nerves.

William pulled my chair to him and kissed me. He said that it was totally understandable. He looked deep into my eyes and said, "Remember, I love you. Whatever he takes is just 'stuff.' He cannot take your happy memories from Sam's childhood or the happy memories from your early years of marriage…and he definitely cannot take your current happiness. Let him go."

I smiled and grabbed him and pulled his face to mine. We kissed. I told him that I loved him. We continued to kiss and then he pulled away.

"Hey, the reason I came in here is that I had this excited voice message from Kristen, David, Susan, and even Artie. They all loved the book. They were so excited that you submitted it, and they can't wait to hear what happens next."

I smiled because I was so glad that they were happy with it. He pulled me up from my chair and suggested that we have lunch. I looked at my watch; I guess I did not realize it was already one thirty.

We went out to the bar, and he asked me what I wanted. Before I answered, he said, "Let me guess, 'tossed salad with grilled chicken, balsamic dressing.'"

I commended him it on a good guess. He asked if I wanted a celebratory IPA to go with it. I said that only if he was sitting, eating, and drinking with me. He assured me he thought that could be arranged. He asked if I was willing to sit up at the bar and if he could work and eat at the same time. He said one of his waitresses, Nancy, had called in sick, so he had to help with lunch rush. I had no problem with sitting at the bar. I offered my services if they were shorthanded: I could help with dishes or bussing tables. He leaned across the bar and guaranteed that I would always have a job there if I needed it.

We ate and talked. He poured a few beers and took food to a few tables. I cleared our dishes from the bar and took them to the kitchen. I scrapped them, rinsed them, and put in the dishwasher. I grabbed a pan and rag to clear a few tables. I started at the back corner and got four tables cleared and ready for the next rush of customers. I looked at the clean dish supply; we had a sizable stack of clean dishes, so I just rinsed these and put them in the dishwasher. I decided I could clear two more tables before I washed and sanitized these.

William came in to see what I was doing. He checked behind me and offered to hire me on the spot. I offered my services for as long as he needed them since I had completed my assigned task for the day by getting the book to the publisher.

He suggested that I take a seat at the bar and relax until the next couple of tables cleared. He said that he would appreciate it if I got those tables cleared and ready and started the load of dishes. He asked how I knew what to do. I laughed and confessed that Larry had given me a quick tutorial the other night when they were swamped.

I sat for a while and cleared four tables and washed the dishes. I unloaded the dishwasher and put them in sanitizer trays and ran them through a cycle. I got the clean dish and silverware bins reloaded. By that time, it was three and the rush was over. William and I both sat at a table and enjoyed a beer. Beverly and another waitress came in for the dinner shift, so they were in good shape.

I offered to stay and help, and he said that they would be fine. It was Tuesday, no specials tonight, so it would probably be slow. Since I was relieved of my duties, I decided to run home and put my laptop and camera away. I wanted to clean the bathroom and make the bed in the spare bedroom for Debbie and Annette. We had the chicken casserole in the freezer, and I had salad fixings on hand. I had bread, and William offered to bring a dessert. I thought we would be fine for tomorrow night. They were not supposed to get there until around four. The plan was to visit and swim then have dinner at the house.

He said that he was going to work until seven, then he would come by if that was okay. It sounded perfect to me. He asked what I wanted him to bring for dinner. I offered to go to the store and get some steaks, potatoes, and maybe some veggies to grill if he was willing to grill. He seemed pleased with the idea. So I had my assignment. I would go to the store and get food for dinner and some breakfast food for Debbie and Annette for Thursday. I was going to pick up some soft drinks and some beer and wine. I knew Debbie and Annette well enough to know they would bring their own beer or liquor if they wanted something specific. I guess I needed to get drink ingredients for the blender; I would have to ask William about that because I wasn't really a "blender kind of girl."

I went to IGA and got the groceries, came home, and put them away before taking a dip in the pool. It was hot and muggy, and the pool felt good. I sat out for a little while to dry. Then I went in and took a quick shower. I put on a sundress and dried my hair. I put on a little makeup and was on my way to the living room when William knocked on the door.

I opened the door and threw my arms around his neck. He admitted that this was the kind of greeting he had looked forward to all afternoon. He kissed me and put his arms around my waist. He worked his hands around to feel my waist and down my dress to pull me close. He stopped kissing me and pulled me closer. He whispered under his breath in my ear, "God, you look beautiful. Your sundresses are going to be the death of me yet!"

I smiled at him and asked if the sundress was better than his T-shirt and shorts, and he just pulled me tighter against his chest.

"It's a very close second. Now let's cook before I do something I shouldn't."

I smiled and led him to the kitchen. I had the steaks in a marinade. The potatoes were washed and wrapped in foil, and I had sliced zucchini, summer squash, carrots, and onions to grill. I stacked the three pans with meat, potatoes, and veggies together. I grabbed utensils and two beers. He carried the three pans, and we walked to the back patio. He started the grill, and we sat at the patio table while it warmed up. I lit the citronella candles to try to keep the bugs away. I asked how the rest of the afternoon had gone. He said that it had been busier than usual, but they were fine for the dinner shift. I volunteered my services to go help and wash dishes if needed. He insisted that my shift at the bar was done for the day.

William put the pan of vegetables and the wrapped potatoes on the grill. He asked why the potatoes were different shapes, and I admitted that I was not sure if he would want a white potato or a sweet potato. I reassured him that I was fine with whichever one he did not want. He said that he appreciated my thoughtfulness.

In reality, it just meant I did not know enough about his food preferences. I confessed that I thought I had seen him eat a white potato with butter and sour cream with steak and I had seen him eat a sweet potato with salmon. He said that I was thoughtful and very observant; he thought I had a future as a private investigator. He liked a regular potato with beef and sweet potato with chicken or fish. I confessed that I liked both, but sweet potatoes were a little less starchy.

"For me it was all about the carbs! I wanted the sweet potato with butter. If I were deathly thin, I would add brown sugar, so odds are you would not see me eating it with butter and brown sugar in this lifetime!"

We put the steak in the outdoor fridge while the potatoes and veggies cooked. He asked if I had downloaded my photos to my laptop, and I confirmed that they were loaded and ready. He said that after dinner, he wanted to have that slideshow I had promised. He checked the vegetables, and they were ready. So he took those off the grill. We kept them covered with foil on the counter. He put the steaks on the grill. He asked how I liked my meat cooked. I would eat a steak anyway, but my favorite was rare. He said that he would do his best, but it was always hard with a grill you were not familiar with. He set his watch to check it after three minutes. He flipped both and set his watch for two minutes. After two minutes, he pulled the steak off the grill and checked the temperature with a meat thermometer. According to the thermometer, they were both a perfect rare.

I had brought two plates, silverware, and napkins down. He fixed the plates while I poured us each a glass of water. We had put two rolls on the upper rack for the last two minutes. He put one on each plate. We sat down to eat. He complimented me on the seasonings on the vegetables and steak. I in turn complimented his cooking because everything was delicious! We ate and talked about the day at the bar, the book, and about tomorrow. I think he was nervous to meet Debbie and Annette, but I indicated that all he needed to do was be himself and he would be fine. I was worried that he might not like them. They were a pair that you had to get used to—an acquired taste. Loud, outspoken, but if they claimed you as friend, they would walk through fire and to the end of the earth for you.

As we were finishing up, he went upstairs to get a tin pan he had brought with him. He brought it along with a can of whipped cream. He put the tin pan on the grill and set the temperature to warm. I decided to put the food up and clear dishes while he did that. I put leftovers in the refrigerator and rinsed dishes and put them in the dishwasher. I pulled out two dessert plates, two spoons, two forks, and napkins and went downstairs. When I got there, he was pulling the tin off the grill. He took the two plates and plated a dessert chocolate chip cookie and added a whipped cream.

He brought them to the table. They looked delicious. I took a bite. If chocolate had *not* been my favorite food group, this would have been great. Since chocolate *was* my favorite food group, this was absolutely wonderful. We ate dessert and put all the dishes and leftovers on a tray to take upstairs. He cleaned off the grill. I was going to blow out the candles, and he stopped me. He took me by the hand, and we sat on the edge of the pool and dangled our feet in the water. He said he wanted to sit outside for a bit before we went in to look at photographs. He took my face into his hands and kissed me. Then he traced his finger around by cheek and down my throat. He kissed my throat and ran his finger down my collarbone, down my shoulder, and down my arm. He kissed me again, and I could feel the heat rise in my face. He grabbed me around the waist and caressed my back. He put his hand on my knee and ran his finger up my thigh. I could feel my heart race, and I stiffened my back. He pulled away and looked at me.

"I told you that your sundress was going to drive me wild. Part of me wants to walk you up those stairs to your bedroom and make love to you. The reasonable side of me remembers that I said I would wait until after the divorce to make sure that our relationship caused no problems for you with your divorce. Then there is another part of me that says that I love you, and I want to do this right. I want to marry you and make love to you on our wedding night."

I took a deep breath and confessed that everything about him was driving me crazy! I was conflicted too. I confessed that part of me wanted to pull him into the pool right here and have a good time on the patio. Another part could go for the waiting until we made it to the bedroom. Yet another side, liked his romantic and caring side, wanted to wait until we got married. I stated that this just meant we *had* to get married, and I might not be able to wait years.

He laughed and pulled my face closer to his. He kissed me and said, "What are your plans for the afternoon after your divorce?" He took a deep breath and pulled away. "No, I must do better than that. How about one month after your divorce?" He reached into his pocket and pulled out a tiny little black box. "Now this is a preliminary gift. I'll put the real one on your finger after the divorce. We can think of this as a placeholder!"

He opened the box, looked into my eyes, and said, "Maggie Mae, will you make me the happiest man on the island and say you will marry me?"

How could he surprise me like this every day? I never thought he would ask me to marry him. When I thought about the way I felt about him, I had no answer other than yes.

I took his face in mine and said, "Yes, because with all of my heart, I love you."

We kissed for a long time, then he pulled away and took a deep breath and put the ring on my finger. I assured him that it was beautiful and no post-divorce ring was necessary. We kissed, and he said, "No, this is an eternity band to remind you how I feel about you. It will fit perfectly with your engagement ring and your wedding band. Now, let's go inside, get some coffee, and look at your photos."

He jumped up and took me by the hand to help me up. He took the dessert tray, I blew the candles out, and we went upstairs.

I went into the bedroom and came back with a sweater. He laughed and asked what I was doing. I indicated I was going to try to stop the effects of the sundress. He shook his head and said, "A sweater won't help because I know what's under the sweater. I will just kiss, hug, and caress you for a month. I might even hold you while you sleep…but I will save the big reveal for the wedding night."

I felt like I blushed from head to toe. He kissed me on the forehead and just laughed.

"I love the fact that you are so shy. You are beautiful, and I love you. The reveal will be fun! Now let's look at your photographs."

I opened the folder with photos from this week. William loved the architectural shots at Middleton Place and from downtown. I liked the water shots from Middleton, the Battery, and the ocean from today. The kites looked great against the bright blue sky. I had a few surprise shots from today. I had taken a few pictures of him working behind the bar and one when he was leaning on the rail of the deck. Those were my favorites. He blushed when he saw the pictures of him. I showed him some shots from the zoo in Columbia and some of my favorites from the state parks around the state. I showed him my Facebook page and added him as a friend so he could look at some of my past photos. I had not added any of this week's photos to Facebook. Part of me wanted to wait until after the divorce.

He complimented my photographs and said there were a couple of state parks that he wanted to visit with me. That would be something fun to look forward to. I knew that he had been up very early today to open the bar, so I suggested that he should go rest up so he could be prepared to meet Debbie and Annette.

CHAPTER 13

The Whirlwind That Is Debbie and Annette (You've Got a Friend)

I was exhausted when I went to bed, and I failed to set my clock. So when there was a knock at the door at seven thirty, I jumped up and went to the door in my pajama bottoms and tank top. When I opened the door, William put his head in his hand and said, "You are going to kill me!" He grabbed me and hugged me. I apologized.

"I either didn't set my alarm or my phone must have died."

He said that he thought my phone had died because he had tried to call before he came over to see me in pajamas. I apologized again and offered to go put on a sweater. He said that it was too late because he knew what was under the sweater! I went to get a sweater anyway, and I put my phone on to charge.

When I came back, he had fixed two cups of coffee. He asked if I had heard anything from the publisher. I opened my laptop and checked my email. There was an email from Susan saying that they loved the draft. I made my way through a ton of spam mail and found a response from the publisher. They said they *loved* the idea of the book itself and the idea of a partnership with the DNR and/or volunteer groups working with the sea turtle protection. I showed the email to William, and he offered to let a foundation attorney look at the contract that had been attached. I appreciated the offer because legal documents usually made my eyes glaze over.

He promised that he would keep me posted. He also said that he would call Susan because she had left five messages. He asked what time Debbie and Annette would be getting in. I was pretty sure they wouldn't get here until three with traffic. He asked what I had on my agenda for the day. I stated that I would come over to the bar and see him around eleven. Other than that, I would probably just stick around here. He asked if I was feeling okay. I insisted that I was fine, just tired because the stress of this weekend was looming on the horizon. He told me not to worry. He asked if I wanted a neck rub.

I admitted that I would love one, but I was not expecting him to do that since I was wearing these sexy pajama bottoms and tank top. He laughed and said that I had no idea how sexy I really looked. I had my doubts that I had jumped up out of a dead sleep and looked sexy, but if he could hold on to those kinds of thoughts, the wedding night would be great.

He grabbed me and kissed me and then walked me to the bedroom. "Okay, one neck rub coming up. After that, I will even hold you while you go back to sleep if you want. I promise, I will not misbehave!"

I laid down on the bed, and he rubbed my neck, shoulders, and back. It was one of the best back rubs I have had in a while. He laid down on the pillow beside me and suggested that we snuggle until he had to go to work. He pulled me close and kissed my forehead. He insisted that I close my eyes and rest, and he promised to wake me up at ten thirty or eleven.

I had no plans to go to sleep, but I wrapped my arm around his waist, and it just felt so comfortable. I had planned to close my eyes for a minute to rest. The next thing I knew, he was squeezing my shoulder and telling me to wake up. He said that he would wait in the living room while I took a shower and got ready. I took a quick shower, dressed, and dried my hair.

We held hands as we walked to the bar. I sat at the bar, and he brought me a cup of coffee. He asked if I wanted breakfast or lunch. I chose breakfast—eggs and toast. While he went back to the kitchen, I checked text messages and emails. Sam sent a message that she would see me at the house Friday around lunchtime. She said that her husband was not coming, but she would be there until the following week. I wondered what that meant. Debbie had sent a text that she and Annette would be there by three thirty. I sent the address to both in a text. There were no personal or work emails that needed any response. Bill had not responded to my text, so maybe he knew that he had ticked me off.

William came out with eggs and toast. He asked if I wanted any bacon, sausage, or grits. I assured him that just eggs and toast would be plenty. I'm watching the calories and all! They were not busy, so he came around and sat with me.

"I had heard from Annette and Debbie, and they would be getting here around three thirty. I also had a text from Sam to say her husband was not coming. He said that maybe he was not able to get away from work. I hoped that it really was just work."

After I finished my breakfast, I got up to go back to the house to wait on Debbie and Annette. I instructed him to add my breakfast to my tab. He smiled and said that my tab was getting to be quite steep. I winked at him and promised to wash dishes to work off my tab if it got too high. He leaned over the bar and kissed me and promised he would keep the job as dishwasher open for me. I had not really noticed, but Roy the fireman was sitting at the other end of the bar.

He looked at William and said, "Hey, I don't get a kiss? How about the option to wash dishes to pay my bill?"

William assured him that both were benefits reserved for special customers.

Roy looked at us both and chuckled, "Man, I'm hurt. I thought we were friends!"

William patted him on the shoulder and said, "Man, we are friends, but we are not friends with benefits!"

I just looked at them both and wished them a good day! I assured William I would call him later.

Roy waved goodbye to me and said, "Bye sweetie, call me!"

I rolled my eyes and just kept walking.

I got back to the house, and I decided I should probably call Nellie and check on the house. I needed to let her know that I would be back Friday morning and that Sam was coming and Bill, and it would probably be wise to tell her about William before she sought out information on her own. I dialed her number, and she answered on the first ring. She asked about the beach, so I gave her a brief overview of the week here. I asked if everything was okay with the house. She said that it had been quiet; no one had been by. I indicated that the alarm company had not called, so I figured it was okay since I had followed her advice and changed the code.

I told her that I was going to be coming back Friday morning and I was bringing a family friend to help pack up some stuff. She did not ask any questions, and I did not volunteer any information. I added that Sam would be coming in Friday afternoon.

She said, "It would be good to see Sam again."

Then I warned her that Bill was coming to get his things Saturday. She did not hide her disgust. She asked if he would be bringing his girlfriend. I guess the question caught me off guard. I indicated that I was sure that he would not be foolish enough to do that because Debbie and Annette would probably be there Saturday to help too. She laughed and said that if she did show up, Debbie would take care of her. I had to laugh. I thanked her for keeping an eye on the house, and I said that I would see her Friday. After I hung up, I could not help but hope that Bill would not be foolish enough to bring Stacey.

I was pondering the thought of Debbie and Annette running interference between me and Bill and Stacey when the doorbell rang. I opened the door, and there stood Debbie and Annette. Each had a small tote bag of clothes, and they were carrying a huge cooler. They put the cooler down, and we hugged. I laughed out loud because only they would bring more beer than clothes! I ushered them inside. I held the door open while they brought the cooler in and put it in the kitchen. They both looked around and said they liked the place. I took them back to the guest bedroom so they could drop off their very small tote bags and purses. I showed them the hall bathroom and the master bedroom. They both said it was cute and comfortable.

Debbie said that her favorite part was the huge screened-in porch. I suggested that they refrain from picking their favorite spot until they saw the backyard. I recommended that they grab their sun

Where I Belong...

hats and a couple of beers and follow me. I walked them down the stairs to the pool and outdoor kitchen. I showed them the restroom and outdoor shower. They both agreed that this was the new favorite part. I opened a couple of umbrellas to shield us from the sun. I told them to have a seat and enjoy a beer. They offered me one, but I was going to stick with water since I knew we would probably end up at the Windjammer later.

I asked them about the drive down. They said it was not too bad until they hit the 199 exit on I-26. I indicated that since all the people were moving in for Volvo and a couple of other plants, the traffic from that point was always bad. I shared about the highlights of my week: the trip to Middleton Place and the aquarium. I told them about submitting the draft book proposal and the fact that the publisher had accepted it. They asked about the status of the divorce, and I gave them an update about the sale of the house and the plans to clear out the house this weekend. They said they would try to come at one point to help. They said that they had to work Friday. Debbie's children were coming in Saturday, and Annette said that she had a family commitment. I assured them that there was no need to worry about coming to help. I felt that between William, Sam, Bill, and me, we could get it cleared out with no problems.

I filled them in on my plans to move here and rent this house from Dave for a while. I caught them up on Dave's offer to let me work for the foundation remotely. They asked if I would be able to afford to do that, and I assured them that I was going to be able to make it work since Dave was offering to rent the place to me for a reasonable rate, and with the settlement from the house, I would be fine.

Annette stood up and looked at me and said, "Okay, so what's the latest with Liam?"

Debbie shot her a glaring stare. "What, you know you want to know too! Do not answer yet. I am going to go upstairs and get a couple of beers. Wait until I come back to respond. I don't want to miss anything."

She ran up the stairs, and I just shook my head. I guess I was surprised we had made it one hour into the conversation without them bringing up his name and asking questions. I stood up and asked if Annette wanted anything to eat. I offered to make some sandwiches. We both were heading up the stairs as Debbie was coming down. I suggested that she turn around and head back to the kitchen with us. I made sandwiches while they sat at the breakfast bar.

Annette looked at me. "Okay, spill it. Are you and Liam getting serious? Tell us everything."

I took a deep breath and decided to just get it over with. "Yes, we are pretty serious. It's been a long time since I have felt this way, but I am pretty sure we have fallen in love with each other. He asked me to marry him, and I said yes."

I looked up at Debbie and Annette, and both looked stunned, and their mouths were hanging open. I leaned over and pushed their mouths closed and suggested we take our sandwiches and chips out on the screened-in porch instead of back to the pool because the porch was a little cooler.

We sat down at the table and ate in silence for a little while. I think they were both in shock. I had never seen these two stay this quiet for this long. Debbie finally spoke. "Well, I never expected that answer. I guess you know that he must pass our test. We have to make sure he is good enough for you."

I divulged to them that I had already figured that was a given. Debbie said, "Well, are we going over to the One-Eyed Parrot to meet him, or is he coming over here? Maybe he can join us at the Windjammer!"

I indicated that we had discussed dinner here and then a trip to the Windjammer.

We finished our sandwiches, and Annette suggested we go for a swim. I cleared the table and cleaned up the kitchen while they went to change into their bathing suits. I suggested that they go ahead and start without me while I changed into my suit. I asked them what time they wanted to go to the Windjammer. I told them I had a chicken casserole, salad, and bread for dinner here. They suggested going to the Windjammer at eight, which was an excellent plan.

I went toward the bedroom to change, and Annette called to me, "Hey, go ahead and text William and see when he is coming over. You know we should go ahead and get the introductions over with!"

I just looked at them and left the room. I knew that this was going to happen. I also knew there was no need for me to be nervous because they would love William as much as I did, but still, it made me nervous. I did not want him to feel like he was going to have to pass some test or inspection. I changed and put on sunscreen. I gathered some towels and the sunscreen. I sat on the edge of the bed and texted William. He called. He insisted that he did not mind being tested by my friends because that just meant they cared about me.

"Just relax and enjoy a swim and the visit. I'll come over at six thirty if that was okay. We can eat, they can grill me with questions, and if I pass, I will go to the Windjammer with you. Now don't worry. I'll bring dessert and see you at six thirty. Now go visit and swim!"

I grabbed the towels, sunscreen, and put on a baseball cap and went down to the pool. They had already jumped in the pool. So I put the things down and got in the pool.

"So did you call 'lover boy'?"

I glared at them and said that I had talked to him and he was coming over at six thirty for dinner. I reminded them that they had to be nice. They assured me that they would be on their best behavior. We floated and talked. We reminisced about high school and college. They asked about Sam. It was a fun afternoon. I informed them that I was going to get out around five thirty. I rinsed off in the outdoor shower and sat out to dry off a bit. They got out and did the same. I assured them that they could continue to play, but I was going to take a quick shower, dress, and get the casserole in the oven. They asked what they could do to help, and I suggested that they could set the table.

I got up to go inside. They informed me that they were going to drink a beer, then they would be in. I went in and took the casserole out of the freezer and went to shower. Man, I hoped they really would be on their best behavior.

I put my dirty clothes in the hamper and hung my suit on the porch. I was getting out the ingredients for a tossed salad when

Debbie and Annette came in. Debbie sat at the bar and talked and watched me make the salad while Annette took a shower. Then Annette switched places while Debbie showered. The casserole was warmed through, so I put it on top of the stove while I warmed the bread. Then I put the casserole back in the oven to keep it warm. Annette put the bread in a basket and covered it with a towel. She and Debbie set the table, and the doorbell rang.

Debbie looked at me, and Annette and said, "Showtime!"

I begged them to be nice. I took a deep breath and opened the door. William hugged me with one arm and handed me the dessert. I took it, and he gave me a kiss. I put the dessert on the breakfast bar. I turned and made introductions, and they all shook hands. I asked if everyone was ready to eat or if they wanted to sit in the living room for a while. Debbie suggested we go ahead and eat because they could interrogate William while we ate.

I shot her a glance, and William chuckled. "Maggie, it's okay. Debbie, Annette, fire away!"

William helped me get the salad and casserole to the table. I asked what everyone wanted to drink, and everyone said water. I was relieved because I thought Debbie and Annette needed to start hydrating if they were going to keep up this pace at the Windjammer. William grabbed five bottles of water from the refrigerator and put them on the table. We sat down, and I started the bread in one direction and the salad in another.

Debbie and Annette waited until we all had salad, and then they started the barrage of questions. "How did you meet? Where are you from? Who is your family? How long have you owned the bar? Can you really make that much money owning a bar? What are your intentions with Maggie?"

He answered them all. I think they were pleasantly pleased to find out who his "people were" and that he had a money source other than the bar. When they got to the question about the intentions, I threw my hands up in the air.

"You have hit him with twenty questions during the salad course. How about we at least get to the casserole first? Besides, his intentions are really none of your business."

They agreed to a short cease-fire while we ate casserole. They complimented us on the dinner, and each got a second helping of casserole.

Debbie cleared her throat and asked if she could ask the question about his intentions now that we were in the middle of the main course. I told her no, but William spoke up. He said that he had no problem answering the question.

He calmly looked at them both and said, "I know that we just met, but I feel like I have known Maggie all my life. I love her, and it is my intention to marry her as soon after her divorce is final as she will let me."

For the second time today, both of their mouths dropped open. I cleared my throat and assured them that they should close their mouths because it was not an attractive look. They closed their mouths, and Annette looked at me.

"So, Maggie, what are your intentions with William and his proposed plan?"

I put my fork down on my plate and looked at her and said, "It is my intention to marry him. Would anyone care for dessert?"

I got up and picked up the salad bowls. William gathered the plates. I pulled out some dessert plates and took the cover off the dessert. "Yum. Chocolate delight!" I scooped up four servings, and William took two to the table while I carried the other two. I brought four spoons and sat down. I was enjoying this second-long silence. The dessert was perfect. Debbie agreed that it was delicious.

Annette looked up, cleared her throat, and said, "Well, I'm thinking you passed the first phase of our inspection and test! Welcome to the family! You will always bring dessert!"

The rest of the meal was spent in small talk. Debbie and Annette asked if I had a game plan for clearing the house this weekend. I admitted to her that I really had no game plan. I planned for Sam to pick her items on Friday. Bill could take what he wanted on Saturday. I only had some things from the kitchen, my clothes, a few paintings, and knickknacks that I wanted. I had a few small pieces of furniture from my mom that I wanted. I assured them that unless they knew of something that they wanted from what was left, I was going to have Habitat come make a pickup. Debbie and Annette both said that they had no room for any more furniture. Then Sunday, I had a group coming by that claimed that they "bought junk." I assured them that I didn't care if they bought it, I just wanted to be able to walk out of there Sunday or Monday morning with the house totally cleaned out.

I asked if anyone wanted seconds on dessert, and they all said that they were stuffed. William helped me clear and clean. I noticed that Annette and Debbie just kept looking at him and then looking at each other. I did not know if I even wanted to know what they were thinking.

William asked if we were ready to head over to the Windjammer. I went to wash my face and reapply lipstick. He said that there was a band playing tonight, so he had called a head to reserve a table for us. Debbie and Annette looked at him and smiled. He said that it helped when you worked down here and you knew the owner.

When we arrived at the Windjammer, we walked over, and William gave them his name at the door. They escorted us in and directed us to a table. Debbie laughed and said that she could get used to the VIP treatment. We took a seat, and William asked what everyone wanted to drink. He looked at me and said he would get me an IPA. Annette and Debbie both said they would have the same thing. He walked over to the bar and came back with a drink for everyone. He said that the waitresses would not start coming around until the show started, which would be nine. I thanked him for getting the drinks and told him that he did not have to do that.

He leaned closer to my ear and whispered, "Don't worry, I will add it to your tab!"

I blushed and kissed him. At that moment, I reminded myself that I was going to have to remember that Annette and Debbie were there. I was so used to having him to myself; I was not going to give them too much to talk about later!

We all talked while we could because we knew it was going to be loud. A Journey song played, and William asked me if I wanted to dance. I admitted that I might be a little rusty, but I would give it a shot. He was fun to dance with—just the right height. After Journey, a Drifters song came on, and we shagged. He was good! I was not the best, but I loved the dance. That was one thing that Bill would never do; I had begged to take dancing lessons. He said that he did not need to know how to dance. So eventually, I went to the lessons by myself. It was a skill that came in handy for foundation dinners. We finished our dance, and I suggested to him that we go keep Annette and Debbie company. By that time, it was time for the band to start. It was a local band, Midnight City. I had not heard them before, but I liked the music. We drank one more beer during the set. Then they took a break. We talked while it was quieter.

William decided it was his turn to ask questions. He asked what I was like in high school and college. They said I was smart and loved science. They informed him that I had dated a band geek during my junior and senior year.

William laughed and said, "What, no football players!"

Annette said that we had our own little circle of friends and did not hang out with the popular football, cheerleading group. He asked if they had known Bill in high school. Annette said that they knew him, but he was not in our circle of friends.

Debbie added that I had come back home after one year of college because I liked to party just a little bit too much. I smiled and insisted to William that that was far enough on that line of questioning. However, Debbie was just getting started. I think the beers from earlier had loosened her tongue entirely too much. She went on to say that I started dating Bill after coming back from college, and we married within a year. She proceeded to tell William about the party we had thrown at our apartment, the one where I requested a Zombie, drank it, and passed out. He looked at me in shock. I shrugged my shoulders and said that I tried to be older and wiser now. "Unlike my two friends here!"

Annette picked up the story. "Yeah, Bill put her to bed. She took off her clothes and then revealed to him that she needed to go to the restroom. He reminded her that she did not have any clothes on and people would see her. Her response was that she was fast and they would not see her. She was actually going to walk across the hall, but he managed to get a pink bathrobe on her."

Debbie laughed. "Yeah, the pink bathrobe story, I always love that one."

My face was beet red. William winked and asked if I still had a pink bathrobe.

I stood up and said, "No, no pink bathrobes. You all may like that story, but it is one that I would like to retire. Now if you do not mind, I think I will step out and get some air."

I got up and went to the restroom and then stopped by the bar to grab a beer on my way to the back deck. I stepped outside. The breeze felt good. I do not know if it was warm in there or if I was just warm because I was mad. I sipped my beer and listened to the music. After a few minutes, William sat down next to me on the bench. He was holding two beers. He nudged me on the shoulder and asked if I was okay. I assured him that I was fine, but I just did not need to hear any more of their stories. He divulged to me that it was a shame because when I left, they had just divulged all my secrets about the Donny Osmond and David Cassidy posters in my bedroom. I looked down and just shook my head.

I looked up at him and said, "Yes, I follow Donnie Osmond on Facebook now, and every now and then, I get a message that he has sent me a message on Facebook or has posted something. Yes, fifteen-year-old me still gets excited when I see those messages coming across my phone. If I had received an actual message at fifteen, I probably would have just passed out."

He laughed. He assured me that I shouldn't feel too bad because he had pictures of Wonder Woman and Heart in his bedroom. I assured him that his secret was safe with me, but unless he wanted it to be broadcasted everywhere, he should not tell Annette and Debbie. He begged me not to give them too hard of a time. He looked at me and asked if he could ask one question. I told him sure.

"If I got you a six-pack and a pink robe, could we see if you could run across the living room without anyone seeing you?"

"Ha, ha, you are so funny. How about if we just skip the robe, I'll just run across the room?"

He pulled me close to him and gave me a kiss. He pulled away long enough to say, "That could work too."

We kissed again. I confessed that I was just so embarrassed. He insisted that I should not worry because he loved me just the way I was! He assured me he would tell some stories that I could hold over his head later. I guaranteed that I would hold him to that!

He said that the band was getting ready to start a second set and asked if I wanted to go back in. I told him that I was fine out here. He took my empty beer and handed me the one he had brought me. He said that the bartender had not put the beer I bought on the tab because I had paid for it. I suggested that he close the tab or Debbie and Annette would drink him into the poor house. He said it was fine because he could handle their tabs. I told him he could go back in, but he said he would rather enjoy the breeze with me. At that moment, I got a text from Debbie apologizing for letting William know my deep, dark secret about my inability to handle a Zombie.

I assured her that it was okay. I indicated that we were sitting outside for a while to get some air. She said that they were going to listen to a few more songs then they were going to head back to the house. I suggested that they let me know when they were ready and we would all walk back.

He asked if everything was okay. I promised that all was well and they would text when they were ready to go. The deck cleared off when the music started. It felt good to have him to myself again. I guess I was getting too old for loud music and crowded bars. I still liked beer but not in as large a quantity as Debbie and Annette. Well, let me rephrase that, I liked it just fine, but I knew that if I drank seven or eight beers, I would not want to hold my head up tomorrow. Maybe I was a little bit older and wiser.

With perfect timing, Debbie texted just as William and I finished our beer. He took my hand, we walked inside so he could pay off the bar tab, and we started walking to the house. Debbie and Annette laughed and talked all the way to the house. I figured that they were probably going to wake somebody up at one point. We went in, and they went to the kitchen for chocolate delight. They asked if we wanted any, but we both said we would pass.

William said he would leave us so we could talk about him. He reassured Debbie and Annette that he was so glad that he had had a chance to finally meet them after hearing so much about them. He said that he would see them tomorrow. I walked him out to the porch. I hugged him and thanked him for the evening. I apologized for the bar tab that I know was probably huge. He said not to worry, that he was sure I could wash dishes or something to work off their tab. I assured him that we would work out a payment plan. He kissed me, and we laughed. We kissed again, and Debbie opened the door.

She looked at William and said, "It's time for Maggie to come inside. Don't make me flick the light on and off to signal for you to go!" Then she went back inside.

I just looked at William. He laughed. I shook my head and said, "Some days, I wonder why we are still friends."

"You are friends because you love each other. They just want to watch out for you, and I appreciate them doing that. Let me know if I passed the final inspection and test! I love you. Sleep well. Will I see you tomorrow morning?"

I was sure that they would need to sleep in. He suggested that I come by to grab some coffee and breakfast while they slept it off, so I agreed to come by around nine.

Debbie, Annette, and I talked for a little while, and then I confessed that I had to get some sleep. They made me promise not to wake them up early. I assured them that I would go eat breakfast with William and then come wake them up for the day of adventures.

As we walked down the hall to the bedrooms, Annette assured me that he had passed the test. "He is a keeper! I am glad you found each other! Sleep well and see you tomorrow!"

They were both pains, but they were my pains. We had remained friends for thirty years. I am glad they liked him because at this point, I was too old to make new friends! I took a shower to get the cigarette smoke smell off. I put my clothes out on the deck to air out. I will wash a load of clothes tomorrow. I was exhausted. It had been a fun day, nerve-racking but fun.

CHAPTER 14

The Calm before the Storm (Patience)

I slept well. I was glad that the introductions between William, Debbie, and Annette were behind me. I guess in the grand scheme of things, they did not tell too many of my deep dark secrets. I got up and got ready. I put my bathing suit, hat, towel, and sunscreen in a tote bag. I was hoping that Debbie and Annette would wander toward the beach when they were ready.

I got to the One-Eyed Parrot at nine thirty. William met me at the door with a cup of coffee and a kiss. They did not open until ten thirty, so it was quiet. He asked what I wanted to eat for breakfast. I assured him that I was not all that hungry. He insisted that I had to eat before Debbie and Annette showed up to start today's drinking. I assured him that I was sure they would be passed out for some time. He insisted that I needed to eat, so I asked for grits with cheddar cheese. He asked Larry to bring a bowl of grits with cheese and a side of bacon. I knew better than to argue! He kept me company while I ate. He asked what was on the agenda for today. I said that we would probably go to the beach for a while and maybe sit out on the patio here to visit—if he understood, I would be paying their tab. He said that I could pay their tab but not my tab. I just gave him a smile and a wink.

He asked what we wanted to do for dinner. I assured him that as far as I knew, they planned to leave right after lunch because they both had to work tomorrow. He smiled and said, "Good, what do you want to do for dinner?"

"How about I come here? I will come sit here with you, and then we can go to my house. I need to do laundry and pack a bag to go to Columbia in the morning."

He asked what time we were leaving in the morning. I assured him that he did not have to go with me tomorrow if he needed to work and that Saturday afternoon or Sunday would be fine. He asked if I was trying to keep him from meeting Sam and Bill. I did want him to meet Sam because she had to give her "seal of approval." Bill was a different story. I did not even want to see him; I did not wish him on William either.

He told me that he would be driving me there in his truck and he could pull a trailer for the furniture. He would bring me back when I was ready to come back, but in the meantime, he would be there to help me.

So Debbie and Annette rolled in around eleven thirty both wearing hats and sunglasses. I wondered how their heads felt this morning. I asked them if they wanted to eat their lunch before we went down to the beach. They gave me a sheepish grin and said they had eaten some chocolate delight. William seemed pleased that they liked it. They had brought a bag with some bottled water. I went to the restroom and changed into my bathing suit. I promised that we would stop back by after spending a little bit of time on the beach. It was hot and the middle of the day, so I knew it would not be a long visit.

We walked down and staked out a spot on the beach. I put on sunscreen. Then we walked down to the water's edge. It was so hot that the water was not all that refreshing. We went back to sit. I indicated that we would be driving to Columbia in the morning, and Sam was planning to get in around three thirty. They said that they were sorry they would miss the chance to see Bill and give him some grief. I suggested that it was probably best they weren't coming. We sat out until about two thirty. It was fun watching the surfers and the people flying kites. As usual, there were lots of dogs to watch as well. The people just down from us were building a huge sandcastle. I knew that Debbie and Annette had to be hot and thirsty. I figured they were both dehydrated after their evening at the Windjammer.

They drank another bottle of water and said they were ready to go if I was ready to go. I told them we could eat lunch at the One-Eyed Parrot if they wanted to. They said that would be great. Then they planned to get on the road to beat some of the traffic.

We went up to the deck but opted to eat inside to get out of the sun. We all ordered cheeseburgers. They split an order of fries. We ordered an IPA and water. They were not too busy, so it did not take too long to get our orders. William checked on us and came by to sit for a few minutes. Annette and Debbie thanked him for all his hospitality and the chocolate delight. He assured them that it was his pleasure and he looked forward to seeing them again soon. He said that he would leave us to visit. I went up to the bar to ask Larry for a check, and he told me that William said it was on his tab. I tried to insist, but Larry and I both knew I was not going to win that fight.

We finished, and I went to tell William that I was going to walk back to the house and see them off. He suggested that I come back as soon as they drove away if I wanted to. I told him I was going to wash a load of clothes, take a shower, and I would come back when I got the clothes in the dryer. He gave me a hug and a quick kiss on the forehead.

They had already gathered their luggage together and stripped the bed. I suggested that they take a shower to get the sunscreen off. They said that they would just change and shower at home so they could beat the worst traffic. I hugged them both and thanked them for coming down to see me and meet William. We agreed that we would all get together soon.

I watched them drive away and then took a shower. Next, I started a load of clothes and cleaned up the kitchen. They had eaten chocolate delight and left a little bit of a mess. I checked emails and texts—nothing new or exciting to report. I did have a message from the publisher that they wanted the individual pictures for the book, so I emailed them and asked if she needed the original artwork overnighted to her. She let me know that she had the .jpg files and said that these would work fine. She said she would be back in touch.

I put the clothes in the dryer and walked back over to the One-Eyed Parrot. I was going to sit at my table, but William motioned me to sit at the bar. I sat down, and he gave me a beer. I told him I was going to sit there and let him work unless he needed me to wash dishes. He insisted that I sit and relax.

I had brought a magazine to entertain myself because I did not want Larry to complain to the management that I was distracting him and keeping him from working. I felt bad that he was going to miss work over the next three days because of me. I sat for about an hour and a half. William asked if I was hungry, but I was still full from my lunch. He suggested that we eat light and turn in early tonight so we could leave early tomorrow. I told him that was fine because I was a little tired from the late night and sitting in the sun today. I do not know why, but the sun always makes me feel drained. He fixed a large salad for us to share with grilled chicken. We left for my place around six.

We sat out on the front porch for a while watching people going to the beach. We ate our salad around seven. It was delicious. He asked if he needed to bring anything for tomorrow, but I thought we had everything we needed at the house. I suggested that we stop at the store on the way in and get a few things because I was pretty sure my refrigerator was empty. He said that would work.

We talked about anything and everything for about two hours. I do not know what it was about being with him, but I always seemed to lose track of time. He told me that he was going to let me get some sleep and he would be here to pick me up at eight thirty. He said that he wanted to stop by the bar to see it was in good shape for the weekend then he would be here. He hugged me and wished me a good night's sleep. Then he gave me one of those kisses that I just did not want to end.

With that, he was gone. I watched him drive away. I went in and pulled the clothes out of the dryer and folded the sheets. I packed a bag and included my laptop. I put the bag and my camera near the door. I thought I might want to take a few pictures at one point. It was ten thirty before I fell into bed. I was so tired that it did not take me long to fall asleep. I did not know if sleep would help to prepare me for what lay ahead tomorrow, but I was hoping it would.

CHAPTER 15

Uprooting a Home (The Winner Takes It All)

I woke up at five and could not go back to sleep. There were too many thoughts rolling around in my head. There were so many memories in that house. There was very little that I wanted to take with me because if I took it with me, it would just remind me of how it ended. How would Bill behave over the weekend? Would he be apologetic and cooperative, or would he make everything difficult? How would Sam feel about removing all the memories from the house that she had grown up in? How would Sam and Bill interact over the weekend? I was almost relieved that Debbie and Annette weren't coming. Then there was William. He was coming to support me and help me. How would Sam react? Debbie and Annette liked him; would Sam give him a chance? Then there was the entire Bill and William dynamic. Would Bill be civil? I knew that William would be unless pushed. Bill could be a real prick when he wanted to be…and I could almost see that happening this weekend. Would Bill bring Stacey? God, please let him have more sense than to bring her.

The more I thought about different scenarios that could play out this weekend, the more I tossed and turned. At five twenty, I just got up. I took a shower and got dressed. I thought shorts and a tank top would be best. I fixed coffee and sat down to attempt to make a to-do list:

1. Sam takes all that she wants out of the house.
2. Bill takes all that he wants out of the house.
3. I take my mom's furniture, my clothes, and personal items.
4. Give a painting to Nellie to thank her for watching the house and always being a good neighbor.
5. Call Habitat to pick up a donation.
6. Call salvage company to haul away the rest.
7. Do not kill Bill.
8. Shield William from Bill.
9. Go by office and take cigars to Dave.
10. Pack up my stuff from my office.
11. Learn how to crochet a turtle.
12. Do not let this list cause me to have a mental breakdown.

Okay. I could do this, right? I called Sam. She picked up on the first ring. She was on the road. She had evidently driven part of the way yesterday so she would get there around two. That was good because I was looking forward to seeing her. I asked if she brought a crocheted turtle. She said that she had packed a few and that she was willing to teach me how to make them. She apologized again that Thomas wasn't coming. He had a few meetings with students that he could not reschedule. She said she was going to stay until Wednesday, either with me in Columbia or with me at the beach. I told her I appreciated her being willing to stay and that I would see her around two thirty. I indicated that William and I planned to leave Isle of Palms between nine and nine thirty. She said that she was looking forward to meeting him. I did not know if she meant it, but I appreciated that she said it.

I sent William a text to make sure he had the cigars for Dave. He responded that he had them packed and he would be there in about thirty minutes. He asked if I had eaten breakfast, but I told him that I would wait and eat when we got to the house. He asked if I slept okay, and I confessed I had slept okay until five. He insisted that I was going to get tired if I had been up since five. I was sure that he was right, but right now, I could not eat or sleep.

He knocked on the door at nine. He came in and took me in his arms. He hugged and gave me a much-needed kiss. He looked into my eyes and told me to *try* not to let this weekend get to me. He assured me that he was there for me. He knew that Sam would be there for me. He said that they would make sure to do their part to make it as civil as possible. I hugged him, and I began to cry. I was not worried about him or Sam. It was Bill that I worried about. He wiped my tears and kissed me again.

"Don't worry. It will be okay, and it will be over soon. You know that I love you, right?"

I nodded my head yes and kissed him. He held me by the shoulders and said, "Now let's go get this behind us."

He picked up my bags and put them in the truck. I locked up the house, and we were on our way. My phone rang, and it was Debbie. She was calling to apologize again that she and Annette would not be able to be there to help. She said that the good news was that Bill would probably live to see another day if they weren't there. She said that the bad news was Bill would probably live to see another day. She said they promised to make it up to me. I was pretty sure that it was probably best that the two of them would not have a chance to talk to Bill. I told her not to worry, and we hung up. William and I held hands and drove toward Columbia in silence.

He told me that I should put my head back and rest. I was able to sleep a little. As we got closer to Columbia, he indicated that he wanted to go by the house and disconnect the trailer before we went by the store. I advised him to take the exit toward West Columbia. I told him the house was on the Saluda River just across from downtown Columbia. We took the exit, and I gave him directions. We turned onto the street, and I pointed to the second house on the left. He backed into the driveway so we could disconnect the trailer.

I got out. I wanted to run in and check the house and use the restroom before going to the store. I would have thought that I would have been happy to see the house, but it just filled me with a sense of dread. I unlocked the door and disarmed the alarm. We walked in. I gave William a quick tour and told him to make himself at home. I pointed out the bathroom right near the laundry room. I went to my room and went into the restroom. I used the restroom, washed up, and splashed some water on my face. Then I went to the great room. William was looking at family pictures on the mantle. I pointed out Sam. He told me he could tell she was mine without me pointing it out. He said that she was like a clone of me. I took that as a compliment!

He took my hand and walked into the kitchen. I checked the refrigerator and freezer. Not much there. He asked if I had a list for the grocery store. He knew me very well. I pulled a list out of my purse. He offered to go to the Food Lion down the road. I offered to go with him, but he suggested that I stay and get a visual of where I wanted to start. He did know me well. I pulled some cash out of my wallet, and he put it back in my purse.

I laughed and said, "I know, it's going on my tab!"

He grabbed me and kissed me and said, "No, this one is my treat."

I started to speak, but he put his finger on my lips to stop me. "Let me do this for you. Now I am going to the store. I'll be right back."

He left, and I went into my room. I knew I had to thin out the stuff in my closet. I decided to label three boxes: keep, donate, and trash. I started with the closet. It was easy. I got rid of all the clothes that were too big. I had lost the weight, but I had held on to the clothes. Now it was time to let them go. Next, I put clothes in the keep box. These were my current size and one size smaller. Next, I pulled out the things that were worn or just not worth saving and put them in the trash box. That took care of the clothes in the closet. Bill could go through his closet tomorrow. He had taken some when he left Wednesday.

Next, I went through the shoes. There were a few pair that I had not worn that I put in the donate box. I had several that went in the trash box. The rest went into the keep box. So my closet was empty except for purses. This was simple; I donated most. I checked to make sure I had not left anything in any of them. I put the keep purses in the keep box. So now my closet was totally empty. I decided to get a bottle of water before I moved to my dresser.

I went through drawer by drawer and threw away old underwear, T-shirts, shorts, and yoga pants. I put the rest in the keep box. I went through scarves and thinned it out a bit. Next was jewelry. For now, I decided to box all these in keep boxes. I boxed up the knick-knacks from the top of the dresser to take with me. Most of these were things Sam had made for me or bought for me over the years. I went through my books on the bookshelf. I boxed the keepers in with the jewelry. I had a good number that I did not want. I decided to leave those for Sam and Bill.

William got back, and we unloaded the groceries. He asked if I wanted him to make a pot of coffee. I told him that would be great. He started it and then came to see what I had been up to. He was impressed that I had gone through a closet, dresser, and a bookshelf in less than an hour. He offered to load the keep boxes on the trailer. He said that he would bring the dolly and load them up. That opened a good bit of the floor space. He sealed the donate boxes and stacked them to free up more space. I asked if he thought it would be okay to bag up the trash items. We could toss those in the middle of the garage. He said that he thought that was a good idea. He bagged items, and he tossed them in the garage.

The doorbell rang. I figured it was probably Sam. I went to answer it and found Nellie from across the street. She had brought a container of cookies. I opened the door and invited her in. William walked out, and I introduced him as a friend of the family who had offered his support in the packing and moving. They shook hands. I thanked her for the cookies and asked if she wanted some coffee. She followed us into the kitchen. William held a chair for her, and I fixed some coffee. William took it to her, and I brought cream and sugar. We sat and talked while we drank coffee. William and I ate one of her cookies. He complimented her and asked if she had put cinnamon in them. She seemed pleased that he could tell what her secret ingredient was.

She got up and said she was going to go and let us get back to work. She eyed William, smiled, and told him she was glad to meet him. We walked her to the door.

I closed the door, and William looked at me. "Friend of the family?"

I told him she was nosy enough without giving her any details she did not need. "Besides, you are my friend. A very special friend!"

He could not argue with that. He asked if I wanted a sandwich. I insisted that I was not hungry, but he fussed that I had not eaten. I gave in and said I would eat a sandwich. While he was fixing them, the doorbell rang again. I went to answer it, and this time it was Sam. She came in, and we hugged for a long time. William walked in and cleared his throat. I wiped a few tears from my eyes and introduced them to each other. William asked if she would like a sandwich before we got back to the task at hand. She said that she would like one after she went to the restroom. She went down the hall to her bathroom. She put her bag and purse in her room. She walked back by my room and said she could not believe I had already emptied the closet.

I told her I had done the dresser too and emptied the books I wanted to keep. I suggested that she go through the books and see if there was anything she wanted. We ate and talked about Isle of Palms, the turtle project, and Tennessee. William took the plates and offered to clean up the kitchen if we wanted to go sit or start some more packing. Sam said that it was probably best if we got busy packing. She looked through the books. She took a couple. I asked her if she thought her father would want any of the books. She said that he might, but she suggested putting them in a donate box. He could look through them and pull out what he wanted. So the bookcase was empty. The bookcase was one that belonged to my mom, so I wanted to keep it. William came in from the kitchen and loaded the bookcase on the dolly and took it to the trailer.

He asked if I wanted to point out the furniture pieces that had belonged to my mom, then he could go ahead and load those in the trailer. He could move things around if we needed him to, but if we could save any arguments with Bill, that would be a good thing.

Sam said she thought that was a good idea. She suggested I get the paintings I wanted too. I wasn't sure if I should do that, but I went ahead and pointed out furniture pieces. Sam offered to help him load them on the trailer. The small round kitchen table and chairs, a small hutch, two end tables, and a small desk. I helped take out chairs. Sam and William walked out the larger pieces and others they loaded on the dolly. There was a hall tree and a cabinet in the guest bathroom. The large mirror over the mantel went to the trailer because it was my grandmother's. I started going through all the stuff that came out of the furniture they moved. I had a box of keep items and the rest went into the donate box. Bill could look through these.

I folded and boxed the brand-new bedspread on our bed. I had picked it. It was mine. William helped me take down the curtains since they went together. I pulled my yearbooks and scrapbooks. I took a box of photos that belonged to my mom and dad's family. I left Bill's family box for him. I had gone through and scanned most of all the photos two years ago, so we would have the digital copy of both families for Sam. There was a rocker in the guest room that I had used to rock Sam. I took that.

There was nothing else furniture-wise that I wanted from the guest room. All the furniture in the master bedroom had belonged to his family, so he would take that. I took the spare TV from the bedroom. He could have the larger one in the great room. I went through the DVDs and took a few that had been mine. I took one DVD player and left the other for him.

I told them I had to sit for a minute then we could go through Sam's room next and she should take any furniture she wanted. If there was a piece we had put on the trailer that she wanted, she could have it. She said that she wanted some of the pieces from her room but no other furniture. I drank a beer and put my feet up for a minute. William came up behind me and rubbed my neck. I moaned and told him that felt wonderful. He and Sam sat down with a beer. If felt good to sit. We had gone through a lot of stuff in a short amount of time.

We were revived a bit, so we moved to Sam's room. She did not want the bedspread, so I put it in a donate box. She wanted the bed, dresser, and nightstand. We unloaded all the content of all the drawers and loaded the bed frame and end tables in her U-Haul. We left the mattress for her to have a place to sleep. William said he would load the mattress and box springs for her on Sunday. William and I took the drawers out of the dresser. Sam sat down and went through the drawers. It was mostly trash, but she found a few treasures from her childhood she wanted to keep. William used the dolly to take the dresser to the U-Haul. Then we loaded the drawers and took them out and reloaded them in the dresser. William put the trash bags out in the garage. Sam took the floor lamp and bedside lamp to the U-Haul. She took a few pictures off her walls. She boxed her scrapbooks and yearbooks and took those to the U-Haul. She put together a donate, keep, and trash box and went through her closet and bookshelf. Again William moved the trash to the garage and stacked the filled and sealed donate boxes. The closet was empty, and the only thing left was a bookshelf and an armchair. She said that her dad could take those if he wanted them. This room was done.

Next, we looked at the spare room. Sam wanted a small curio cabinet. Neither of us wanted the knickknacks, so we put in a donate box for Bill to look through them. There was not anything in the closet because we had cleaned it out a couple of years ago. This room was done.

So the bedrooms were done. The bathrooms were next. We cleaned out the medicine cabinets and threw away a lot. I pulled out all the towels and sheets that I wanted. Sam took sheets that would fit her bed. I threw out some towels that were worn out, but William pulled them and said the animal shelter could use them. So he boxed them, marked them for the shelter, and put them on our trailer. I boxed the things from my office: scanner, printer, filing cabinet. William boxed what he could and took them all out to the trailer. I took the prints and lamps from my office. I loaded them on the trailer. When I looked at the trailer, I thought I was taking too much. William said that if it was mine and I wanted it, I should take it.

I walked around. The den had to be done. I was going to leave the contents of that room to Sam and Bill. I would like to take some of the photos from the mantel, but I would let them take what they wanted. I pulled what books I wanted and left the rest. The kitchen had to be done. I did not want to touch that right now.

Sam asked about the attic. Luckily, we had cleaned it out six months ago. The only thing up there was Christmas decorations.

I told her that maybe after we emptied out more of the house, we could pull those boxes down for her to take what she wanted. I said the garage was all Bill's crap. We had coat closets to go through and a storage closet in the hall.

I looked at the clock. It was eight. We had been packing since eleven. Sam had started at two thirty. We were all tired. I was pretty sure I was going to be very sore. I felt like it was time to stop for the night while I could still move.

William asked if we wanted Chinese food or pizza. Sam said that pizza would be good so they would deliver. Sam called and ordered.

William finished loading a few things on the trailer and in the U-Haul. Then he locked them both. We locked the garage. William suggested that we each take some Tylenol. I asked Sam to look through the kitchen cabinets to see if there was something she wanted. She took a few mugs and a couple of serving bowls. She asked for an old cookbook from the church and one from her school. I told her they were hers for the taking. We each started a box, and she stacked them in the corner. There were a few things I wanted, but I decided to let Bill go through them first.

I rechecked my text messages to see when Bill was coming tomorrow. He had sent another text message to say that he would be there at eleven, so I guess he realized that he needed to be there before three. Good! We agreed that we would eat pizza. Take showers and go to bed. The pizza arrived by eight thirty. We ate and called it a night. I had left towels in each bathroom. There were sheets on the beds. I told William he could sleep in the guest room with me. I promised that I would keep my hands to myself. He said that he would like to sleep with me, and we could cuddle tomorrow because he was too tired tonight. It sounded like a good deal to me.

Sam overheard us, and she laughed. "Good grief you two. It is 2021. You know you can sleep together."

I told her that we had decided to wait. She asked if we were waiting for the divorce to be finalized. I nodded my head yes and left the "until we get married after the divorce is final" part out.

William signaled me to take a shower first. I made it a quick one so he could have hot water too. I lay down on the bed while he showered. That was the last thing I remembered. I woke up when he put cover over me. He lay down, and I rolled over and nestled my head on his shoulder. He put his arm around me. He kissed me and told me to go to sleep. I was too tired to argue. I did manage to say that I had set my alarm for nine before I fell sound asleep. I do not think I moved all night. It was probably a good thing because when I woke up at eight and moved, I hurt all over. I went to stretch my foot and a charley horse caught my calf. It was all I could do to stumble out of bed and try to stand up.

William was sound asleep because when I jumped up, it startled him. He jumped up and asked me what was wrong. I apologized for waking him up. I told him it was a charley horse. It finally eased off, and I walked around to stretch it out. I went to the bathroom and took a potassium to help.

William asked if I was okay. I hugged him and said that I had just worked some muscles that had not worked in a while. He hugged me and pulled me back in the bed. I asked him if he was sure it did not bother him to be this close and "not be close." He said that he loved holding me and we had plenty of time to be that close later.

I asked him if he had changed his mind about the marriage thing, and he said never. He said that as soon as the divorce was final, we were setting a date, and he was going to put a real engagement ring on my finger. I told him not to worry about that because the ring he gave me was perfect. He assured me that he was not worried, and he would put the ring on my finger because he wanted everyone to know that we belonged to each other.

I asked him if he wanted to go ahead and get up before the alarm went off. He squeezed me tighter and said he was happy right where he was. I told him that I did not know what I had done to deserve him, but I was certainly glad I wandered into the One-Eyed Parrot.

He said that he was glad I had wandered in, too, because it was meant to be! He held me and caressed my arm and side until the alarm went off. When it went off, I sat up to hit the snooze. He pulled me closer and said we can kiss until the snooze goes off. He rolled over so he was leaning over me and kissed me. He ran his finger down my neck and shoulder. He pulled me closer and ran his hand down the side of my leg. I pulled away and told him that he was driving me crazy.

He said, "Maybe we needed to consider getting married sooner."

I told him that my divorce hearing was set for two weeks from Monday, and I had no idea how quickly you could get a marriage license after a divorce.

He said, "I called an attorney friend, and he had said that the final decree terminated the marriage, so technically, we could walk away from the divorce hearing, get a marriage license, and get married that afternoon or the next day. Although I do not want to get married at the courthouse. I want a preacher to marry us. We can get married at the gazebo at Battery park or we can get married on the beach. I picture you in a white flowing sundress carrying hydrangeas and roses. I would like to have a few people there. We could have a reception at the bar."

I sat up and looked at him. "Wow, you have given this a lot of thought."

He said, "Yes, I have thought about it a lot because if I don't, I think about the wedding night, and if I think about the wedding night, you would be here right now with no clothes on."

I blushed and said, "I do want to marry you. I don't know if it's practical to say we are getting married the day after the divorce, especially if you want a few people there."

He said that he could go along with that reasoning. He asked if I wanted to get married at the gazebo, on the beach, in a church, or somewhere else like his house or Susan's house.

I told him that I really liked the idea of getting married on the beach at the end of the boardwalk. Then we could walk up the boardwalk to the bar for the reception.

"Okay. We have the location. How about a date? How would you feel about August 14?"

I asked what prompted the August 14 date.

"It's my birthday, and you becoming my wife would be the best present ever."

I asked him if it was not just that he did not want to remember another date, and he furrowed his brow. "So August 14 is your birthday, how old will you be?" I had been dreading this number because I was pretty sure he was younger than me.

He looked at me and said, "It's just a number, but my number will be forty-six."

My mouth dropped open, and he asked what was wrong. "I knew you were younger. I will be fifty on November 14."

He said that he had no problem with that and asked if I did. I told him I guessed that it was not a problem. My mom had been five years older than my dad.

"Good! Fifty, you know we have to have a party!"

I assured him that we could celebrate privately but no crowds! He smiled and said, "We can decide closer to November. I think a party and a private celebration may be in order."

The snooze went off, and I cut it off. He stood up beside me and picked me up and hugged me. He took my face in his hands and said, "I think this has been a very productive morning! We have a plan, we have a date, and we have a location. Now we have to discuss the honeymoon."

I told him that I was supposed to start working for Dave and the foundation the week after my divorce. How could I ask for time off for a honeymoon?

He said, "How about if you just volunteered for Dave's foundation, volunteered for my foundation, did volunteer work for the sea turtle group, and worked at the restaurant to work off your tab? Do not answer. Just think about it. You know that I will support whatever you want to do."

"So you gave me all this to think about this morning when Bill will be showing up at eleven? How will I be able to concentrate?"

He looked at me and said, "Well, if you are thinking about a wedding, wedding night, and a honeymoon, he won't bother you!"

That was a good point. I told him that I would think about it and we would discuss it after we got through today. We both dressed while we talked. Now we headed to the kitchen. He cooked some eggs and bacon. He put some biscuits from the deli in the oven to warm. I fixed a pot of coffee.

Sam walked in as we were finishing. She sat down at the breakfast bar and winced in pain. "So is anybody else as sore as I am?"

We all agreed that we were sore and today was going to be a tough day. I put the Tylenol bottle on the bar so we could all drug up to prepare.

The doorbell rang at ten forty-five. I went to answer the door. It was Bill. He brought doughnuts. I looked in the driveway and saw that he had just brought his car. I asked how he was going to take furniture, and he said he had a truck coming at eleven fifteen. I closed the door, and we walked to the kitchen. He and Sam hugged. He turned and stared at William. I introduced my "friend of the family" to Bill, and they shook hands. I offered him bottled water in the refrigerator or coffee, and I asked him where he wanted to start. He said he would start with the bedroom furniture.

"I am taking that since it was from my family."

I told him that I figured he would. I asked him to look through a few boxes of books and knickknacks from my bookcase. He said that he would look at those after they started moving furniture out. He walked to the great room and asked if anybody wanted the furniture. Sam said she did not want any of the furniture. I told him that I did not want it. So he said he would take the furniture from the great room. He asked about the dining room. I told him I figured he would want it since his parents had given it to us and I had taken the table from the kitchen. I let him know that I had taken the pieces from around the house that had been my mom's and that Sam had taken her bedroom suite. I told him that he, of course, should take the furniture and contents from his office, and he was welcome to the furniture in the spare bedroom. He said that he would take it.

The doorbell rang, and he went to let the movers in. He showed them the two bedrooms, the great room, the dining room, and his office. They said that they would start with the bedrooms. I suggested that William and Sam to move their bags into the closets so the movers would not pick up their stuff. Then Sam, William, and I started moving books and knickknacks off the furniture in the living room. When the movers emptied the furniture from the bedrooms, Bill went through the boxes of books and knickknacks. He took a few books, a lamp, and a couple of framed pictures. He said that we could have the rest or give it away. Sam and I each took a lamp and some pictures. Sam and William took the things out and put them in a box on the trailer and one in the U-Haul.

While Bill's movers took his great room furniture, he went through his closet. He packed things to take and then filled a box for donations. We stacked the donation box in the garage. I asked Bill if he wanted any of the prints on the walls from around the house. He took three and left the rest. Sam did not want any. I took two Charleston prints and a couple of beach scenes. The rest, William and Sam boxed up for donations. Bill went through the boxed items in the great room and took a few items but left the rest. Sam took a couple of bird figurines. I took a couple of figurines and wrapped the rest and sealed it for donations. William put it over in the corner since the room was empty now.

I asked Bill about the china in the dining room. He said that he wanted it because he thought Stacey would like it. I winced a little, and Sam and William both looked at me. Bill apologized.

"No need to apologize, you and your movers can pack that up. I will take the dishes from the kitchen. I'll put your coffee mugs out on the counter for you."

He got the movers to pack up the dishes. Then the movers took the dining room furniture and loaded it on the truck. Bill packed up the things from his office while they finished the dining room. Then the movers got the furniture from his office. They loaded his boxes from the dining room, great room, and the two bedrooms.

By this time, it was three thirty. Bill told his movers to go unload at his house and come back tomorrow for items from the garage and tool shed. He looked at me and asked if I was going to want anything from outside.

I told him I wanted the deck furniture since I had just redecorated the deck. I relinquished all the tools from the garage, tool shed, and his grill. I asked him if he wanted anything from the kitchen besides his coffee mugs. He said that he wanted the air fryer and the canister set because they had been his mom's. I got a box for him to load them up. He said that he would get them tomorrow because he was going to go home and help with the unpacking. I asked Sam and William if they wanted a doughnut. Sam grabbed three out of the box and handed the box to me. I handed them to Bill and told him to take these because I was sure Stacey would like them.

"Touché. Well played, Maggie. I will see you tomorrow." He went over and hugged Sam and nodded to William. "It was nice to meet you, friend of the family."

With that, he was gone. In four hours, he had pretty much cleared out the house. William put his arm around me and asked if I was okay. I hugged him and said I was fine but would be even better after his second haul tomorrow.

I looked at the two of them and said, "I know we must pack this kitchen, but what if we took a break and fixed something to eat?"

William said, "There was some fruit the kitchen. We have chips and cookies. I bought beer and Diet Coke."

Sam added, "We have three doughnuts and some grapes. It's a regular smorgasbord!"

William asked what we wanted. He told us to sit and he would bring a tray with a variety.

I looked around the house and said, "Unless we want to sit on the floor, we are going to have to sit on the patio."

He suggested the floor since it was so hot outside. We agreed.

I went to the refrigerator and pulled out three beers. I retrieved three frosted mugs from the freezer. I poured the beers and looked at the bar. "Oh, look, he missed the three barstools, we can sit here!"

Sam made a face and said that she was sure he would get the barstools tomorrow.

It felt good to sit. It felt even better to eat. I thanked William for fixing the food and helping with the packing yesterday and today. He said he was glad to help. I asked about the donation boxes. I told him that a Habitat truck was coming by at five today, and they could take what we had packed.

"As soon as I finish my snack, I will go see if I can add more to the donate pile. The trash, we can either call the junk truck to pick it up or we can take it to the dump tomorrow. I just thought about it. Sam, you packed your mattress in your U-Haul and Bill took the other two mattresses... I guess we sleep on the floor tonight."

William suggested that we bring the lounge chairs in from the patio. Good thinking on his part!

I boxed up some more items for donations and filled a couple more bags with trash. I took a few more framed photos from around the house. His office was empty. The spare room was empty. Sam's room was empty. The dining room was empty. The Habitat truck showed up at four forty-five. William had moved all the donation boxes to the garage, so they loaded them onto a dolly and onto the truck. There were a couple of random chairs, an end table, and a coffee table that they took. They gave me a receipt and left. Sam and William offered to take the trash to the dump. I asked Sam to call the junk truck guy to see if by any chance they could stop by. Luck would have it that they were making a pickup about five miles away and said they would stop by at six.

William gathered all the trash bags at the end of the driveway. They came, collected, and left. The house felt better without the added clutter. Now I really did have to go through the kitchen. I started a box for Bill's things. I added his air fryer, the canisters, and the coffee mugs he had collected over the years. I put the dishes in a box for me. I packed my coffee mugs and glasses. I used towels to cushion everything. I asked Sam if she wanted anything. She wanted the wok and a waffle iron.

William put a frozen lasagna in the oven. He pulled a big bowl out of the cabinet and made a salad. He found some frozen string beans in the freezer. He put those on the stovetop on low to cook. He said that it would take about ninety minutes for the lasagna to cook. We could pack a few more things until it was ready. Then we could wash and pack the pots and bowls after we cleaned up. He said that he would leave a frying pan out to fix eggs in the morning and then we could pack that. I had to smile; he either understood my "to-do list structured brain" or he was just like me. Either way, I loved him for doing all that he did to make this easier.

Sam and I went through the cabinets and pulled silverware, utensils, pots, pans, and small appliances that we wanted. Bill could decide what he wanted, and the rest could be donated or trashed. I had recently cleaned out the pantry, so there was not a lot in there. I figured Bill could take that since he was close to home. There would not be anything in the refrigerator after we ate dinner, breakfast, and packed sandwiches for the trip to Isle of Palms.

William and I went ahead and swept off three lounge chairs and brought them inside. He loaded the rest of the patio furniture in the trailer. He asked about the little statues in the flower beds and flags around the patio. I told him I wanted them. There were a few potted plants that I wanted, so he put those in the bed of his truck. It was seven thirty, and I was exhausted. I told them that I thought we had done more than enough today. William locked the trailer and the U-Haul. We closed the garage door and went inside. Sam said she was going to take a shower. I sat at the bar, and William went to the refrigerator for two beers. He checked the freezer and brought me a frosted mug. He collapsed on the chair beside me. He leaned over and kissed my forehead and worked his way down to my lips for a long overdue kiss. He put his arm around me and said that we had done some good work today.

I told him that he had gone above and beyond, and I apologized for Bill's sarcastic remarks I had heard him make directed at William and those that I am sure he uttered out of my earshot. William said that it was fine, that in a couple of weeks, we would not have to deal with him again.

He cleared his throat and looked at me. "So since we are getting married August 14, is there any reason to move your things into Dave's house now and then have to move them to my house, which will become our house, in August?"

I had not thought about that. Tomorrow we planned to go by and see Dave and take him his cigars. I could come back to Columbia to get my things out of my office next week or when I was here for the final divorce hearing.

I looked into William's eyes and said, "Well, I guess I need to talk to him about the beach house and the whole volunteer for the foundation thing. I need to think about all of that. I guess you are right about this stuff though. No need to unpack it twice. I guess a lot of this crap I don't even need to take with me."

He told me that these were my things that I wanted. "After twenty-seven years of marriage, it's not too much to ask to take things that you want from the house. You are welcome to put everything in the house. We will make it our house. I think your patio furniture will look great on the screened-in porch and patio."

I hugged him and whispered, "You know I love you, right?"

He kissed me and whispered back, "I know, but it's always nice to hear. I love you too."

Sam came in and fixed a glass of Diet Coke. "Well, that shower helped. I feel somewhat revived! We accomplished a lot yesterday and today. Dad really cleared out the house quickly with the help of his moving team!"

I had to laugh. Only Bill could work it so he did not have to exert a lot of effort in this situation. I bet he would hire someone to come take his place at the final divorce decree if he could work it out. After his sarcastic "goodbye, friend of the family William" remark, I half expected him to bring Stacey with him tomorrow. When the thought crossed my mind, I subconsciously shuddered. Both William and Sam asked what was wrong. I told them it was nothing and that I was thinking how tomorrow could go.

Sam's mouth dropped open. "You don't think he'll bring Stacey, do you?"

"At this point, I would not put it past him, but there no need to worry about it now. We would deal with it tomorrow."

William asked if we were ready for dinner. Sam said that she was starved. I told him I thought I would drink one more beer and then take a shower. He put the string beans on warm and cut the oven off. He looked at Sam and said that it was ready if she wanted to go ahead and eat. I thanked him and insisted that he relax because he had moved a lot of heavy boxes and furniture. He said that we would all feel this one tomorrow!

Sam ate a bowl of salad. She asked me if I was okay, and I told her that I was fine, just exhausted. She said that she was sorry that her dad had hurt me with the comment about Stacey loving the dishes. In the grand scheme of things, it was really nothing. She said that I did a really good job of not chewing him out when he said it. She looked at me and asked if she could ask me a question.

I told her to ask away.

"You and William. You just met, right? It feels like he is a part of the family if that makes sense."

I smiled. "Yes, I met him last Friday when I went to Isle of Palms. I know what you mean about him feeling like a part of the family. I hope that this doesn't upset you, but I love him."

She looked down for a moment to collect her thoughts. "Mom, you and dad haven't been close for years. What I see between you and William is the way it is supposed to be. If he makes you happy, I am happy. Just do not get pregnant like Stacey, okay!"

When she said that, I almost spit out my beer.

She looked at me and said, "Just kidding!"

We both laughed. William walked in as we were laughing and asked if we could share the joke. Sam looked at me and said that I could tell him but she would not.

I cleared my throat and told him that Sam wanted us to be happy but I couldn't get pregnant like Stacey. In true William form, he said, "10-4. We can make sure that doesn't happen!"

Sam fixed a plate of lasagna and string beans. William got another beer. I told him to go ahead and eat while I took a shower. He said that he would wait. I went back to the bedroom and washed my face. I rummaged through my tote bag and found a tank top, baggy T-shirt, and yoga pants and, of course, clean underwear. I jumped in the shower. I could already feel some soreness settling into my lower back, arms, and legs. More Tylenol would be needed tonight. The good news was that we only had the kitchen, garage, and shed to go, and most of the stuff was Bill's. I finished my shower and got dressed. I towel-dried my hair and pulled it back. I took the towels and washcloths and picked up dirty clothes to wash a load. William walked back to check on me, and I asked for his clothes to add to the mix. I started the load of clothes, and he said he would fix us a salad.

He asked if I wanted beer or Diet Coke. I told him I wanted a glass of water and one more beer.

We sat down to eat. Sam had finished her lasagna and beans and was working on some of Nellie's cookies. She thanked William for fixing dinner. She said that she was going to go into the great room and call home to check on Thomas and the dogs.

We ate in silence. I think we were both too tired to talk. We finished our salads and ate some lasagna and green beans. Frozen lasagna was always good, but this tasted exceptionally good. I think it was because we had worked so hard. William texted Larry to check on the restaurant and then set his phone aside. I asked William if he was done with his plate, and I rinsed, and he loaded the dishwasher. We decided to wash the load and pack them away. I found paper plates in the cabinet that we could use for breakfast and lunch. I wiped down the countertops and went to put the clothes in the dryer.

It was already nine thirty, and I said that I thought I was going to go ahead and go to bed. I rationalized that the quicker we got started tomorrow, the quicker it would be done. I texted Dave about coming by to see him tomorrow afternoon. He said that he wanted to stop by to see us at the house. I told him to come by anytime.

I tried to get comfortable in the lounge chair. I did not see how it would be possible; however, I do not remember anything after kissing William good night. I woke up at six and got up. William's lounge chair was empty, and I found him in the kitchen. He and Sam were drinking coffee and eating a doughnut. He looked at me and handed me a cup of coffee. I told him that he was a saint! He asked if I wanted the last doughnut, but I thought I would rather eat some of Nellie's cookies! I grabbed a cookie, took my coffee, and went to get dressed. I emptied the dryer and folded clothes. I put Sam's clothes on her lounge chair and ours on our respective chairs. When I got back, William had cooked eggs and bacon. I sat down to eat. William had already unloaded the dishwasher and boxed up the dishes. He had them labeled to go in his trailer. I told him that he had been a busy bee and asked what time he got up. He said he got up at five. We decided we were going to drive back to Sullivan's Island tonight. To disconnect the trailer. Sam and I would drive to Isle of Palms and stay at Dave's house. We were ready for real beds. I loaded the cleaning supplies from under the sink and from the bathrooms into a box. I put them to the side. I would give the kitchen and bathroom a quick clean before we left.

Bill showed up at eight thirty; I guess he was ready to get this finished as well. He started with the shed and garage; well, I should say his moving crew started with the shed and garage. They were finished with that in about an hour. He looked through the boxes of items from the kitchen. He took a few pans and casserole dishes and added them to his box with the air fryer. He took that box to the truck. He said that he did not want anything else. We labeled the rest of the boxes as donation and put them on the front porch.

William said we could call Habitat or we could drop them by Goodwill. I asked Bill if he wanted the food from the pantry and freezer. He took the canned goods and the frozen meat and frozen vegetables. I put the flour and baking supplies in a box to take with me. We packed our clothes in our tote bags and put them in our vehicles. William put the lounge chairs onto the trailer. Then we did a final walk through. The only things left were the food in the refrigerator and the box of cleaning items. I had a broom, a mop, and a vacuum too. Bill offered to take the donation items to Goodwill, so we loaded the boxes on the back of his moving truck. He asked the guys to stop by Goodwill and he would make the donation on the way to his house. I told him that I would give it a clean and then we were leaving.

We each said we would call our attorneys and the realtor to say it was ready. We said our awkward goodbyes. He hugged Sam, and he was gone.

I decided to drink a bottle of water and get busy cleaning. William offered to vacuum the carpet, and Sam volunteered to sweep kitchen, laundry room, and bathrooms. I cleaned the bathrooms and kitchen. Sam mopped the floors. We stood back and looked. I think it was clean enough for someone to buy "as is." It was noon, and we were done! William asked if we wanted to get some lunch before we got on the road. I told him I wanted to go to Pizza Joint for one last time! Sam and William said they had worked up an appetite and pizza would be good. We locked the U-Haul and trailer, and we rode together in the truck to get lunch. I called Dave to make sure he did not stop by while we were at lunch. He said he would stop by Pizza Joint and join us.

We sat down and ordered a large "Big One" pizza and Diet Cokes. Dave came in and hugged Sam. I suggested that he hug me another day because I had been packing boxes and cleaning. He asked if we were done, and William told him it was all loaded. Dave asked how it went with Bill. I said that it was fine, that he had brought a moving crew to load the furniture from the great room, dining room, master bedroom, spare bedroom, his office, the garage, and the shed.

"Damn, did you two get any furniture?"

Sam said that she took her bedroom suit and an end table and chair. I told him I got the kitchen table and chairs and a few pieces that were my mother's.

William added, "Plus we got this really great patio set for the porch and deck."

I do not know if Sam suspected where the conversation was going, but she excused herself to use the restroom. When she left, I cleared my throat and told Dave that I would not be staying in the beach house after August 14. He asked where I was moving. William cleared his throat and said that I would be moving in with him after we got married. Dave's mouth dropped open.

I added that Sam didn't know all our plans, and Dave promised not to mention anything. Dave started to speak a couple of times and stopped. Then he finally said that he could tell by looking at us that we were meant to be together. He asked what this meant about working for the foundation. I told him that it probably meant that I would not be working for him but that I wanted to volunteer to help with fundraisers and functions. He said that he totally understood. He said that he hated to lose me, but as long as I was willing to help train Amy and volunteer, he would take what he could get! He looked at William and said that maybe this would mean that the two foundations could work on some joint ventures. William said that he would be open to that happening.

Sam came back, and we switched to small talk. I knew I had to tell her, but just not today. I reached in my purse and handed Dave a small box. I told him that it was a small thank you for letting me stay at the beach house and being so understanding about work. He opened the box and hugged me. He was almost giddy. I had not expected that reaction to cigars. He seemed so excited because that it had been years since he had smoked a good cigar, and now he had six of them! He said he could hardly wait to get home and try one out! We visited a little longer, and he left to go smoke.

I told him I would talk to him this week and I would see him when I came to town for the divorce hearing—two weeks from tomorrow. We paid our bill and went back to the house. I checked the mailbox one last time even though I had forwarded the mail to the beach. We walked through and checked the shed, garage, and house one last time.

I walked across the street to thank Nellie for the cookies and tell her goodbye. I took her a painting of the Columbia Skyline to thank her for watching over the house. I hugged her neck and thanked her for everything. I told her that I would check on her occasionally. She said that she liked my young man. I just looked at her. I assured her that he and I had just met. She told me that she believed me, but she could tell that we were meant to be together.

"It's funny. You and Bill were always like two puzzle pieces from two different puzzles. You just did not fit. But you and William, it is a perfect fit. I know you two will be very happy together. I can tell Sam likes him too."

I hugged her and asked how she could be so wise. She insisted that she learned everything from being so nosy and keeping a watchful eye on everything! I blushed and told her I was so glad she was that observant. William came over and shook her hand. She told him to take care of me and that she was sure she would see us again. She said she was long overdue for a trip to the beach.

We walked back to the house. Sam and I took one last look. We looked in the attic and realized that we had forgotten the Christmas totes. William went up in the attic and handed them down to us. I was glad we had cleaned out the attic last summer. The Christmas boxes were all that was up there. William loaded them on a dolly and rolled them out to the trailer. I figured that Sam and I could go through ornaments and divide them up and trash what we did not want. He closed the door and locked it. William had already hooked the trailer up. He asked Sam if she wanted to follow him. She said she would.

He said, "We are getting on 26 and staying on it until 526 to Mount Pleasant."

I told her to text if she had any problems or needed to stop. We looked at the house. She wiped away a tear, and I hugged her. New chapters in life were exciting, and we had some exciting times ahead of us. She said that she knew that there were good things ahead.

We got in our cars. William grabbed my hand and pulled me in close for a kiss. "Here's to the next chapter!"

CHAPTER 16

Back Where I Belong (Here Comes the Sun!)

The traffic was not too bad. We stopped at William's house, and we decided it was best to leave the U-Haul there because there was not a lot of parking at Dave's house. William unhooked the trailer and put it in his stand-alone garage. Sam put her luggage and computer bag in William's truck. He drove us to Dave's house and helped us get Sam's bags upstairs. He told me he was going to go check on the bar. I knew he had to be tired. He said that he was fine. He suggested that we come to the One-Eyed Parrot for dinner.

It sounded like a good idea. I showed Sam her room and told her to make herself at home while I went out on the front porch, look at the mail, and drink a beer. She came out to join me and brought one of her crocheted turtles. It was adorable. I asked if she thought she could teach me to make one. She told me that she would show me tonight or tomorrow. As I sat there, I realized the dull headache I had been feeling yesterday was on my left ear. I knew that my allergies had been acting up since I had been here, and I knew it was because I had not taken my allergy medicine every day. I went in to take some medicine and came back. Sam asked what was wrong, and I said that my ear was bothering me.

We sat and enjoyed the breeze. There was a wind chime next door that was so soothing to listen to. We talked about Tennessee. She was enjoying her class schedule. She admitted that the class she taught the other day and all my talk about sea turtles had made her miss her marine biology classes. She had talked about going back to school to get a master's in marine biology, but that was not something she could easily do from Chattanooga. She admitted that she had toyed around with the idea of coming back to South Carolina and going to the College of Charleston. She said she was still formulating a plan.

I asked how Thomas felt. I knew he was from Chattanooga, and it might be hard to get him to pick up and move. She said that was still part of the formulating process. I promised her that I supported her whatever the decision.

She leaned forward with a serious look and told me that she hoped I knew that she supported me whatever my decision was. I asked her what she meant.

"Mom, it is obvious that you and William are serious. I know you said you were waiting until after the divorce was final, and I respect you both for that. What are you going to do after the divorce is final?"

I figured I might as well just say it and get it over with, like ripping off a Band-Aid. "Well, we were thinking we might get married. Would that bother you?"

She did not even look all that surprised. She said, "I had talked to Nellie, and Nellie had told me about her theory that you and Dad were mismatched puzzle pieces and you and William fit together perfectly. The more I see you two together, the more I see it. I think you two would be very happy together. Any idea when this marriage will take place?"

"August 14."

"Wow, Mom, that's really soon. It's a month away."

"I knew it was soon, but we were just going to get married on the beach and then have a small reception for family and friends at the One-Eyed Parrot." I asked her if she thought I was crazy.

She laughed and said, "No more than usual. I am happy for you, Mom! I like William!"

I looked at my phone. It was almost seven, so I suggested that we walk down to the bar for dinner. I added that since I was tired, it needed to be an early night. She said that she was tired, too, and looked forward to a real bed! We got there, and William waved and motioned toward "my table." We sat down.

I laughed and told Sam that I had sat here for three days trying to write the turtle story. William stopped by and asked what we wanted. I said that I just wanted a small salad and a Diet Coke. Sam said she wanted a burger and fries. He insisted that I needed more food than just a salad. I just did not feel all that hungry. He asked if I thought I was getting sick, and Sam piped up that my ear was hurting. I was sure that I would be fine because it was just allergies. He told me that if it got worse, he could call the doctor here on the Isle of Palms. I thought I would be fine, but I probably just needed to get some sleep. I told Sam that I was going to go back to the house. I insisted that she stay and asked her to bring my salad in a to-go container. I said that I would leave the screen door open, and I could either leave the back door open or put a key in the plate under the fern.

She said that she would eat and stay for a little while and check emails. She would not be late because she was tired too. I told William to put dinner on my dishwashing tab, gave him a hug, and turned to go. He said that he would walk me out.

We got outside, and he spun me around to hug me. It made me a wobble a bit. "Are you sure you are okay?"

I told him I was fine, just tired. He kissed me and made me promise to call if I feel worse, even if it was later tonight. I promised him that I would. I turned to walk home praying I would not walk like I was as dizzy as I felt. I thought if I just took some decongestant, I would be fine by morning. I went upstairs and unlocked the door. I put the key in the plate and went inside. I fixed some water and took some medicine. I brushed my teeth, washed my face, put my hair up, and got dressed for bed: frog pajamas and a long sleeve baseball shirt. I did not check emails or Facebook or anything. I just lay down. I heard Sam come in and looked at the clock. It was ten. I did not get up because I wanted to stay under the covers. I must have turned the AC down too low because I felt cold.

There was a tap at my bedroom door, and I expected to hear Sam, but it was William. He whispered that he wanted to check on me. I told him I was okay, just cold. I heard Sam saying something about it being warm in here. The next thing I knew, William was kneeling beside me with his hand on my head.

"You are burning up. Do you have a thermometer?"

I told him that I was sure it was nothing, but the thermometer was in the green bag sitting on the bathroom counter. It was one of those forehead models, so he checked my temperature. It beeped.

"Hmmm, well, it is not nothing, you have a fever of 102. Does your ear still hurt? Do you hurt anywhere else?"

I told him that my ear still hurt, just a dull throb. My neck hurt under my ear, and that was all. He asked if the Tylenol was in the bathroom, and I signaled toward the medicine cabinet. He went to get the bottle and spotted the water bottle on the bedside table.

"Let's get some Tylenol in you to try and get that fever down. Your glands feel swollen in your neck. Here, let me help you to sit up."

I sat up, but when I did, the entire room was spinning. I was pretty sure that I wasn't going to be able to sit up for long or I was going to get sick. He gave me two Tylenol and helped me to lay back down, but he propped me up on a second pillow.

"When you lay back, does the sick feeling go away?"

I nodded my head yes. Sam asked if there was something she could do. He asked her to get a bowl with ice and a washcloth. He wanted to try to cool my face and neck down. He asked her to get the cloth cool and put it on my forehead while he went to call the doctor. I told him it was too late to call him.

"I'm calling the doctor or I'm taking you to the ER. It's your choice." He dialed the number. Dr. Morris answered on the first ring, William could tell from the background noise he had not awakened him. He explained the situation and indicated where we were. He said he would come take a look.

"It sounds like a bad ear infection. I'll give her an antibiotic shot and a shot to help bring the fever down. I am just down the road at Acme Seafood. I will run by the office, get my bag, and some medicine, and I will be right there. Try to keep her under lots of cover with a cool cloth on her face until I get there."

William asked Sam to get another blanket out of the closet. He reapplied the washcloth. Sam put the second blanket on me. In about fifteen minutes, there was a knock at the door. Sam went to let the doctor in and brought him back to the bedroom. William got up so he could check on me. He took the cloth off my head and felt my glands.

"Definitely swollen."

He called my name to wake me up. He introduced himself and said he was going to check my throat and ears. All I could do was nod. I could not keep my eyes open. He called my name and told me to say "Aww." He held my mouth open and looked at my throat. He said it was fine. He checked my nose—not too congested. He checked the right ear—it is a little red. Then he checked the left ear. William asked him how it looked.

"It's a pretty bad infection. Very inflamed. I'm guessing she has allergies?"

Sam told him that I had taken allergy shots for years, but now I just took Zyrtec or singular every day. William remembered that I had commented the other day that I had forgotten to take it for a few days. Now that the cloth had been off my head, he rechecked my temperature. The forehead one said it was 101. He called my name and informed me he was going to put a thermometer under my tongue just to double-check. He ordered William to sit and hold it and talk to me to try to keep me awake.

He got up to get the two syringes out of his bag. He grabbed the thermometer and checked. It was a little over 101. He asked William if he had given me any Tylenol. William looked at his watch and said that he had given me two about thirty minutes ago. He indicated that he was going to give me an antibiotic shot to jump-start the healing. He was also going to give me a higher dose of a medicine to reduce the fever.

"We need to get that fever back down below 100. I want you to give her two Tylenol in four hours if her fever is still 101." He gently rolled me on my side lowered my pajamas, told me that it was going to sting, and jabbed me with two shots.

I remember saying "Ouch, that hurt." I think I remember him apologizing. He said that the fever should break within the hour but to keep an eye on me. William indicated that he would stay. Sam said she would help too.

He said that I would feel lousy in the morning, but by tomorrow night, I should feel almost 100 percent. He said not to worry about food but keep water and juice in me.

"And if she gets up to go to the bathroom, help her because she may be dizzy until tomorrow night. It's the fluid behind her eardrum."

It was weird. I heard everything they said, but I felt like I could not open my eyes.

William thanked him for making a house call. The doctor said he would call at eight in the morning to check on me.

"Call me before if you need me."

Sam walked him to the door and thanked him. William told Sam that he would stay with me while she got some rest. She said to call her if anything changed. She went to get a fresh bottle of water and put a straw in it. "Maybe you can get her to drink some water."

William pulled the cover up and lay down beside me. I rolled over onto his arm, and he made sure I was under both blankets. "There you go. You get comfortable and get some sleep. That will allow that medicine to start working."

I tried to answer, but I felt like I was deep in a hole or a pit, and I just could not open my eyes or talk. It felt weird. I just gave in and went to sleep.

I woke up a little while later trying to pull the cover off, and William was trying to get me to stay under the cover. I told him I was too hot. I was drenched with sweat. He said the good news was that this probably meant that the fever had broken. He got the thermometer to check my temperature. It was down to 100.

He smiled and said that it was going in the right direction. He said that he would compromise and take one blanket off. He asked if I wanted a cool cloth on my face.

I told him I would get up and get it, and he indicated that I would not because I still might be dizzy. He got a washcloth and a bowl of cool water, and he wiped my face. He got the bottle of water and indicated that I needed to drink some water. If felt good because it helped to cool me off. I asked him what time it was.

He looked at his watch and told me it was two thirty. I had been asleep for three hours. He asked how my ear felt.

"It feels better. I am sorry that you must be here so late. You should go home and get some sleep because I know you have to be tired from moving all that furniture and boxes out of my house."

He said that he was fine and that he had slept for two hours. He told me that I had scared him when my fever was 102.

I told him I just remembered going to sleep at ten. Then I remembered hearing his voice and Sam's voice and someone I did not know. He said that was Dr. Morris.

"You mean to tell me you know a doctor who makes house calls?"

He said, "It helps when you have lived here all your life and you have gone to school with people and their kids have worked with you! You need to try to go back to sleep."

I moved to stand up, and he stopped me. "What exactly do you think you are doing?"

I told him I needed to go to the bathroom. He informed me that he would help me stand up slowly and walk with me to the restroom.

"You are *not* going to the bathroom with me."

"You can fuss all you want, but I will help you because Dr. Morris said you have fluid behind your eardrum, and it can cause you to have vertigo. I am not going to let you fall down."

I knew I would not win this battle, and besides, I did feel a little dizzy. When I stood up, I grabbed his shoulder to steady myself. That was when I got the "I told you so." He walked me in and made me promise to hold on to the cabinet. He said he would stand right outside the door but he would be there to help me walk back to the bed.

I was able to maneuver pulling down pants and holding on to the cabinet and sitting then standing up; there was a little wave of dizziness but not too bad. I maneuvered pulling up my pants without falling. I washed my hands and splashed water on my face. I looked at myself in the mirror. I let go of the cabinet long enough to brush and put my hair back up in a band. My face looked very pale. I felt the need to brush my teeth. I opened the door, and there he was to walk me back. He asked how the dizziness was. I told him that if I moved slow, it was not too bad. I sat down and then laid down.

He asked if I needed anything. I insisted that I was fine and I needed him to go home. He said that I could just let it go because he was staying. He felt my forehead and checked my temperature. It was 100.5. He figured it was from moving, but he got me two more Tylenol just in case.

He told me he would go back to sleep if I would go back to sleep. I agreed to his deal because the long trip to the bathroom had worn me out. He smiled and caressed my face. He assured me that he would be there when I woke up. I thanked him. He covered me up with one blanket, and it was just a few minutes before I was asleep.

I woke up at seven, and he was not there. I heard him talking to Sam in the living room. He must have heard me stir because he was there before I could sit up. He asked if I wanted some coffee. I told him I would rather have a Diet Coke if we had one. Sam came in and said she would get the Diet Coke while he checked my temperature. It was 99. He said that was a good sign. I sat up, and my head felt much better. I stood up to go to the restroom, and my personal Florence Nightingale was there. William stood outside the door while I repeated the process from last night. My balance was much better.

Sam looked over at the nightstand because the phone kept receiving text messages. She asked if it was his phone, and William said that it belongs to me. Sam picked it up to see who kept texting. It was her dad. She knew she should not look, but she looked anyway. She read message after message of him accusing me of sleeping with William. The more she read, the madder she became. William asked if something was wrong. She said that it was her dad but she was going to take care of it. She said that neither of us should have to deal with him being a jerk. She started to erase the messages, but William told her to leave them because I should see them later, just not right now. She did not erase them, but she did put my phone on silent. She took the phone to the living room and called her dad. She wanted him to think it was me because she wanted to hear what he would say.

She dialed, and he answered right away. He made an insulting comment just like Sam knew he would. She responded, "Dad, this is Sam. How dare you type and say those kinds of things to Mom. She has not done anything wrong. She and William made the decision to wait until the divorce was final. How about you, Dad? How's Stacey today? How is that pregnancy going? Oh, I guess you didn't think about that. I guess you forgot you told me she was pregnant. Guess what, Dad, everyone knows because she has posts on her Facebook page. All the world knows that you and Mom are getting divorced in two weeks so you can be with your girlfriend who is four months pregnant with your baby. You see, Dad, if you had waited until *after* the divorce, you would not be expecting a baby with a girl who is half your age. A girl who is younger than me. So you see, I do not appreciate you texting Mom and calling her names. You are my father, but I have lost all respect for you. Do not call Mom again, or I will call her lawyer myself and get him to take care of this situation. I may call him anyway. He needs to know. I think this would cross some line bordering on harassment."

With that she hung up. She turned around, and William and I were standing in the doorway. William smiled at her and said, "You go, Sam! Do you feel better?"

Sam sighed and said, "Yes, I actually do. I am sorry, Mom. I should not have read the text messages, but it kept buzzing. When he said what he said, I had to call. He shouldn't be allowed to talk to you that way."

Just then, the phone buzzed again. Sam looked down and saw his text. "Sorry. I was wrong."

I looked at Sam and thanked her for standing up for me and for William. "I guess I better see those texts if I am going to call the attorney."

Sam handed me the phone. I read them and just shook my head. William asked if he could read them. I showed them to him. He read them and thanked Sam again for standing up to him and me. He turned his attention to me and told me that I had had enough excitement for the morning.

"Here, I will walk you to the sofa so you can have a change of scenery. Would you like some scrambled eggs or anything?"

I told him I was not hungry but I would like some water. Sam brought me a bottle and sat beside me on the sofa. I insisted that I wanted him to go home and get some rest, but he said that he was fine. He said that he still had a bag with a change of clothes, so he was going to take a shower if it was okay with me.

I told him to take a shower, eat breakfast, take a nap, whatever he needed to do. He said that he would shower and eat. Then he was going to make sure that Larry and Stewart had the bar covered for lunch. He planned to stay here today.

Sam said that she would watch the patient while William showered and checked on work. Then she said that if I was feeling okay, she would like to borrow the car and drive into town to go by College of Charleston.

I told her she was more than welcome to take the car because it sounded like I would be sitting *here* for a while. I asked if I could have my phone. Sam and William looked at each other and said that they thought phone privileges were okay, just not walking around without a spotter!

William went to take a shower, and I told Sam I was fine if she needed to do something in her room or kitchen. I was going to call my attorney just to let him know what was going on, but I had no plans to move from the sofa. She went to her room to get dressed to go to C of C. I dialed my attorney. I shared the events of the weekend, packing the house, and Bill's sarcastic comments and the text messages this morning.

I disclosed that Sam chewed him out on my phone when he had made a crude reference when he thought it was me on the phone. I told him that Sam had reprimanded him, saying he had no right to make comments about me and William when we had made a commitment to wait until the divorce was final. I added that she went on to tell him he was the one that had been selfish and had gotten his girlfriend pregnant. I told him when she was done, she had hung up on him, and he had sent an apology.

He asked me to forward the emails. He would call his attorney so Bill would be made to understand that he had to keep his distance. After this outburst, he should not call or email me.

"The next time you will have contact is two weeks from today at the hearing."

He told me not to worry, but he suggested that I save any emails or text messages in case we needed to document anything. He said that he was glad that we had been able to get all the furniture and personal items out of the house. He would contact the realtor to get that finalized.

I told him that while I had him on the phone, in the spirit of full disclosure, William had asked me to marry him. We had not been intimate and would not be intimate until after the divorce, after we were married on August 14. He said that was good to know. That was one month after the divorce, and everything should be fine since, as Sam had pointed out, Bill had already gotten his girlfriend pregnant four months ago. He told me to hang in there because we would be done with Bill in two weeks. I thanked him for his help and hung up.

I was just about to stand up when William walked in. "Maggie Mae, what are you doing?"

I knew I was busted, so I just sat back down and said, "Liam, I was waiting for you to come help me stand up!"

He laughed and came to help me up. He hugged me and kissed me. "I am so glad you are feeling better. What do you need?"

I told him that I wanted to go to the restroom and get some more Diet Coke. He walked me to the restroom. The dizziness was much better, and my neck did not even hurt anymore. We walked to the kitchen, and he put more ice in my glass and filled it with Diet Coke. I looked in the fridge and found bagels and cream cheese. He told me that he would take me to the sofa, and he would fix the bagel and bring it to me. He put it in the toaster and put some of the softened cream cheese in a small cup. He brought it over to me. I thanked him and suggested that he get some breakfast. He put some grits on to cook and fixed himself a cup of coffee.

His phone rang, and he answered. It was Dr. Morris calling to check on the patient. He gave him a report, and he said he was very glad to hear I was better. He said he wanted to come by this afternoon and look at my ear. He said he might give me another shot instead of prescribing pills for ten days. He said the shot worked faster without being as tough on the stomach for so many days. William assured him we would be right here. Dr. Morris said that he would text before he came by. He was hoping to come by at four.

William fixed his grits with cheddar cheese and bacon. Then he came and sat by me on the sofa. He turned the TV on so we could catch up on the news. It felt like we had been removed from the world all weekend. Sam came out and asked if we needed anything. I told her I could not think of anything. William asked if I would like some tomato soup and a grilled cheese sandwich for dinner, which actually sounded pretty good at the moment. He got up to check my pantry and then asked Sam to get a large can of tomato soup. He said he would "jazz" it up! She said that she would get it and bring it home.

Sam said that she was going on a tour of the science department and meet with a marine biology counselor. I told her to take her time and enjoy the campus. I indicated that my keys were hanging on the hook by the door.

When she had backed out of the driveway, William looked at me and asked what was going on. I told him that she was considering transferring to College of Charleston to get a master's degree in marine biology. "She said the class she taught on sea turtles last week and all my talk about the turtle conservation program here had made her miss marine biology."

William asked what that meant about her husband. I told him all she had said was that was part of the process of formulating the plan.

"I do not know that they are having any trouble, but maybe with both teaching, they have drifted apart. Or maybe it is just that she is homesick. Maybe he would move with her. I just don't know."

I told him that I had called my attorney to let him know about Bill's comments this weekend, the text messages, and Sam's response to him. "He said he would call Bill's attorney to make sure that Bill was made aware that he would have no contact with me until the day of the final divorce decree."

I also let William know that I had filled my attorney in about us and our plan to get married.

William perked up and said, "Okay, if you are talking to the attorney, it's definitely happening, right?"

I told him yes. He said that he appreciated the update. William leaned forward and kissed me. "You know, Maggie Mae, I love you very much. I will be glad when your divorce is final so we can be together."

I kissed him and said, "Me too."

He asked if I was still feeling okay. I assured him that I was. He suggested that I take a nap or at least lay down because I did not need to get too tired. He said that I would probably be back to full strength tomorrow, but I would have to be careful in the sun after two powerful doses of antibiotic. I told him I wanted to sit here with him for a while. He told me to let him know when I was ready to lay down and he would strip the bed since I had sweated off all that fever. I closed my eyes and put my head on his shoulder.

He called Larry, and he said that everything was fine at the bar. William told him to call if he needed anything but he would be here with me especially since the doctor was coming back. Larry said that he would call but not to worry. William hung up. He leaned his head against mine, and we rested.

He grabbed my hand and said, "You know, you have to get to feeling better because we need to put your furniture in the house."

I told him we would deal with that after Sam left on Wednesday if that was okay with him.

"That is fine. We also need to use your 'super list-making skills' to plan for the wedding."

I told him we could do that tomorrow. That seemed to please him. It made me happy too!

We napped for about an hour on the sofa. William got up and told me to lay down on the sofa for a bit. He went into the bedroom. I assumed he was stripping the bed. He put fresh sheets and a clean blanket on the bed. He took the dirty sheets and blankets to the laundry room. He washed the sheets and a few towels. Then he put the blankets on to wash when the sheets went in the dryer. He pulled a load of towels out of the dryer. He left the basket in the living room. He woke me up to check my temperature. Still 99. Good news. He brought me some water. He asked if I wanted to use the restroom before I lay down for a nap. I told him I felt like a twelve-year-old.

He insisted that he was just taking care of me because I had to be well for some very important plans he had for me. I stood up, and he stayed close in case I was dizzy. I was fine. He walked me to the restroom and waited outside. I came out and got back in bed. I told him I wanted to take a shower, and he said we would have to check on that with Dr. Morris. He wanted to make sure I was stable on my feet before I got in the shower unless I wanted him to stand in there with him. I blushed and told him I was not quite ready for that! He said that it was fine, he could wait until August 14. I smiled and kissed him. He ordered me to get some rest and he would be back to check on me.

He fixed himself some coffee and folded the towels. He checked in on work. All was well. He called his attorney to fill him in on the divorce/wedding plans. He said he would check on the process for a marriage license but that we should be able to just go get one right after the divorce decree was filed. He called his sister to check in. He told her that I was napping and recovering from an ear infection.

Then he asked her how she would feel if we got married on August 14. She squealed into the phone, and he suggested that she had to stop because dogs from miles around could hear her high-pitched squeal. She said that it was wonderful news and she would do whatever we needed to help. She told him to give me a hug and tell me to get well soon so we could plan. William suggested that maybe we could get together Friday or Saturday to discuss wedding plans.

Okay, so I had told Sam and Dave. William had told Susan. Next thing I had to tell Debbie and Annette. Not today, maybe tomorrow. He lay down on the sofa for a short nap before Dr. Morris texted.

The vibrations of William's phone woke him up. The text from Dr. Morris said he would be there in ten minutes. He shook his head to wake up and checked his phone. It was four fifteen. William came to check on me, and I was still sleeping. He felt my forehead, and it still felt cool. I woke up when he touched me. He asked how I was feeling.

"I think I feel better. My head doesn't feel tingly if that makes sense."

He checked my temperature. It was normal. He said that Dr. Morris was on his way.

"I need to use the restroom before he gets here, and I want a shower!"

William said that we would ask the doctor about a shower when he got here. He walked me to the restroom, and then we walked out to the living room.

Williams said, "You are walking much better. This morning, you walked like you were just a little drunk. Now it's a normal walk."

I sat on the sofa. The doorbell rang, and William let Dr. Morris in. He walked in and said, "Well, Maggie, you look much better than you did last night. Today, you are in the land of the living!"

I told him I felt much better. He checked my throat, nose, and right ear. All good. The lymph node was less swollen. Then he checked the left ear.

"This is much better. Not quite as angry and inflamed. Is the dizziness better?"

I told him it was much better. He said that the fluid was gone from behind my eardrum. He checked my temperature, normal.

"Maggie, it looks good. Please make sure that you take your allergy medicine every day. That way, the congestion will not build up. When it builds up, it goes to your ears or your sinuses."

I promised him I would take it. He said that he was going to give me one more shot of antibiotic but no shot of medication for fever. He directed me to stand up and pull down my yoga pants just a little. He gave me the shot.

He said, "What, no 'ouch' from you today!"

I told him I had no memory of last night's shot. I asked him if I could resume regular activities. He said to be cautious but go ahead. I asked if I could take a shower. He said to be careful not to get water in my ear and to be careful so I did not fall.

William promised him that he would be there to catch me if needed. Dr. Morris said that I would be fine to go out tomorrow, just no pool or ocean water in the ear and not too much sun. William thanked him for coming by and asked him to send a bill for him to pay.

William walked him to the door and found me in the bedroom gathering a change of clothes and a towel. He walked with me to the bathroom and started the shower. He offered to help me undress, but I told him I could do it. He said he would be outside the door. I started the shower and went to step in. I felt a little shaky. I asked him if he would come hold my hand while I stepped over the tub while keeping his eyes closed. He said that he would. He came in with eyes closed and held his hand out. I stepped over the tub, and he peeked. I fussed at him, and he apologized.

He said that he just needed a quick peek. He pulled me toward him and kissed me. "You are quite beautiful. You have given me something to look forward to. Now shower and be careful. I'll be sitting right here in case you need me."

I showered and stopped the water. I put my hand out and asked him to hand me a towel. I wrapped up in the towel, and he held my hand while I stepped out.

"See, I didn't peek that time! Your clothes are on the bed. I will step outside. Call me if you need me."

I dressed and came out to the great room. As I walked out, Sam was coming in. She said I looked much better. She went to the kitchen to take the tomato soup to William. I sat on the sofa. I lay down for just a bit. William fixed some grilled cheese sandwiches and warmed the soup with added milk, pepper, and rosemary. I told him that everything smelled delicious. He asked if I was ready to eat, and I said that I was. He brought me a tray with soup, a sandwich, and a glass of Diet Coke. It really was delicious. He and Sam fixed their plates and joined me in the great room.

I asked Sam how her visit went to College of Charleston. She said it was a great visit, and she really liked their Marine Biology Program. I asked if she had decided what she was going to do. She said that she had to weigh out all the pros and cons. She was not going to rush into anything. She said that the adviser said that a January start date might work best with my timetable.

We finished up. I thanked him for dinner. I told him it was perfect. I did not realize how hungry I was until I started eating. He reminded me that I had not eaten my salad last night and had only eaten a bagel this morning. He stacked the plates and bowls and took the dishes and trays to the kitchen.

I insisted that he had babysat long enough. "I want you to go to your bar and check on Larry and Stewart. Then I want you to go rest. I am fine. Sam and I are going to sit here and visit because she leaves for Tennessee on Wednesday."

Sam smiled and suggested that if I were up to it, she would teach me to crochet a turtle.

I looked at William and said, "See, I will be making turtles, you go work and rest."

He reluctantly agreed to go to work and then home. He told me he would call later to check on me. "I'll let you, ladies, visit tomorrow, but I can bring you lunch or you can come by the bar."

I told him that sounded like a plan. Sam asked if we could all go to Shem Creek Bar and Grill tomorrow night. William said that sounded like a great idea. I agreed. I sighed, and William looked at me. "You are thinking of days gone by and the Trawler Restaurant, aren't you?"

I looked at him and asked how he knew that I was thinking about the Trawler. "If you have spent any time at Shem Creek in the '80s, you can't help but remember the Trawler Crab Dip."

The thought of it just made my mouth water. He winked at me and told me he had a recipe that was close! With that, he leaned over and gave me a kiss, and he was off to work.

Sam went to her room and brought out her sample turtle, several crochet hooks, and several skeins of yarn. She asked if I wanted to stick with the traditional greens or make our turtles multicolor.

She had a pretty yarn that was a mix of blues and greens. I said we should start with that one and a traditional green. She sat beside me. We each took a hook and a skein of yarn. She started a few stitches and showed me what to do. She wanted me to get a basic stitch down pat, and then we would work on the actual turtle shape. She could talk while she crocheted; I was not quite ready for that yet. It was a simple pattern though. We worked, and she talked, and by five thirty, we each had made a turtle! I was so proud of my accomplishment that I took a picture and sent it to William. He was impressed with my mad skills.

Sam went to the kitchen to get us some water. I asked if she would put on a pot of coffee. She laughed and said, "Well, you must be feeling better!"

I assured her that I was and that one beer might be in order with dinner. She started the coffee. I got up to use the restroom, drank some water, and we started our next pair of turtles. By the time I started my third one, I could talk a little bit while I crocheted. We talked about her job at the University of Tennessee. We talked about the degree program at College of Charleston. I did not ask any questions about her marriage or whether her husband would come to Charleston if she moved. I figured when she was ready, she would tell me.

Sam asked about the wedding plans, so we talked about those for a while. She told me that she knew I would have to make a list of everything we had discussed when my hands were not busy crocheting. I knew she was teasing me, but she was right. I indicated that I also had to call Annette and Debbie and let them know. I knew that they would be mad if I kept it from them too long.

We continued to make our turtles. We decided to branch out and make some blue ones, red ones, yellow ones. By seven thirty, we had about twenty turtles. She suggested we take a break and think about dinner. I told her that I had a few frozen entrées in the freezer, a frozen pizza, and maybe corn dogs. I knew that I needed to buy groceries. She laughed and said I needed to start eating healthier. I knew she was right, but I liked to keep the fast-food stuff on hand for a quick meal on the go. I had come down here for a vacation, and I did not want to cook.

We decided on pizza. It was obvious that pizza was not only my favorite food group but Sam liked it too! We each put a slice on a plate, grabbed a beer, and settled back on the sofa. She turned on the TV and asked how I felt about a movie night. She suggested *Mamma Mia* 1 and 2. I felt that musicals with ABBA music would be a great girls' night in! Sam went and grabbed two more slices and gave one to me. We finished our slices and paused the movie so we could each have a bathroom break. When I came back, Sam was on her phone. Evidently, William had called to check on me. She reported that we had made twenty turtles, had pizza and a beer, and were in the middle of a *Mamma Mia* marathon. She told him good night and passed the phone to me.

"I won't keep you. I just wanted to make sure you were feeling better, and it sounds like it's a good evening. I am so glad that Sam is there to watch *Mamma Mia* with you so I don't have to!"

I laughed. "What, you aren't a chick flick sort of guy? This could be a deal-breaker!"

He quickly added, "Oh, for you, I would watch *Mamma Mia* 1 and 2, but only for you! No deal-breakers here! I love you. You guys have fun."

Sam and I watched both movies and sang along to our favorite songs. We decided we better go to bed so we could make more turtles tomorrow before lunch at the One-Eyed Parrot and dinner at Shem Creek. My ear was still a little tender, but I felt so much better. I rolled over, and that was the last thing I remembered.

Things were back to normal on Tuesday because I woke up at six thirty. I got up, took a shower, made the bed, and went to the kitchen. I put a pot of coffee on. At seven, Sam walked out and went straight for the coffee. I asked her if she slept well. She said that she did expect for sea turtles singing ABBA songs. I told her that tonight we had to be careful what we watched so the dreams would not be so weird. She grabbed a bagel, and I grabbed a banana. After our light breakfast, we were both saving calories for lunch and dinner; we sat down to make more turtles. She made them very quickly, and I had definitely picked up speed. We had a music channel on for background noise. She introduced me to a band called Greta Van Fleet out of Michigan. I really liked their music. I could close my eyes and picture a little bit of Led Zeppelin, Freddie Mercury from Queen, and Rush.

My phone rang at eleven. It was William checking to see if we had survived the movie marathon. I confessed that we had watched both movies and sang along. I told him I was feeling good today, and we were working on more turtles. "We had plans to head that way by eleven forty-five for lunch."

He said that it was overcast and a little cooler, so we should sit under an umbrella on the back deck. I told him we would see him in a bit.

We stopped after we finished the current turtle. We freshened up and got ready to walk to the bar. I put two turtles in my purse to show William. We sat outside and enjoyed the breeze and shrimp and grits. William sat with us a while, but he had to work the bar because they were busy. We decided that we would go to the grocery store to get Sam some snacks and drinks for her ride home in the morning. We went and got pedicures and sat and drank some coffee. We decided to go back to the beach house, sit on the porch, and make a few more turtles until William picked us up to go to dinner at Shem Creek.

I told Sam that I was going to call the publisher next week and see where we stood on working out a deal with the coastal state park gift stores. I was going to need to find a way to attach a turtle to each book. I would have to figure that one out.

Sam reminded me that I needed to make a wedding list from all the things we listed last night. I told her that I would make it now so she could help me remember: dress, William's outfit, flowers, music, guest list, reception, photographs, reception music, and food. I asked Sam if she would be my maid of honor. She said that she would love to, but she asked about Debbie and Annette, and I told her they would fight over it. I would just give them a "job" at the wedding.

We finished about ten turtles, and we were talking wedding when William walked up. He smiled and said, "Well, that's the kind of talk I like to hear!"

Sam laughed and asked him what he wanted to wear, khakis or shorts? He suggested khaki shorts as a compromise. We made a note and marked that one off the list. He asked if we were ready to go to dinner. He thought we better not go too late since Sam had to get an early start for Tennessee tomorrow.

I put our turtles in the box on the coffee table and locked up. We were able to get a table near the bar quickly. We ordered a beer and crab dip to get started. Then we each ordered a shrimp and scallop dinner. They had a guy playing the piano, so the atmosphere was nice. William asked if we wanted to get the U-Haul tonight and park it at the beach house and I would just bring Sam over to get it in the morning. I told him that at some point, I would need to go through the stuff on his trailer. He said that there was no rush. I suggested to Sam that we look at the Christmas decorations later unless she wanted to take it all with her. She groaned and said later was fine.

We finished dinner, and William drove us back to the beach house. He hugged Sam and told her that he looked forward to seeing her in August. She told him that she was glad to have the chance to meet him this weekend and said that she was glad he was going to be part of the family. Sam went inside and left us on the porch to say good night.

She turned and said, "Now you two, don't stay out here too long. Don't make me signal you with the porch light!"

William said, "Yes, ma'am, I won't keep her out here long. No need to signal."

We sat and talked a few minutes. I told him I would come by to see him at the bar in the morning if he had already left his house by the time we came to get the U-Haul. I hugged him, and we kissed good night.

"Maybe we can look at that wedding list tomorrow night. Susan offered to help. She loves planning weddings."

"I would love her help, but remember, this is going to be very small."

He laughed and said that was his plan, too, but once people got involved, it might grow a bit.

"Hey, we haven't been down to the beach to check on turtle hatching. Shouldn't that be happening soon?"

He said that we could go down to the beach tomorrow or Thursday night and check to see what the volunteers were up to. He said that hatching season was May until October, but the peak was early July. I told him I would like to get involved and help the group. He said that Susan would be thrilled and would sign me up for as much volunteering as I wanted.

"I guess turtle-hatching season will affect a beach wedding on August 14."

He said, "It would mean we could not hold a wedding on the beach later in the day. We will have to look tomorrow night or this weekend to see where active nests are, and it may affect the exact location."

At that moment, the porch light flickered. He laughed and kissed me and went to his truck.

I went in, and Sam laughed. I told her we were just talking about the wedding. I grabbed us a couple of beers, and we sat on the porch and talked about the sea turtle nesting implications for the wedding location. She said that she had not even thought about that. I admitted that the thought occurred to me this afternoon while I was crocheting.

"We will figure it out."

I assured her it was not going to be a big wedding, so it would not require a lot of planning. I declared that I would not let people know about it other than her, Dave, Annette, and Debbie until after the divorce hearing. The hearing was in twelve days. She asked if I had called Annette and Debbie. I told her I would do it tomorrow. We talked until about ten thirty. Then Sam said she was going to pack her bag and get some sleep. She said that she wanted to get on the road by eight thirty, so I said I would drive her over to William's house at eight fifteen. I kissed her good night and told her I would see her bright and early in the morning.

It felt like I had just put my head on my pillow, but when I rolled over, my alarm was going off at six thirty. I got dressed and went out to fix some coffee. Sam was already out there with a pot of coffee brewing. I asked her if she wanted any breakfast. She said that she was going to eat a bagel and that was enough. I asked her why she was up so early, and she said that she just could not sleep because she had so many thoughts rolling around in her head. I understood that feeling all too well.

She said that she just kept replaying her conversation with her dad in her head, then she had to decide about graduate school. She just had a lot to think about. I told her that I was not going to pry, but that if she needed to talk, I was there to listen. She said that she appreciated it. I asked her if she wanted to go ahead and get the U-Haul. She said she thought it might be best to get on the road early to beat the traffic.

We each fixed a cup of coffee in a travel mug. I helped her grab her bags, and we left for Sullivan's Island. We got there around seven thirty, and William's truck was still there. I helped Sam put her things in the cab of the U-Haul. We hugged. I told her to call when she got home, and with that, she was on the road.

I had really enjoyed having her here to visit. Part of me hoped she would move here. I felt like Isle of Palms/Sullivan's Island were home at least for me. I did not feel at home when I was in Columbia over the weekend. I felt that this was where I belonged. I was standing there in deep thought watching her drive away when William put his arms around my waist. I was so lost in my thoughts that I had not heard him, so it startled me.

He apologized for scaring me and gave me a big hug. He asked if I wanted breakfast. I told him a cup of coffee would be good. He took my hand, and we walked up his stairs. It was hard to believe that after August 14, these would be *our* stairs. Exciting and scary all at the same time. No matter how scary it felt, this did feel like where I belonged.

CHAPTER 17

When Time Stands Still (Anticipation)

William and I did not do anything too exciting over the next few days; we just enjoyed each other's company. I think I was still a little tired from clearing out the house in Columbia and getting sick with an ear infection. We ate together, took a few walks on the beach, watched some movies. We met with Susan and talked a little bit about the wedding. I wanted it small. I wanted it on the beach, but I did not know if the turtles would cooperate. I really wanted to have it around four when it was not quite as hot. She was still formulating a plan if the turtles were hatching.

The publisher and I had worked out a deal with the state parks to put forty copies of the book in each coastal park: Edisto, Huntington Beach, Hunting Island, and Myrtle Beach. I had an additional two hundred copies that I was going to make available to the Sea Turtle Groups along the coast. The publisher was going to keep 20 percent from each sale. I agreed to keep 10 percent, and the parks and conservation groups would keep the rest. After I paid for yarn for the turtles and crocheted them, I was not really making anything, but that was okay. We had decided to design a bookmark with some of the artwork from the cover of the book that the publisher would have printed, and I would attach a turtle to the bookmark.

I had called Debbie and Annette the day after Sam left to check on them and to let them know about my plans to get married. They asked for details about how it went in Columbia at the house. I told them that Bill had made a few sarcastic remarks, but the worst comments were sent via text the next day that Sam had intercepted.

"After she finished chewing him out, all he could muster was sorry. There had been no word since. I was enjoying the silence from him."

They were excited about the idea of the wedding. I told them it was going to be small, and I asked them to keep quiet about it until after the divorce was final. They promised.

I had touched base with the attorney, and the sale of the house was going through on the Wednesday before the divorce hearing, so there would be a check for each of us there. He said the hearing would be at the Richland County Courthouse on Main Street at 10:00 a.m. He said I could come to his office at nine fifteen, and we would ride together.

William helped me go through the things in the trailer. The kitchen items, we put in his kitchen. We hung a few pictures in the living room and bedrooms. We placed my mom's furniture pieces around the house, and he offered me a spare room to set up an office. I told him I did not need a lot of space if I was just doing volunteer work with the two foundations. We decided to split his office in half, and he set up my office on one side. That will work well for those times when we were working on foundation events together. As we went through things, I found more to donate, so we boxed those items up and took them to Habitat. I just put the Christmas decorations in a storage room. I told him I would let Sam go through it all later.

He had a closet that was as big as a bedroom, so I had plenty of space for my clothes. I went ahead and put the clothes from the trailer in the closet at his house. I would move my things from the beach house right before the wedding.

I guess I was trying to stay extra busy so I would not think about the divorce hearing. I helped at the bar a couple of days; after all, I needed to work off my tab. So I washed dishes; I even waited tables a few times. William and I went on a moonlight cruise of the Charleston Harbor. It was so beautiful. We took a trip to

McClellanville one day so I could take pictures. The old buildings were great. We found a café on Main Street for dinner.

Finally, it was the Friday before my hearing. William helped me pack up my clothes and personal items from the beach house, and I took it to his house. I guess I could have stayed at the beach house until August 14, but I just wanted to get all my things in one place. I cleaned the kitchen and bathroom. I mopped and vacuumed. I dusted and stripped the beds and washed the linens and put them away. William helped me complete a walk-through to make sure it was in presentable order to turn back over to Dave. We swept the porch and deck. I packed a bag and included a dress outfit for court.

We left around midday to go to Columbia. I dressed up so I would be presentable to go by the office. We visited with Dave for a while, then I cleaned out my desk and files. Dave gave me some information about the next foundation event. It was not until November, so I could start working on it with Dave and Amy (who had taken my job). I gave Dave the keys for the beach house and thanked him again for his generosity. I told him I had done a mail forwarding order to William's house, but if it were okay, I would check the box for a while to make sure nothing slipped through.

We had made plans to meet Debbie and Annette for dinner. We went to Terra. We went back to Annette's after dinner to visit. We talked wedding plans. I told them we were set for August 14.

"We were only having about twenty people at the wedding, and we had decided to have it on the back deck at the One-Eyed Parrot. That way, we would not interfere if the turtles were hatching and moving to the sea. We were going to have a reception inside with a few more people, all very casual."

Annette had started dating an attorney in Columbia, and she asked if she could bring him. I insisted that it was fine. Debbie laughed and said she would be looking for someone to date at the wedding or reception. They asked about what I was wearing. I told them I knew I wanted a sundress, but I had not found "the dress" yet. I told them that William's sister was working on the details and she and I would be emailing an invitation Tuesday (after the divorce). We made it an early night because they both worked all day. We had rented a pontoon boat to go out on Lake Murray on Saturday. I was looking forward to having a chance to attempt to fish. Then we could swim and relax.

We had a hotel room for Friday, Saturday, and Sunday nights. We just did not want to crowd Debbie or Annette. It just seemed like we had not had any time for just us lately. William said that he wanted to talk about honeymoon plans. So I had my wedding planning notebook. I opened it up to a new page, and we discussed options. William offered a trip to Ireland, and even though we both wanted to make the trip, we agreed that maybe some place less exotic would be fine for a honeymoon. The plan was to spend a good bit of time doing all the things that we both thought about entirely too much! He asked if I wanted to go to someplace in state or out of state. I told him for the honeymoon, in state was fine. He asked if I wanted lake, beach, or mountains. I suggested that since we lived at the beach and we were going to the lake tomorrow, the mountains might be fun. I asked how he felt about the Oconee, Table Rock, Devils Fork area. I told him the cabins at Devils Fork and Oconee were both great. Devils Fork was booked. He suggested a hotel in Clemson. That way we could tour the campus, go to Oconee, Devils Fork, Table Rock... We could do all that on our timetable. If we woke up and wanted to just stay in, we could just stay in. I told him that I liked the idea. He said that he would book a hotel tomorrow.

We watched a movie on TV. I could not talk him into *Mamma Mia*, but I did talk him into *Iron Man*! We went to sleep early so we could meet Annette, her boyfriend, and Debbie at the Marina by nine. We both slept well and woke up before the alarm.

We dressed for the lake and ate breakfast at the hotel before heading out to Lexington. It was a nice pontoon. We loaded a cooler of drinks, and Debbie loaded a cooler with food. We had beach towels, sunscreen, fishing supplies, and I had my camera. Annette's new guy was very nice. His name was Tim, and he was a family law attorney. He was from Lexington, and he had spent a lot of time on the lake, so he was appointed as driver. We rode around for a while, then we anchored and fished a bit. We caught nothing; well, there were a few that we caught, but they escaped.

After fishing, we parked the boat on an island and got out to sit in the sun for a while. We walked and explored. We grilled burgers while we were there, and we ate. We had a great time just talking. Everyone seemed to get along well. We headed back to the marina at around four. We gathered trash off the pontoon and swept it out. We filled it back up with gas and turned in the keys. Annette, Debbie, and Tim were going to the skyline club to dance, but I told them I thought we would take a rain check. I would have loved to dance, but I had gotten a little sun, and I really just wanted to take a shower and relax. William said that he would rather have the alone time with me but that we would go dancing soon.

We both showered and got into comfortable clothes back at the hotel. We ordered room service and turned on the TV for background noise. I downloaded my photos, and we looked at them. The sun on the lake was beautiful today. I was able to capture a few waterfowl too. I had some shots of the group. William told me that he had been thinking about my photos and had an idea for a fundraiser for either his family foundation or Dave's foundation. He said that we could ask photographers to submit artwork and create a gallery show. People could buy or bid on photos as a fundraiser. I told him that was a definite possibility because there were enough artists in Columbia and Charleston. He said that he did not necessarily mean professional artists; he thought amateur photographers would be good too. I thought it sounded like a good idea too.

I asked him what he wanted to do tomorrow. He asked about the zoo. He said that he had never been to one. I told him we could go to the zoo, eat lunch there, and then we could walk around downtown. I confessed that I always loved to take pictures at the zoo on the botanical garden side. He suggested we turn in early. I put my camera battery on to charge, and we turned in.

As usual, we both woke up before the alarm. We showered and dressed. We got bagels and coffee downstairs and headed to the zoo. It was crowded, but not too bad for a summer day. We looked at the animal exhibits and walked through the aquarium. We sat for a while and drank a Diet Coke. I told him I was not hungry, but we should stop if he was hungry. He said that he could wait until later. We took the tram over to the botanical garden side so I could take pictures. We took the garden trail that led through the woods back to the river and to the foot of the bridge. We took the tram back and walked to the car.

We ate at a little diner on Main Street, and then we walked around the statehouse grounds and the Horseshoe at USC so he could have a state capital history lesson. I took pictures at both places. After that, we went back to the hotel to freshen up. I was exhausted; we had walked five miles. We decided to go to bed early. I could feel myself starting to get tense. I had to be at the attorney's office by nine fifteen.

William said he was going to drive me there and wait outside with a celebratory cup of coffee. I told him I might need to go to a bar for a shot or two. He said that it could be arranged!

I figured out what I was wearing tomorrow. I took a shower and lay down on the bed while William checked in at the bar. Everything was fine. Somewhere along the line, I fell asleep. William covered me up and cut off the light.

CHAPTER 18

It's a Wrap! (Go Your Own Way)

Well, again, I woke up before the alarm. I tried not to toss and turn because I did not want to wake William up. Today was the day. We would meet in court, sign some papers, and walk away from a twenty-seven-year marriage like it never existed. Well, we had Sam to show for it, and if we were honest, the first ten years were good years. We would each walk away with a check from the sale of the house. Bill would start his life with Stacey and their new baby, and I would get to start a new life with William. I sighed to myself, but it was not really to myself because William sat up and asked me if I was okay.

I told him I was fine, and I apologized for waking him up. He said that he had been awake for a little while thinking about court. He hoped it would be quick and painless. He asked if I wanted him to go with me, but I felt that it would probably be best if he did not go. I suggested that he wait at my attorney's office.

He looked at the clock, and it was six thirty. He said, "I guess technically, we could go get breakfast, but how about you come over here and let me just hold you for a little while? Then we will get dressed and go downstairs for breakfast." He kissed my forehead and told me that everything would be fine. I knew it would be; I just wanted it to be over.

He told me that he had been hunting online last night and found a dress. I had to chuckle. "You aren't thinking of wearing dresses now, are you?"

He shot me a look. "Of course not, I don't have the legs for it! I was looking for the wedding." There was this white maxi dress with a small blue floral print on it. Anyway, it made me think of hydrangeas and, well, you. Do you have any idea what you want to wear?

I told him that I knew I wanted a casual sundress with a jacket or wrap, a maxi length was fine. "If I could find one with a blue floral print, maybe you could wear a blue shirt with your khaki shorts."

He suggested that we go look this afternoon or tomorrow.

"I didn't think you were supposed to see me in the dress. Isn't that bad luck?"

He said, "I don't have to see you in it, but I think I can see it on a hanger."

I told him that we could go today after this morning's hearing was over.

We got up and got ready. I brought a business suit from work. I had lost a little weight because the pants were baggy. That was a good way to start the day! William put on shorts and a polo shirt. I wished I were going to be with him instead of a courthouse. We went downstairs and got a light breakfast and headed for the attorney's office. His office was over on Lady Street; parking could be an issue. We found the building, and after circling the block, we found a parking space. We went upstairs. My attorney greeted us. I introduced him to William. I told him William was going to wait here for us to come back. He said the hearing was at ten, and we should be finished by ten forty-five. I sure hoped he was right. My attorney suggested that William wait in the conference room because it was going to get too warm today for him to wait in the truck.

We walked down to his car and drove over to the courthouse on Main Street. We parked, and I took a deep breath. He told me not to be nervous. We went in the building through security and went upstairs to the courtroom. Bill was there with his attorney. There was a pregnant girl sitting beside him who looked like the "Stacey from Facebook." I looked at my attorney and told him that it must be my lucky day.

He said that he was surprised that his attorney let her come. At nine fifty, the bailiff let us in. We took a seat at one table while Bill and his attorney sat at another. The judge came in and called the court to order. He read over the papers and called Bill to the stand.

I whispered to my attorney, "Please tell me I don't have to testify."

He told me I would not have to since it was not contested. Bill had started the paperwork, so he was testifying. The judge asked a few questions. Bill answered. The judge made a few comments. Then he asked if the house was sold since that was a stipulation of the divorce. Bill's attorney stated that it had sold for $500,000. The judge gave the breakdown, and after expenses were paid, Bill and I would each receive $235,000. The judge granted the divorce degree. He adjourned, and my attorney went up to a clerk's window to get the decree stamped and dated. The clerk gave him two checks, one for him (his fee) and one for me. I am assuming that Bill's attorney did the same thing. I asked my attorney if we could go, and he said we were free to go.

He asked if I wanted to speak to Bill. I had hoped to get out of there without any interaction, but that was not to be because Bill and Stacey walked up. Bill wished me the best for the future.

I really was at a loss for words. I just looked at them and said, "Good luck!" My attorney grabbed my elbow and lead me to the elevator. I guess he was afraid I would say something worse. Bill just stood there with his mouth hanging open, and I heard Stacey say, "What does she mean by that?"

As we turned to get in the elevator, Bill said, "She means she wishes us good luck that's all."

Stacey looked at him and said, "I kind of think she was talking to me."

I grinned, but luckily the elevator closed before they saw it.

My attorney chuckled and leaned over to me and whispered, "They are probably going to need all the luck they can get!"

We drove back to the office, and I felt like a weight had been lifted from my shoulders. I was divorced, and I had the paperwork to prove it. He was free to be with his new family, and I was free to start my life with William.

We parked and went upstairs. I walked into the conference room, and William stood up to hug me. "Maggie Mae, how did it go?"

"Liam, it was fine!"

My attorney shared that Bill had told me he wished me every happiness.

William looked shocked and said, "Oh no, Maggie. What did you say? Were you nice?"

"I was very nice. I looked at the two of them and simply said 'Good luck.' I think that was nice enough under the circumstances!"

"The two of them? You mean to say that Bill brought Stacey? What an idiot."

I kissed William again and turned to my attorney and thanked him for everything. He told me to stay in touch and let him know if I needed anything. William shook his hand and grabbed mine and walked toward the door. We got in the truck, and he pulled me close for a kiss. I always enjoyed his kisses, but somehow without the weight of Bill and Stacey in the mix, his kisses felt that much better!

He started the truck, and we headed out. I suggested we try a bridal or dress shop in Mt. Pleasant or downtown Charleston. He said we could try Charleston first, get something to eat, and then hit Mt. Pleasant if we needed to. I told him I needed to stop by the bank to get the check from the settlement deposited. We held hands and made our way back home. I had been dreading this day for three weeks, but it was over in forty minutes. In a way, it was sad that a long marriage could be dissolved that quickly, but if I were honest with myself, it had been dissolving for years.

He kissed my hand and said, "You know we have a lot to do if we are getting married on August 14."

I told him that with Susan on the case, I was sure we would not have any trouble getting everything done.

We drove to the market and parked. He asked if I wanted lunch first. I told him yes; I wanted a celebratory lunch! We went to Tommy Condons. While we sat there, I did a search for dress shops. There were several on King Street and Meeting Street. I might even find one in the shops at Charleston Place. I did not want to spend too much, but I did have the money in my account! We finished eating and started walking. The first shop did not have anything dressy, and it looked like the clothes were for younger women. The next shop was a bridal shop. I did not want an actual wedding dress. The next shop had lots of cute sundresses. They had some designer names. I picked up one. William liked it, but I did not like the price tag. He said to get what I wanted.

"How often do you get married?"

I laughed and said, "Well, me? I get married twice!"

I took several back to try them on. He asked if I was going to model them. I told him I had not decided yet. I tried on the first one, and it just did not fit right. The second one was solid white. I did not think I wanted to go that route. The last one was off-white, and then it had small flowers all over it. The colors reminded me of hydrangeas and roses. The salesclerk came back to see if anything worked. I showed her the floral dress. I told her it was for my wedding on the beach. She said that was perfect.

I asked if she had a wrap or shawl that went with the colors of the flowers either the blue, lavender, or pink. She brought a couple of options. She had a shawl that was a perfect blue. She agreed that it was perfect together. She asked what kind of shoes I wanted. I told her espadrilles that tied on the leg and had a low heel. She measured my foot and brought a pair. I tried them on. It was the perfect outfit. She said to wrap it up and not let him see it until the day. She asked what he was wearing. I told her khaki shorts and a pastel shirt, a blue that matched this dress. She told me they had both in the shop next door. She went out and got William and took him next door. She asked him his sizes. She pulled a pair of shorts and a shirt and asked him to try them on. He tried them on, and she said they were perfect. She told him to buy them and she would wrap them up so they would be a surprise on the day.

He stayed to make the purchase, and the salesclerk and I went back to get my dress and shawl boxed up. She boxed the shoes. She rang them up, and William walked in and paid for them. I insisted that I would get them, and he insisted that he was taking care of it. The salesclerk told me to never argue with a man who was buying you a dress. I kissed him and thanked him. We walked to the truck. He suggested we stop by his house for something. We went in and went out on the deck. The sun was low in the sky, and it was just so beautiful. He came out and stood behind me with his arms around my waist.

I leaned back against him and said that it was so beautiful. He told me that I certainly was beautiful. I blushed and said that I meant the sun setting in the sky was beautiful.

He said that he still meant me. He turned me around to face him and kissed me. "I am so glad you found your dress. I know it will be beautiful. There's just one more thing you need to make it official." He reached in his pocket and pulled out a ring box and opened it. The ring took my breath away.

I said, "It's beautiful, but you didn't have to give me another ring."

He reminded me that the first ring was just a placeholder for this ring and that the three rings would be on my finger on August 14. He looked at me and said, "Maggie Nelson, will you marry me?"

I smiled and said, "I will be happy to marry you."

He pulled me closer and kissed me. Then he put the ring on my finger. I flung my arms around his neck and kissed him.

"When did you get this ring?"

He said that he had contacted a jeweler two weeks ago. He had sent pictures of samples. "I measured the ring from your finger when you weren't wearing it and got him to size it. Does it fit okay?"

I told him it was perfect. He suggested that we go see Susan because she was dying to see the ring on my finger. He said that we could get her to look at the two outfits and she could get the flowers to match. She can get started tomorrow on the planning.

"I want you to relax and enjoy your wedding. I want to enjoy my wedding. Let's let her plan."

I was so happy at this moment that I would not think of arguing. We kissed again, and then we called to see if Susan was home. She was and said we better come by now. William picked up the two bags from the dress shops so Susan could get an idea of color. We drove to Susan and Artie's house. The kids were probably in bed. Susan came running out to the truck before we could get out. I held my hand out, and she just started squealing! Then she started jumping up and down. She asked us to come in. William said he did not want to wake the kids. He handed Susan the two bags and told her that they were our wedding outfits. We had not seen each other's outfit. The salesclerk matched the shirt to the dress. William asked her to look at the dress and match the flowers. Susan said that she remembered I wanted hydrangeas and roses. She asked if she could add tulips. I told her that would be fine. She was so excited that she started to squeal again. William hugged her. Artie was there, and he congratulated us both. He was a lot more subdued that Susan. William told her that we could talk tomorrow about plans. Susan asked if she could come by the bar tomorrow to look at the deck and get an idea of what we were looking for. He told her we would be there.

With that, we went back to the house. I changed into pajamas. My ring even made my pajamas look fancy. He hugged me and asked if I liked it. I told him that I loved it. He asked if I was hungry, but I assured him I was too excited to eat. He did suggest we try to get some sleep to be prepared for Susan.

We propped up on pillows and turn the TV on. He held me and kissed me. He ran his finger my arm. These two weeks were going to be another countdown; this time, it was a countdown to the happiest day of my life. The day I would become Mrs. William Riley. I could not help but squeal myself. William just laughed and kissed me.

CHAPTER 19

Wedding Bells and Forever (A Thousand Years)

We were only going to have about twenty-five people at this wedding, but the way Susan was planning, you would think we had rented out a huge church for one thousand people. William and I went to the courthouse and got a marriage license on Tuesday. Susan had taken over, and I was very glad! She had invited everyone to the wedding. The wedding was going to be held on the back deck of the One-Eyed Parrot. She had found an arch that she was going to cover in flowers. She was going to put tulle and garland around the deck rail. All the tables and umbrellas were going into storage.

    She had a family friend who was a photographer who will be taking pictures. She had another friend who will be making the wedding cake. She had some high school kids from church who will be playing a keyboard and violins. I said that violins on the deck of a bar might be too much. She told me not to ruin this for her! William reminded her that it was *our* wedding, but I gave in and said violins would class up the deck!

    Sam was going to be my matron of honor. Larry was going to be William's best man. The pastor from their family church was going to conduct the wedding. We were going to church Sunday, and he required counseling to conduct the wedding. I was looking forward to going back to church.

Susan took care of the wedding details, and William did what he called the fun stuff. He had the honeymoon suite booked at a hotel in Greenville. We were going to be there for a few days, and then we were going to Clemson, Oconee State Park, Table Rock, and Devil's Fork. He said we could enjoy the great outdoors after we spent a few days indoors enjoying being husband and wife.

Dave and his wife were coming. He had told Annette and Debbie that they could stay at the beach house. Sam and her husband were going to stay at a hotel on the Isle of Palms. Susan had arranged for a caterer to use the kitchen at the bar. Larry said that he and Stewart would oversee anyone using the kitchen. We had invited a few more people to the reception—people from around town, some of the regulars at the bar, and friends of William. I had Dave, Annette, Debbie, Sam, and her husband, and I had invited Nellie to come. Her son was driving her down for the wedding.

I told Susan she needed to go to a yoga class to relax because she was so stressed out. She made me go too. It was fun, but it just proved that I was in very bad shape. We did one class, and I was sore for two days. That made Susan decide we had to go to another class.

On Monday before the wedding, William and I went to a ballroom dance studio to practice our waltz since it had been a while since we had danced. William had arranged for a DJ at the reception, so we practiced the shag, swing, two-step, and a few line dances. Man, and I thought the yoga made me sore! It was fun, and we decided we were going to start dancing a few times a month.

I got my hair trimmed about a week before the wedding so it would be cut but not *look* cut. Susan scheduled me a spa day on Thursday before the wedding. I got a pedicure, manicure, facial, and massage. While I was there, I got my legs and underarms waxed. That was my first time and last time to get anything waxed. That hurt. Susan suggested that William should get his hair cut and get his beard trimmed. She wanted him to cut it off, but I put my foot down. Some things do not need to change.

We went to church the Sunday before the wedding and a couple of counseling sessions. I really liked the pastor. He expressed the concerns that I knew he would—you know, the ones about us getting married after only knowing each other for six weeks. The pastor said he would agree to conduct the marriage ceremony because he had known William long enough to know he did not jump into anything blindly. I still did not believe we were doing it either, but I also could not picture me spending one more day without him. I used to laugh at people who talked about soulmates, but I truly believe we were meant to be together.

Susan, William, and I worked on odds and ends for the wedding. Debbie, Annette, and Sam got in on Thursday. Susan put them to work putting together a few favors to go on the tables. Now Susan had William's crew wax the floor inside. She covered the tables with tablecloths with a flower arrangement and candles on each one. The DJ would be in the back corner. The cake and punch would be in the other back corner. There would be a buffet line along the back wall. There was a section of floor over in front of the DJ that was open and ready for dancing.

She had it all decorated by Friday night. The bar was closed Friday and Saturday for the rehearsal/rehearsal dinner and the wedding/reception. We had the rehearsal, and then we had a simple rehearsal dinner out on the deck. Everything was perfect. Susan had done a wonderful job.

I stayed at the beach house with Annette and Debbie on Friday night. Susan said that we could not stay in the house together even if we were not doing anything before the wedding night. She said that she had put too much work into this to have us spoil it with bad luck. William did sneak over on Friday night to give me a kiss. He told me he could hardly wait to see me walk down the aisle. We kissed again, and he went home. Larry and Stewart had offered to take him out for a bachelor party, but he said he wanted to feel good for his wedding day. I had told Debbie, Annette, and Sam the same thing.

Sam's husband was driving in later tonight, so when he got there, he was checking in to the hotel right down the road from the One-Eyed Parrot. Sam said that she was going to go over to the hotel when he called. He got in around nine thirty, so I walked her over. I hugged her and told her I would see her in the morning.

Debbie said she would take the couch because I needed a good night's sleep in the bed. She was not going to risk being yelled at by Susan because she had deprived me of my beauty sleep. I went to bed at ten. Debbie and Annette stayed up for a little while. They might not feel good for my wedding!

I woke up at seven and lay there for a while thinking about all that had happened in six short weeks. Maybe the island *is* magic? I met William, I got a book published to help save turtles, Sam might be moving back, and I was getting married! Oh yeah, and I got a divorce and sold a house.

I fixed breakfast and coffee. All the others were still asleep. I told Debbie to go get in my bed so she could sleep. She just put the pillow over her head and stayed where she was. I sat on the porch to drink my coffee and picked up my phone. I had a text from William. "She said we couldn't see each other, but she didn't say we couldn't talk." I smiled and dialed his number.

He answered on the first ring. "Good morning to the future Mrs. William Riley!"

I laughed and asked him how he slept.

"I slept terrible. I cannot sleep without you in the bed anymore. I am used to reaching over and touching you."

I had to admit I had missed that too!

"Do you remember when we are supposed to get there? I don't want to call Susan. She'll fuss at me."

I laughed and told him we were doing all the pictures after because we cannot see each other. So we will get there right before the wedding.

"When you go out on the deck, Susan will lead me into the bar until the music starts for me to come out. Sam will be in there with me. Larry will be with you outside. I am glad it is not any later than four. This is going to be a very long day waiting for the wedding."

He said that he had already put our suitcases in the car. We talked a little bit longer. I told him that I had better go start getting ready. I had to shower, dry my hair, and put on makeup. He told me he loved me and he would see me soon.

I stripped the bed. Dave had said just to strip sheets, not to worry about washing them. Annette and Tim got up and fixed some breakfast and drank coffee. Debbie had started to stir. She ate, and then we all sat out on the porch with coffee. We talked for a while, and then I went to take a shower. I washed and dried my hair. It was one, and I thought I better eat a little something. I ate a peanut butter sandwich, and then I brushed my teeth. I put on my dress, and then I started working on my makeup. Then I got my shoes on and my shawl.

Everyone else was getting dressed. Sam showed up. She looked so pretty. Susan had picked a solid color sundress that was a baby blue. Thomas was with Sam. It was so good to see him. I gave him a hug. He said that I looked so pretty. It had probably been six months since I had seen him. I was glad he had come down. I hoped he would move to Charleston with Sam. Thomas said that he was going to walk over to the bar. Debbie, Annette, and Tim said they were going to join him.

There was a knock at the door. I opened it to find Susan. She looked pretty in her royal blue dress. She said that it was time to leave. Sam and I got into Susan's car. She drove to the One-Eyed Parrot. She parked, and we all went inside the bar. William and Larry were outside on the deck with the guests. Susan pulled our bouquets out of the refrigerator. I had never seen flowers this pretty before, hydrangeas, white roses, and pink tulips. Every color emphasized a color in my dress. Sam's bouquet had hydrangeas and tulips. Her blue dress matched the hydrangeas perfectly. I had to say, Susan was good! The music from the keyboard and violin filled the air. I had to admit, the One-Eyed Parrot had never looked so good. The old place dressed up nicely. Maybe William should consider hosting more weddings. Susan could be the official bar wedding coordinator. I had to chuckle. Sam and Susan both looked at me. I told them the place was so beautiful I was just picturing more weddings being scheduled here.

Susan smiled and said, "As long as it's not a wedding for you or William, that will be fine. The place does look pretty good if I do say so myself."

The song finished. Susan opened the patio door, and they started another song. She went and stood near the railing. She nodded to Sam to march in. Sam walked toward Larry and William. William winked at her. Then the wedding march started. I stood and listened for a bit. First, because it was a short walk and I wanted to hear more of the song; second, because I wanted to pinch myself that this was really happening. I looked at Susan, and she nodded. I stepped out on the deck and walked toward William. He looked so handsome in his blue shirt and khaki shorts. Susan had a pinned a white rose on his shirt. Larry was in khakis and a pink shirt. He looked very handsome too. Maybe he should wear pink button downs more often to work behind the bar!

William was grinning from ear to ear. When I stopped beside him, he took my hand and leaned over and told me I was beautiful. I whispered to him that he looked handsome and wished him a happy birthday.

The pastor talked a few minutes and read a couple of scriptures. He talked about us finding each other and that everyone felt like we had already known each other a lifetime. Then we exchanged vows and rings. He did not even have to finish the "you may now kiss the bride" sentence because William was already there. Our guests laughed. The pastor introduced us as Mr. and Mrs. Riley and invited everyone to step inside for a celebration. We stayed outside for a few pictures and a few kisses. Then we joined everyone inside.

Several other guests had arrived for the reception. For our first dance, we had decided to go a more nontraditional route. We waltzed, but it was a faster waltz to Greta Van Fleet's song "You're the One." Then everybody danced. We visited with everyone and then danced some more. We cut the cake and had our toast. William tossed the garter, and Roy the fireman caught it. I had to laugh. Susan handed me a smaller bouquet to toss. I tossed it, and Debbie caught it. She looked over at Roy and winked. He smiled, and they danced. William and I looked at each other and smiled. The thought of those two together was amusing.

William and I walked by, and I said, "Be careful!"

Roy said that it was not very nice of me to warn Debbie about him. I winked and told him I was actually warning him!

Debbie smiled and said, "Yes, probably good advice!"

William looked at the two of them and said he thought they were a pretty good match for each other. We took a few more pictures and visited with everyone. We thanked Susan for all her hard work. Sam hugged us both and told us how beautiful it all was. Debbie and Annette both hugged me and said that that they were so happy for us. I promised them we would get together after the honeymoon. Debbie said that she would come down to visit us and her new fireman. Annette just rolled her eyes.

William got everyone's attention and thanked everyone for being there to celebrate our special day. Tanya, one of the waitresses, came in from the deck and whispered something to William. He grabbed my hand and led me to the boardwalk and called for everyone to come watch. He said the sea turtles had hatched and were making their way to the ocean. We all gathered at the end of the boardwalk and watched as they all made their way to the ocean to start their new lives. William hugged me and whispered that it seemed only fitting that the sea turtles would make an appearance at our wedding.

William turned and faced our guests and finished his speech. "Again, I want to thank you all for being here today to celebrate our special day. We kind of got to celebrate a special day for the sea turtles as well! Please dance some more, eat some more, and drink some more. But I think I am going to take my wife and begin our new adventure."

Everyone applauded and followed us back to the bar and out to the front to watch us get in the car. Someone had decorated the car with bright flip-flops and koozies; I guess this was the beach version of cans hanging from the back of the car. I think I liked it. He opened the door and helped me in. Then he got in and grabbed my hand.

He kissed me and said, "Mrs. Riley, are you ready for the next step in our adventure?"

I leaned over and kissed him and told him that I was ready to start one of many adventures that we would have in our lifetime together. Then we drove away. He stopped at his house, and I figured he was stopping to take the flip-flops and koozies off. He got out, took them off, and put them in the back of the car and then walked around and opened my door. He took my hand and said, "We can start the Greenville portion of our adventure tomorrow, but tonight, we celebrate here in your new home, Mrs. Riley."

I looked into his eyes and said, "Tonight we celebrate in *our* new home, Mr. Riley!"

EPILOGUE

I had no idea how much my life was going to change when I stepped into the One-Eyed Parrot six weeks ago to find a place to retreat to attempt to write a children's book. I walked in thinking I was going to spend a couple of weeks at the beach to recover from the end of a marriage; instead, I found a whole new life. I found my matching puzzle piece!

Once in an argument many years ago, Bill had told me that I was miserable, and I was good at it. Until I stepped onto the Isle of Palms for this adventure, I had not realized how true his statement had been. I had been so unhappy for so long that I did not remember what happiness felt like. Here with William, I had found out what I had been missing for so long.

I had no idea what twists and turns lay ahead for us or for Debbie, Annette, or even Sam and Thomas. I was sure there would be good times and maybe some sad times. I just knew that with William by my side, we could face anything together.

ABOUT THE AUTHOR

Judy LeGrand was born in Sumter, South Carolina. She always liked to write. It all started with diaries as a child, progressed to blogs, and even a few local magazine articles. A high school English teacher told her she should be a writer, but she didn't know where to start. She has worked as a secretary, a youth director at a couple of local churches, and now as an executive assistant. She attempted to write her great American novel several times, but that "bucket list" item eluded her until one night she had a dream that woke her up because it felt so real. She decided to type it up like a journal entry, and adding to that journal entry became a daily routine. She did a good bit of her writing sitting at the Pizza Joint in Columbia, South Carolina, with her laptop in a corner booth. Four months later, *Where I Belong* was finished!

Printed in the USA
CPSIA information can be obtained
at www.ICGtesting.com
LVHW091553110624
782912LV00001B/148